ALSO BY DANNIE MARTIN

The Dishwasher

Committing Journalism

IN THE HAT

DANNIE MARTIN

SIMON & SCHUSTER

SIMON & SCHUSTER
Rockefeller Center
1230 Avenue of the Americas
New York, NY 10020

This book is a work of fiction. Names, characters, places, and incidents either are products of the author's imagination or are used fictitiously. Any resemblance to actual events or locales or persons, living or dead, is entirely coincidental.

Designed by Deirdre C. Amthor

Manufactured in the United States of America

10 9 8 7 6 5 4 3 2 1

Library of Congress Cataloging-in-Publication Data

Martin, Dannie M.
In the hat / Dannie Martin.
p. cm.
ISBN: 978-1-4516-3664-2
I. Title.
PS3563.A72328615 1997 97-11962
813'.54--dc21 CIP

ACKNOWLEDGMENTS

Many people must be acknowledged for helping me get *In the Hat* into print.

Ed LeClair, my friend and typist for over ten years, who never said no to me, though he probably should have.

Jan Sluizer, who almost single-handedly kept me out of the joint, gave me a place to live time and again, and housebroke me enough to do it.

Richard Lee Bostic and "Big Al" Perryman, my two heroes. Blair Guthrie, who was a victim of murder July 3, 1995. His spirit remains untouched.

T. D. Bingham and Barry Mills are two good friends who are locked up twenty-three and one-half hours a day.

Crissie, and her man, Eddie Shay. Friends Deakon and Shelly Proudfoot. My favorite youngsters, Melissa, Gary, and Alissa Bradley—all their support is appreciated.

Peter Sussman, my first editor, and good pal. Harry Kreamer, who was even willing to discuss philosophy with me. Randy Daar, an excellent lawyer and a perfect friend. Jake and Laurie Rohrer and Sandy Close, who have always rooted for me.

Thanks also to my editor at Simon & Schuster, Bob Mecoy, and his assistant, Pete Fornatale, for their faith in me.

Last but never least, my literary agent, Fred Hill, whose belief in my writing has never wavered, and his aide, Irene, who puts up with me.

Thanks so much to you all and to the many others who supported me along the way. There's no way I didn't need each and every one of you. No man is an island.

TO SEVEN ANGELS

Jackie Costa

Jo Anne Guthrie

Jennifer Guthrie

Janie Kreamer

Julie Martin

Janet Sluizer

Joann Thomas

Seven J names that would have been OK with Jesse James

EXHIBIT 16

Duly marked as evidence by H. Martin Torres

He lost her so unfairly
That it robbed him of his mirth
Until his feet, mired in vengeance,
Stalked this bitter earth.

A note, obviously part of a poem.
Found in Grady McCall's (aka The Stepper)
personal property after his demise.

CHAPTER 1

When Vernon Coy woke up he was lying between Paula and Curly on their big heart-shaped bed. It was five in the morning and his hangover was attacking him with cotton mouth, a full bladder, sand-filled eyeball sockets, and a bigger-than-usual headache. Proof again that you have to pay when you party.

He slid over Curly, who slept peacefully on her stomach, and eased his foot gently onto wall-to-wall carpet, trying not to move his head too much. Naked, he stepped carefully down into his sunken living room. All he could think of now was the bird, Gatorbait, waiting in his cage on the back porch. Vern went out the door and took a long, satisfying piss in the grass by Gatorbait's cage. The rooster clucked and moved about in his cage until Vern was done.

"Hey, big brave fella," Vern said to the rooster in a loving tone.

Gatorbait was a game rooster with offbeat coloring for a fighting chicken. He was a cream and rusty red color with brown spots on his breast. Vern gave him a couple kernels of corn. He didn't want him eating heavy before his fight in the afternoon.

As he looked at the chicken, he thought about the promise he had made Paula and Curly that he wouldn't fight any more chickens. Ever. It hadn't been a hard promise to make at the time. He had lost over one hundred thousand dollars in the year just past betting on chickens.

Today's fight was very likely to cause a nasty scene. Especially after the drunken stunt with his brother's alligator. Vernon looked out at the pond where the beast was already getting ready to sun himself in the early-morning sunshine. Only the San Joaquin Valley in August gets this hot this early.

Vernon had loved his chickens, but they had let him down too many times. The night he had drunkenly vowed to quit betting chickens, he had snatched all nineteen of his chickens out of their training cages and put them in a pen with the gator.

"Colonel Sanders is here! Come and get it!" he said as he threw them over the fence. He'd put a roll of chicken wire over the top of the pen so that the birds couldn't get out. Paula and Curly had followed him around begging him not to do this cruel thing, but he was too far gone on mad and whiskey. These were no ordinary chickens. They were fighting roosters. A strain he'd developed over the last five years, using Georgia cocks and Filipino hens from the best fighting stock around.

By the next day the four-foot gator had killed and eaten five of the birds and had crushed two more, presumably to let them age a bit. He was not only hungry but also mean and ornery as hell. Vern had inherited the gator along with Curly when his brother, Weldon, was sentenced to sixteen years in prison for armed robbery. He turned away from the gator.

When he walked back into the house to call his friend Melvin,

Curly was up making coffee. Vern's house looked like an awful mess from the outside but was well furnished with every modern amenity on the inside. He liked it that way. Curly turned her cheek up for a kiss. She looked gorgeous in a white chemise.

"You don't want my breath right now, hon," Vern told her.

"Well, kiss my ass then, honey," she said, and raised the chemise enough to show off her smooth white ass. She took off before he could swat her.

Melvin's groggy voice came on the line just as Paula entered the kitchen, sleepy-eyed and grouchy-looking. Paula and Curly lowered their voices, so he raised his to be sure they could hear him.

"You heard me, Melvin. Be here by seven and bring your knives," he said to the sleep-laden voice.

When he hung up he averted his eyes from the window overlooking the gator pen, remembering how the roosters fought one another as the gator stalked them. He had loved the chickens dearly and his conscience bothered him now.

"Get some of this mess picked up!" he yelled at the women in the kitchen as he made his way to the bathroom to take a cold shower.

"Fuck you, Vernon," Paula yelled back from the kitchen.

"Yeah, we ain't fucking maids," Curly added.

A pair of pantyhose and two silk briefs hung drying from the shower curtain rod. More undies hung from the towel rack and a plugged-in hair dryer rested in the middle of the floor. A curling iron and plastic bag of big black curlers lay on the toilet lid. Vernon dreaded the cold shower he knew he had to take. Cold showers were torture, but they got the job done.

"It looks like a goddamn fucking whorehouse in here!" He screamed as the first jet of icy water hit his face and chest.

"Goddammit, Vernon, you'll wake the neighbors!" Paula

yelled back. He began singing at the top of his lungs. "'Don't call me, woman, I won't be around. I'm lookin' for somethin' that's never been found.'"

"Vern, you fucking idiot! It's five-thirty, for Christ sakes!" Paula screamed.

"Get your lazy ass in gear, woman. We got things to do!" he yelled back as he squirted shampoo into his hair, then realized he still had on his hair net.

"Shit!" he exclaimed and adjusted the nozzle until some warm water mingled with the cold.

The cold shower and a couple aspirin had taken care of his headache. He left the shower and looked intently into the full length mirror on the outside of the shower door.

"Damn, you're beautiful," he said to his red-eyed image. The bloodshot eyes were all that marred the animal that peered back from the mirror at him as he began to carefully comb his hair. He squeezed Close-Up toothpaste—the color of his eyes—onto a brush and began brushing the fur from his tongue.

His wavy wheat-blond hair had a reddish tint in the sun. Lately he'd taken to cutting it shorter and combing it straight back. Curly called it his "low-rider" look.

Paula was out in the kitchen with Curly when he went into the bedroom for his Levi's and T-shirt. A pair of old comfortable brown rough-cut cowboy boots completed his outfit. He walked through the living room again and back to the kitchen.

Paula put a saucer in front of him with two pieces of wheat bread toast on it when he sat down beside Curly. As he reached for the strawberry jam, he could feel them both looking at him.

"Get me some coffee, hon," he said to Paula, who walked to the stove, poured him a cup, sat it in front of him and went back to staring balefully in his direction with her arms crossed across her chest. He knew that was bad news.

He jammed and ate both pieces of toast in dead silence, Curly sitting across the table, and Paula standing. Neither moved or spoke, just stared holes through him. Curly finally broke the ice as he drained the last of his black coffee.

"Vernon, tell us you ain't going to no chicken fight," she said.

"Don't make me lie, girl," he replied.

"Well, then tell us you aren't going to enter a chicken," Paula put in. She always said "aren't" instead of "ain't."

"Don't make me lie, girl," he said again.

He watched the shaft of the morning sun coming through the kitchen window. Like a lover, it held Paula and shone through the chemise. There was a small triangle at the junction of her thighs where they didn't quite touch each other.

"Your legs sure look nice in that sunshine, hon," he ventured.

"Then tell us you aren't going to bet any money," she responded, uncharacteristically ignoring his compliment.

"I'm betting it all, girl," he responded. There was no use trying to duck the issue.

"Vern, I must of fucked one hundred Filipinos this last week and now you're going to take the money and give it to one Filipino with a tougher chicken than yours?" Paula inquired in a menacing tone.

"Ain't no chicken in the world tougher than Gatorbait," Vernon replied, looking at the sunlight on the floor to avoid her burning eyes.

"You fucking, lying asshole," Paula said and stormed out of the kitchen. The door of the bedroom slammed and shook the whole house.

"Vernon, you told us you would get rid of all the chickens and that you wouldn't lose any more money on chicken fights. You gave us your word. How can you do this?" Curly asked him in almost a whisper that sounded loud in the slipstream of Paula's wrath.

"Don't start that shit, Curly, you know exactly why I have to do it. You saw what I saw last night," Vern replied, and looked directly into her blue eyes. He was tired of being talked bad to by whores.

Last night during the party Vern and Curly had walked out back to smoke a joint. The sun was just going down and there was an awesome fight going on near the gator's pond. There was one rooster left and as the gator lunged for him with jaws open like *Tyrannosaurus rex*, the rooster flew up and banged at the gator's head with his spurs.

Vern could have sworn one of the gator's eyes was shut.

"My God," Curly wailed as the two animals waged war near the sun-dappled pool of water. It had once been a goldfish pond, but the gator had killed or eaten every living creature. Vern figured Weldon hadn't given him a lot of love and affection when he was home, and the gator was growing up.

Vern ran to the pen, jerked the gate open, and began chasing the rooster. Curly began screaming when one of Vern's legs went into the pond. Paula brought out some people and they helped him catch the rooster and get him in a small cage.

"I do understand and it's okay, just don't tell Paula I said it," she whispered. Vern looked at her and she was smiling. The smile framed by her curly blond hair and cornflower eyes was the nicest thing he had seen for a while. Once again Vern reminded himself of how lucky he was to have her.

It was true that he was breaking a solemn oath, but he didn't see anything else to do. True, he had lost big money betting on his fighting chickens. Money that Curly and Paula had sold their bodies to obtain. Like all degenerate gamblers, he had kept thinking that he would finally come up with a King Kong chicken and get even. It never happened. Some won a few, but they all got killed pretty early in the game. Along with his bankroll.

"Here's three hundred for us to party on tonight if Gatorbait loses," Vern said, pushing three one-hundred-dollar bills across the table to Curly.

"I'll hang on to it, hon, but he won't lose," she answered, taking the money, getting up, and walking to the bedroom. They could both feel Paula sulking in there.

Vern poured himself more coffee and sat back at the table. He did intend to quit fighting chickens, but if this chicken could whip an alligator, Vern had to see the rooster that could bring him down.

CHAPTER 2

Melvin Nix drove up in Vern's yard at 6:45 and parked his pickup. He wasn't happy about being rousted out of bed this early and left his tape deck playing so he could hear the last of an old Johnny Rodriguez tape. Melvin hated these new country stars like Randy Travis and the "Thousand Points of Light" bunk they sold to the public.

"A thousand pints of shit," he would say when Travis or George Bush's name came up in a conversation. Melvin disliked Republican presidents and New Wave country singers. But since he was a liberal, everyone else in the world was okay with him. He could even tolerate niggers, queers, and bulldaggers if they didn't try and hang out with him. Each to his own and the devil take the hindmost was the way he looked at things.

Right now he was looking at Vern's yard. It was a fucking mess. The grass was a foot high right around the driveway and four feet high everywhere else. The house was on a three-acre parcel and round chicken cages stuck up like saltshakers all around the house and fields. They were all empty. An old push mower sat in the weeds near the driveway where someone had made the last push a few years ago. Weeds grew up between the rusty blades.

Melvin, himself a neat and clean man, had always marveled at how Vern's house looked so rundown from the outside. Inside, the sunken living room with its overstuffed leather couches was beautiful. But Vern even used an old-style cooler instead of air-conditioning. Said he liked it better and didn't want to look ostentatious, whatever that meant.

Melvin speculated on the chicken cages. They were the only things in good shape around the house. Vern had taken good care of them. They were individual training cages, built round and six feet high. Their food and water dishes were on a shelf four feet above the ground so that each rooster had to fly up to eat or drink. It was a method of making their wings strong. Other owners used different training methods and cages.

But Melvin knew a couple who used Vern's system and wondered if he might be able to make some money. It was a cinch he could if Vern would sell the cages cheap enough. Melvin figured he would. Vern was sick of fighting chickens, a fact that made him very curious about why Vern had called him. He turned the ignition all the way off and headed for the front door.

Curly and Paula were still in the bedroom when Melvin walked into the kitchen and poured himself a cup of coffee.

"Did you bring your knives?" Vern asked him as he sat down at the table.

"Yeah, I brought 'em, but I thought you quit the chickens," he replied.

"I did, but I got one chicken left and I'm fighting him today," Vern told him. Melvin didn't reply and just went on sipping his coffee.

"Let's roll!" Vern yelled toward the bedroom.

Curly and Paula came out of the bedroom, both dressed in designer jeans, tight T-shirts, and high heels. Melvin noticed that Paula's eyes were puffy, as if she'd been crying. They both smiled at him and he put the coffee cup down and followed them out of the house. There was never any dawdling in this crowd. When they got ready to go, they went. Vern switched the cooler off and locked the front door after they all got outside. Then he walked around the house to pick up the chicken.

When he walked back around the house with the cage they all stood there looking at the vehicles. Paula's one-year-old Blazer sat beside Vern's Lincoln Town Car.

"We'll take the Blazer," Vern said and started toward it.

"I don't want no chicken shit in my car, Vern," Paula wailed, and looked as if she might begin crying. Curly put an arm around her and Vern stopped.

"Okay. We'll go in Melvin's pickup, then," he replied and put the cage in Melvin's truck bed, placing it close to the cab in the hopes that Gatorbait wouldn't get too much wind.

"If you fight like I think you will, I'll buy you your own air-conditioned van to ride in," Vern whispered to the chicken as he sat the cage down.

"What did you tell that fucking chicken, Vern?" Curly asked as he turned around.

"Probably told the fucker he loved him. He sure hasn't mentioned nothing like that to me in a while," Paula answered her.

Vern slid in behind the wheel of Melvin's Dodge without replying. These bitches were so sassy this morning he didn't want to deal with them. When one asked him some smart-aleck question and the other answered for him, about all he could do was ignore them both. Paula slid in next to him and Curly sat in Melvin's lap by the door.

The interior of the truck was hotter than the shades of hell. Vern rolled down his window and put the air conditioner on after he cranked the motor. Curly was fiddling with the radio, looking for a country station as they drove out the driveway. A new house had been built on the property next door. It was a beautiful two-story ranch-style affair trimmed in redwood. A lawn had just been laid and sprinklers were spraying water over the neatly trimmed grounds.

"Looks like you got some upper-class neighbors," Melvin remarked.

"Yeah, I may have to hire someone to mow my lawn," Vern responded.

He didn't know who had bought the property. The house was much flashier than those usually found in this west Fresno neighborhood. Years ago it had been cotton fields, fig orchards, wineries, and cotton gins, with working people's houses interspersed here and there.

In the decade just past the developers had come in, building condos, apartment complexes, and more family homes. Vern had bought his three acres cheap when it was still a semi-industrial area. Lately he'd been getting about one offer a month for his property, but the thought of selling never entered his mind. Coming from a large family of poor dust-bowl Okies had instilled in him a fierce desire to own land. Now that he had some he planned to keep it until he died. It would be a nice gift for his kids if he had any by then.

"What time do we have to be at the chicken fight?" Paula asked.

"It starts around noon, hon. Why?" Vern asked.

"I've got a trick waiting at the Park Motel, so let's swing by there. It's that claims adjuster who comes up from LA. He referred a friend here in Fresno and the guy called last night. I told him I'd come by this morning before checkout time."

"Did you call the guy in LA to see if he referred him?" Vern asked.

"Yeah, he did," she replied.

"Well, we'll stop by there on the way," Vern said as he pulled into a 7-Eleven store parking lot. They all got out and went in.

Melvin brought his cooler from the truck and they bought a case of Budweiser and some crushed ice to keep it cool. Curly and Paula ran around like two kids, buying peanuts and sodas while a clerk from India or Pakistan or somewhere watched them with a hungry gleam in his eyes. They had a very powerful effect on most of the men they encountered.

Vern swung the truck into the parking area of the motel.

"What room is he in?" he asked as he shut off the motor.

"I'll have to check at the office," Paula said as Melvin and Curly got down to let her out. They all watched her as she walked into the office, then came out and went around the corner.

"How long do you think she will take?" Melvin asked when Paula disappeared.

"How long does it take you to fuck, Melvin?" Curly asked in reply.

Vern couldn't help but admire the way she answered questions with a question when she was in a bad mood.

"Hell, I don't know." Melvin sounded exasperated.

"Then how in the fuck are we supposed to know how long it takes a total stranger to fuck?" Curly rejoined sarcastically.

"Goddammit, Curly, lighten up on Melvin," Vern ordered, and before Curly could reply, Paula came walking back up to the truck.

Melvin and Curly got down again to let her in.

"That was quick, babe. Could be a new world record here," Curly quipped as Paula climbed into the pickup.

"I didn't trick him," Paula replied as Curly and Melvin got back in and Melvin slammed the door.

"Why not?" Curly asked.

"He had a dick like a Shetland pony. It must of been sixteen inches long," Paula said.

"Aww, come on," Curly exclaimed.

"Well, it was way longer than them rulers they gave us in eighth grade. And it looked like one of them Sears and Roebuck flashlights the police wear in their belt. I told him no fucking way. Not for a hundred, not for two hundred."

"What room is he in?" Curly asked.

"One-oh-four," Paula replied as Vern began backing the truck out. He had to slam on the brakes when Curly opened the door and jumped out. She was around the corner before anyone could say anything.

"How long do you think she will take?" Melvin asked.

"Ordinarily about five minutes, but she'll probably nurse this one along as long as she can," Paula said and looked over at Vern and smiled.

He was glad her mood was becoming lighter. But no one could stay in a bad mood around Curly very long. He didn't want them picking at Melvin, which was one of their favorite pastimes. Melvin was going to tie the fighting knives on Gatorbait and Vern wanted his mind to be on the job.

Tying knives on fighting chickens is an art. Melvin Nix was legendary among chicken fighters. Even the Oriental chicken owners admitted that he was the best. He was the first white man to ever reach that plateau in chicken fighting. It was a heady honor in a business where one slightly altered angle of the knife would kill your chicken and your bankroll at the same time.

Curly came back toward the truck with her happy prance, blond hair bobbing with every step. When she climbed back onto Melvin's lap, she handed Vern a hundred- and a fifty-dollar bill.

"Put this on Gatorbait," she said as he started the pickup.

"Keep it for our party, hon," he replied and shoved her hand back. She stuck the money in her purse behind the seat.

"That was really quick, Curly," Paula remarked as Vern drove toward the highway.

"He was too hot, you must of got him really steamed up. He came before it was all the way in. But you weren't lying. It was longer than one of those rulers they gave us in school."

"Did you get his phone number?" Paula asked.

"Hell, yes. I made him repeat it twice," Curly said, and they all laughed.

"Melvin's got a hard-on," Curly exclaimed, and twisted around in his lap to look at him.

"That's bullshit," Melvin yelled, his ruddy face turning a beet red.

"That's probably a nose inhaler in his pocket," Paula chimed in, turning Melvin's face even redder.

"Goddammit, I ain't telling you bitches again, leave Melvin a-fucking-lone. You are trying my fucking patience," Vern said in a low but dead-serious tone that turned the atmosphere in the truck cool as a walk-in icebox. Something in his manner let them know how important this chicken fight was to him, and they all took refuge in silence. Paula leaned forward and turned the volume up on the radio as Curly and Melvin pretended to study the passing scenery outside their window.

The radio and low hum of the air conditioner were the only sounds for ten miles or so. Then Vern gazed in the rearview mirror and exclaimed "Ah, shit!" as he decelerated and eased the truck to the shoulder of the highway. Paula glanced back and saw a highway patrol car easing to the shoulder behind them with blue and red lights flashing.

"Police!" she said softly for the benefit of Melvin and Curly, who kept looking straight ahead.

"Anyone got any dope on them?" Vern asked as he pulled to a stop.

"I got them pills I brought for Curly and Paula, but there's no way I can get at them," Melvin said.

"Well, just sit still. I think it's a woman and she's by herself," Vern said, gazing intently into the rearview mirror.

"We doin' the abused wife?" Paula asked, rubbing at her already reddened eyes.

"Oh, hell, yes," Vern said, as he hit the button to let his window down just as the female officer appeared at his window, clipboard in hand.

"What seems to be the problem here, Officer?" Vern smiled at her.

Curly glanced over at Paula when Vern said that. The look told Paula that what Vern said wasn't entirely original. The glance Paula gave back said she agreed. They often communicated like this without saying a word.

"Your driver's license, please!" the officer demanded, ignoring Vern's cliché.

"Proof of insurance and registration," she intoned when Vern handed her his license. Melvin reached around Curly and rummaged in the glove box until he found the papers and handed them to Vern, who passed them on to the policewoman. She studied them for a minute and said, "Whose truck is this?"

"It's mine. I'm Melvin Nix," Melvin said from behind Curly.

"Just a minute," the cop said and walked back to her car with the papers. Vern watched in the rearview as she picked up her two-way radio and began calling in the information. After three or four minutes she walked back up to Vern's window with the papers attached to a clipboard. He saw her take a hard look at Gatorbait in his cage. Vern could see patches of sweat on her khaki shirt.

"You can't ride four in the front seat of a pickup and none of you have your seat belts fastened," she said to Vern.

"Well, we didn't have any choice about riding four," Vern replied, and glanced over at Paula, who by now had tears running down her cheeks from her reddened eyes. Looking back at the officer he went on: "My sister here was getting beat up by her husband again. He's been drunk for a week now. I had to go and get her and my car's in the shop so I borrowed Melvin's pickup."

"The last time he beat her up he broke her jaw and three of her ribs," Curly chimed in.

"I don't let nobody just take my pickup. I go where my pickup goes," Melvin said.

Paula, not to be outdone, let out a big sob and dropped her head into both hands. The awful racking noise she made sounded like she was gagging.

Vern looked directly into the police officer's green eyes.

"We're taking her to Livermore to a battered women's shelter and she don't like it there," he explained, and Paula began sobbing louder as Curly rubbed her back, saying, "There, there, it's okay, honey."

"Can't one of you ride in the back?" the cop asked, and Vern could see a softening around her eyes.

"Well, we could, but her pet chicken is back there and it gets very upset around anyone but her," Vern replied.

"I was going to mention that. It looks like a fighting rooster to me," the officer said.

"Oh no, it's a banty. They do look like fighting chickens a little, I guess. But I never saw a real fighting chicken," Vern replied.

The cop stood back and looked at Gatorbait, alongside the beer cooler, then stepped back up, leaned into the open window, and said to Paula, "Do you want to press charges against him, girl?"

Paula shook her head no and went on sobbing.

"We already pressed his face up against the ground a little," Melvin said.

"Shut up, Melvin!" Vern and Curly said at the same time, but Vern saw a twitch of a smile on the officer's plain lips.

She took the papers from her clipboard and handed them back to Vern.

"You fasten your seat belt, at least. You guys can go on, but there's no guarantee you won't get stopped again before you get to Livermore," she said.

"Thank you, Officer," Vern said, taking the papers and fiddling with the seat belt, trying to figure out how it worked.

"Drive careful," the cop said, and walked back to her car.

"I will, and thanks again," Vern said to her back and rolled the window back up.

"Did you hear that shit?" Paula asked Curly when Vern got back on the road.

"Yeah, he said he never saw a real fighting chicken before." Curly laughed, and they all began laughing.

"Melvin, you damn near went too far with that violent remark," Vern told him.

"Hell, she looked like she was in the mood for revenge," Melvin replied.

"If she'd believe Vern never saw a fighting chicken, she'd believe anything," Paula said.

The mood was lighter as they passed Madera, California, and went up the old 99 highway toward Modesto. Vern kept glancing back at Gatorbait to make sure he was okay. He began to get apprehensive and edgy again as they passed Modesto and he began looking for the turnoff to the chicken fight. He finally saw it and turned on to a road that ran along a canal bank.

There was a peach orchard on the left where they turned off and Vern stopped on the canal road for a piss call. Curly and Paula headed toward the tall weeds by the ditch while Melvin opened the cooler and extracted two half-quart cans of beer. They busted the suds and drank while Gatorbait watched them and clucked.

Vern saw Paula looking at the peach orchard as she walked back up the ditch bank to the pickup. Then she looked at him and they smiled at each other as he raised the beer can in a small toast as if to say, "We've come a long way, girl."

When they were kids they had picked a lot of peaches in orchards just like this one. Neither of them would ever forget the excruciating labor for little money, or the way the peach fuzz got on a sweating neck and itched and burned like hell. Shared memories like this formed the basis of their love like terrible but precious secrets. They each knew exactly what the other was thinking in moments like this, but they never discussed it unless they were alone.

As they continued on down the canal road, Vern saw Curly squirming around in Melvin's lap. She was determined to tease him, even though she'd obeyed Vern's verbal order to leave him alone. He was wondering whether he should say something to her when the peach orchard ran out and they arrived at the chicken fight.

CHAPTER 3

Soledad prison sprawls on a verdant expanse of land near Salinas, California, in the southern part of the Salinas Valley. Salinas is the lettuce capital of the world. The place where prisoners die on the vine is near some of the most fertile land in the country. Sugar beets, tomatoes, beans, and cotton are among the crops that grow nearby.

Soledad was the third maximum-security prison to be built in California. San Quentin was the first and Folsom the second. Unlike those walled fortresses, Soledad was enclosed by double fences with gun towers at each corner. A gauntlet of rolled razor wire lies between the fences and barbed wire tops them off.

The hallway at Soledad Central Facility is a quarter of a mile long from east gate to west gate. The west end leads out to a big recreation yard with ball fields, a weight pile, handball courts, and a running track. The east gate leads out to the prison industrial area where factories make paper towels, shoes, and other items for use in prisons.

Everything else, from the large cellblocks to the mess hall, laundry, gymnasium, chapel, and isolation units are connected to the hallway at right angles. The cellblocks are three tiers high and each tier has a row of thirty cells facing thirty cells directly across a common walkway. Between the cells of the first tier are card tables. There is a guard's office and TV room near the front of each cellblock.

Cells that were built for one person now hold two people. The cellblocks hold 360 men instead of the intended 180. At all times except the wee hours of the morning or on weekdays when convicts are out of the blocks on work assignments, the cell houses are as noisy as a gorilla cage at feeding time. Weekends are the worst.

About the time Vern pulled into the chicken fight, his brother, Weldon, stood in front of his cell at the end of the first tier in C cellblock. He was trying to ignore the noise and looking out the window at the end of the cell house. The view wasn't much but a fence and a field beyond, but the sunshine looked good. A black convict walked up and interrupted his reverie.

"Hey, Coy, the cop callin' you down there," the man said.

Weldon looked toward the front of the block past the various card games in progress. The cop was waving at him. He felt his pockets to make sure he wasn't carrying anything illegal and walked to the front of the building where the guard waited by the door to the hallway.

"Lieutenant wants to see you," the man said, pointing to the door of the block lieutenant's office. The guard was a small, dark-complected man dressed in the khaki uniform of California corrections officers. His name was Guzzi, but convicts referred to him behind his back as "Mickey Mouse," because he had large protruding ears and a nose and facial features that vaguely resembled the cartoon character. Weldon opened the lieutenant's door, went in, closed the door behind him, and stood in front of the desk where the lieutenant was signing some papers.

"Have a seat, Coy." The lieutenant glanced up and waved toward a folding chair in front of the desk. He was a big, beefy man with a short haircut that looked like wheat stubble with streaks of gray. Middle age seemed to be bettering him. His nose looked like a raw potato with big whiskey and cigarette veins under the skin.

"I'll just stand, if you don't mind," Weldon replied. He felt uncomfortable being alone with the lieutenant in his office. The man finished signing the papers and looked up at him.

"The building officer tells me you got too much paperwork in your cell. It's a fire hazard, you know."

"Yeah, well, I'll get rid of some of it," Weldon said.

"You do that," the lieutenant replied and reached for his cigarettes in a shirt pocket.

"Have one," he said and threw the pack of Camels on the desk. Weldon fished an unopened pack of Camels from his own shirt pocket.

"Have one of mine," he replied and threw his pack onto the desk. He picked up the lieutenant's pack, put it in his pocket, and turned to go. It was a ritual they had played out many times.

"Wait until I go off shift at four," the lieutenant said as Weldon went back out the door.

"I will," Weldon replied, knowing that was a goddamn lie and knowing the lieutenant probably knew it was a goddamn lie.

Mickey Mouse was up on the third tier shaking down someone's cell as Weldon made his way past the card games to his own house at the end of the first tier. The cell contained a double bunk, two lockers, and a sink and toilet. That left very little room for anything else. Boxes of legal papers and other odds and ends were pushed under the lower bunk and clothes hung all over the cell on makeshift hangers. A four-legged wooden stool sat next to the rear wall. The stool was used to help Weldon's cell partner climb up and down from the upper bunk.

He took another quick look out of his cell door to make sure Mickey Mouse was still up on three range, then grabbed the stool and twisted one of the legs off. The stool leg was hollow and held a syringe, and a roll of cash money that belonged to his cellie. Weldon shook out the syringe and fitted the leg back onto the stool.

He cleared a place on top of his locker and laid the syringe there alongside a metal spoon, a Q-tip, and a book of paper matches, then filled a glass with warm water at the sink. As he made the preparations he glanced out the cell door window to make sure Mickey Mouse was still up on the third tier and saw his cell partner, The Stepper, walking up to their cell.

"Get on the point," Weldon told him as he reached the cell.

"I got it," The Stepper replied and leaned against an unoccupied card table in front of the cell.

He could relax a little now that The Stepper was watching out for the man, but he saw his hands shaking as he tore the cigarette pack open and extracted the two little glassine-wrapped spheres that looked like black marbles.

As he unwrapped the cellophane on one of the little balls, the vinegar smell of the tar heroin wafted to his nostrils and almost made him gag. Using a single-edge razor blade, he cut off a match-head-size piece of the tar and put it in the spoon. It was gummy and stuck to every surface it touched.

Dannie Martin

He squirted some water out of the syringe onto the dope in the spoon, then held three paper matches under it until the tar dissolved into a thick black water. Dropping a piece of cotton from a Q-tip into the sludge, he put the tip of the needle into the cotton and drew the black water up into the syringe.

The residue in the spoon looked like a dirty bathtub that a greasy mechanic had just bathed in. The smell of vinegar filled the cell. Weldon was using a standard diabetic insulin syringe. He tied a long sweat sock around his left biceps and tapped the needle into a protruding vein above his elbow. Then he pumped his fist and eased the plunger back. A tendril of blood eased up into the barrel of the syringe like a red mushroom and he slammed the plunger home.

By the time he pulled the needle out and put a finger on the drop of blood easing from the hole it left, he could feel the warm balm of the drug taking hold at the base of his skull. It crept around to just behind his eyelids and relaxed them until the upper lids began to droop.

"*Ahhh,*" he exhaled, as the opiate took hold along his spine and rushed like smooth oil into his achy, craving joints. The iron-and-cement cell began to take on a warm, soft glow. This was the feeling he'd craved, chased and sought after, ever since he'd first felt it at the age of fourteen. The chase was hard and brutal but well worth it.

The cellblock noise was softer now. He looked out the cell door at The Stepper as he drew water into the syringe and squirted it into the toilet, cleaning it out.

The Stepper was seated at the table now, calmly playing solitaire with a deck of cards. He didn't look at all impatient or like anyone acting as a lookout. Even nearby convicts didn't realize he was watching out for someone. That was one of the things

Weldon liked about the old man. He was smooth. He also knew exactly where Mickey Mouse was and what he was doing.

"Do you want a taste?" Weldon asked him through the window in the cell door.

"Yeah, fix me up one," The Stepper replied.

"I'll be a few minutes. I got to make up some papers," Weldon said.

"Go ahead. The Mouse is going house to house on the third tier shaking down. He'll be busy for a while," The Stepper said, without looking up from his game of solitaire.

Weldon cut another piece and put it in the spoon. He was a bit surprised because his cellmate usually declined heroin, preferring weed or prison-made wine. He then used the razor blade to cut three squares off of an empty Tang bag. The bags were made of a tinfoil-like paper and were excellent repositories for tar heroin. Regular paper couldn't be used for tar because the gummy substance would soak into it.

He cut three more chunks from the ball of tar, put them on the squares, and folded each into neat little packages. Each ball had been a gram, so he figured he had about a gram and a half left for himself. Not a bad feeling at all.

He cleaned up everything except the dope in the spoon on the locker and put the gram and a half along with the syringe back into the stool leg and screwed the leg back onto the stool.

"Come on," he told The Stepper, who got up and entered the cell, unscrewing a state-issue ballpoint pen.

He took the filler out of the pen and snorted the liquid in the spoon up into one nostril, then held his head back for a minute so it wouldn't run back out. The length of the pen allowed some of the liquid to run back into the spoon and he snorted that into the other nostril.

"The buzzards know we are up to something. They will be

down here any time now," The Stepper said, still sniffing to ease the dope up into his sinuses.

"I know it," Weldon replied.

The buzzards he referred to were the other heroin addicts in the cellblock, who seemed to have radar antenna that let them know when someone had dope, and they would usually flock to the place where it was. Weldon and The Stepper had semidiscouraged them by trying to explain that flocking around was like telling on someone. When that didn't work, they tried subtly threatening them. But some would come anyway on some pretext or other.

Weldon looked at the old man standing before him, eyes becoming red and pupils pinned from the heroin, and saw himself in thirty years if he lived that long, which was highly unlikely.

The Stepper still had more hair than Bill Clinton, although it was snow-white. A small, neatly trimmed white mustache adorned his upper lip. It reminded Weldon of one that David Niven wore in old movies. The Stepper was sixty-seven years old now but didn't look a day over fifty.

He was a tall, rangy man, and the age showed more on the skin of his hands and arms, limbs that were covered with bluish old jailhouse tattoos that had faded over the years and run together in indecipherable symbols and letters.

His weather-beaten tanned face made his blue eyes as startling as poppies in mud. He was the best handball player in Soledad and spent a lot of time out on the windy yard. Beating youngsters at handball was his favorite pastime.

He was standing there cleaning the spoon with a piece of wet toilet paper he had dipped in cigarette ashes. The ashes scoured the burn marks off the spoon. When he was done he put the spoon back on the locker, reassembled the ballpoint pen, and followed Weldon out of the cell.

"Here they come," he told Weldon as they sat opposite each other at the card table and picked up the cards and began shuffling.

"I see 'em," Weldon replied.

Brian Ward and Jack McDaniels, the shot callers of the Duboce White Boys gang, were sauntering down their way from the other end of the crowded cellblock. Brian, dark-complected, and Jack, blond, both had large handkerchiefs, carefully ironed and folded, tied around their foreheads so that the tails of the handkerchiefs hung just so down their backs. The Aryan Brotherhood had initiated the fashion at Old Folsom Prison in the early seventies. It had been the cool look for gangs and wannabes ever since.

They were both medium-built men and weight lifters in their mid-twenties. They wore tank tops over their prison-issue denims. They reminded Weldon of two of Vern's fighting chickens making their way through a barnyard.

Weldon watched them approach and was thinking about how the Duboce White Boys, or DWB, became a band of vicious white thugs that originated on a street named Duboce in San Francisco that divides the Tenderloin from the old Mission District.

The members now were from all parts of the state. But Weldon knew the two men who had started the clique. Alan Younger, called "Young Alan," and Timothy Jones. They both lived in San Francisco and still called the main shots in the gang.

The rumor around the joint was that they now made a lucrative buck by charging illegal aliens tax for the right to deal tar heroin in San Francisco. If Weldon knew Alan Younger as well as he thought he did, the prison leaders like Brian and Jack weren't getting much, if any, of that swag. They reminded him more of panhandlers than gang leaders.

As much time as Weldon had done in his life, and it was a lot, he couldn't figure out all the configurations, motivations, and alliances of these new-breed gang members. "Dope babies and crackheads" is the way The Stepper described them, but there was a lot more to them than such a bottom-line analysis.

The three major gangs had come into being in California prisons in the late fifties and early sixties. The Mexican Mafia, the Aryan Brotherhood, and the Black Guerilla Family. These gangs had strong codes of honor they lived and operated by.

Though they were deadly and feared by convicts, at least everyone knew how to get along around them. Many of them had been friends of Weldon's and The Stepper.

But the newer gangs like the Duboce White Boys or the Sacramaniac Nazis were hard to understand or deal with. Most of the older gang members from the Mexican Mafia, the Aryan Brotherhood, and the Black Guerilla Family were locked down at Pelican Bay now and these upstarts held sway. They had no compunction about killing for small reasons, or pressuring people into sodomy and the like. Things that were never done in the old days.

Weldon and The Stepper held them in contempt but tried to live with them.

Brian and Jack sat down at the empty chairs on either side of the table as The Stepper dealt out a gin rummy hand.

"Looks like you two birds is doin' okay," Brian said.

"Yeah. Looks like you both full a that gow," Jack put in.

"We had a taste," Weldon replied, as he put his hand together and sorted the cards into pairs and suits.

"Hope you got a slam for me and Jack," Brian said with a smile.

"Could be I do," Weldon replied and placed a king on the discard pile.

"Hey, man, Little Joe Hamilton went home from Pelican Bay last week. I talked to him on the phone this morning at his mom's house," Brian said.

"Good for him," Weldon replied. Little Joe, like Brian and Weldon, was from Fresno. Weldon had known them both since they were kids. He liked Brian but had always felt uneasy around Little Joe, who had been sent to Pelican Bay on suspicion of committing an unsolved murder at Folsom Prison.

Little Joe was somewhat of a mad dog and a coward as well, Weldon expected. He had once killed his best friend because the gang had ordered him to do it. The Stepper told Weldon Little Joe gave him the creeps, a feeling Weldon shared.

"Well, he wanted you to hook him up with Vern and he ain't too happy you wouldn't even put in a word with your brother. He feels kind of disrespected about that."

"I don't hook people up with Vern, and Vern don't like dope addicts. Shit, he don't even like me most of the time and I can't help it if Little Joe feels disrespected."

"Yeah, if he's got all them bad feelings, he should hook up with a shrink," The Stepper added.

"You're burglarizing our conversation here, Stepper," Brian said, and he and Jack looked at the old man, who gazed steadily back at Brian.

"Here," Weldon said, taking a paper out of his pocket and sliding it over to Brian, who grabbed it.

"You guys go slam. There's enough there for you both and let me and Stepper finish our gin game."

"Okay," Brian said, as he and Jack got up to leave.

"But you know, Weldon, some of my tip gets mad that you never kick them down anything."

"That's your clique and your problem," Weldon replied.

"Okay, man, okay. And thanks, huh?"

"Don't mention it," Weldon said as they sauntered off.

"I can't get over how those guys still like to think they are taking something when you give them something," The Stepper said, watching Brian and Jack walk away.

"Ah, they know better. Besides that they always turn me on when they hit," Weldon said.

A voice came over the speaker announcing a ten-minute hourly movement. The cop unlocked the front door of the cellblock and convicts began streaming in and out. Weldon put his cards down and stood up.

"I'm going to the yard," he said.

"Okay," The Stepper said while gathering up the cards, then added, "You know, it's driving them guys crazy tryin' to figure out how you get that stuff in here, and I been livin' with you damn near a year and I ain't even figured it out."

"Keep working on it. You'll figure it out," Weldon replied and headed for the yard.

As he walked down the west gate ramp to the yard, he looked to his left at the corner gun tower. He could see the guard sitting up there behind his gun rack. There was a tower at every corner of the yard and nothing but open fields beyond the double fences.

A bank of pay telephones was on either side of the yard and convicts were lined up waiting. Even here the convicts were divided. North Mexicans and blacks used one bank of phones and south Mexicans and white gang members used the other. He thought about lining up to call Curly, but knew she wouldn't be home this time of day on Sunday.

He saw Yay-Yay walking around the track and moved onto the track in the opposite direction so that he would meet him. About forty convicts were walking around the running track in groups of two and three mostly. They all walked counterclockwise and some looked at Weldon funny as he went by them the other way, as if he were intruding.

"Hey, Cowboy," Yay-Yay said, when Weldon met him. Weldon had on a pair of cowboy boots when he met Yay-Yay in a holding tank as they were being booked into the Fresno county jail. Yay-Yay had called him Cowboy ever since. They had shared the same jail tank and went to Vacaville together for evaluation before being transferred to Soledad.

Yay-Yay was thirty-six years old, the same age as Weldon. He had been arrested for selling heroin in Fresno but was from El Paso, Texas. He'd only lasted a few months in Fresno before he got caught.

"Nothing but sneeches here," he told Weldon in the holding tank. He called snitches "sneeches."

Yay-Yay got six years for selling drugs and Weldon got sixteen for armed robbery. Not long after they arrived at Vacaville, Yay-Yay had killed another convict for stealing a pair of sneakers from him. Just went in the man's cell at breakfast time, stabbed him to death and took the shoes back.

He was arrested for that and plea-bargained for ten more years on a manslaughter charge. So now he was also doing a sixteen-year sentence. He was a tall, slim man who looked more Indian than Spanish and didn't look dangerous at all. But no one ever stole anything from him again. He had worn his recovered sneakers to court.

"I've got some cheeva for you and Big Mac. I'd like you to find him and give him his. I need to go in on the next movement and write Vern and Curly a letter," Weldon said as they walked along the track together.

"Man, you just made my day. Go on and give me Big Mac's. I think he's in the block, but I'll find him for sure," Yay-Yay said.

Weldon took a book of paper matches from his pocket and

handed it, along with the two papers, to Yay-Yay, who lit up a cigarette, passed the matches back, and kept the dope.

"You having any problem with them Dirty White Boys?" Yay-Yay asked.

"Nah, you know Brian is my homeboy. Some of 'em mumble because I don't give them nothing, but fuck that. I ain't Santa Claus," Weldon replied.

"Man, just remember no matter how tight you are with them guys they still owe their first loyalty to the gang," Yay-Yay said.

"I know that, man. They're all about halfway fuckin' crazy."

As Weldon walked back toward the cellblock, he was puzzled about Big Mac. Julius McFadden was his name and he was the shot caller for a gang called Monster Crips from Los Angeles. They called him Big Mac because he was six foot four and weighed three hundred pounds. Almost none of it fat, and he was quick as a cat on his feet. He worked out daily on the weight pile and bench-pressed 550 pounds. He was good-natured but could be mean as a snake if the need arose. He'd asked Weldon to meet him on this movement and never showed up. That wasn't like him at all.

He loved heroin and Weldon gave him a shot every time he got any. The few white and Mexican cons that knew of his friendship with Big Mac didn't appreciate him being friendly with a black, especially a black gang member, but Weldon had been around prisons all his life and knew a couple things about survival that they didn't know. He also understood a few things about the Crips that most people, including the authorities, were slow to pick up on.

They were more than just a ragtag bunch of gang bangers, which is how they had begun. They controlled the sale and distribution of crack cocaine all over the United States. Los Angeles Crips pretty much ran that show. They were the new kids on the block in organized crime and they were getting better at it each day. They were here to stay and they were building an enormous power base, whether anyone liked it or not.

In the real world he and Big Mac would be like CIA moles to one another. They were homeboys because Big Mac had lived in Fresno as a young man and, being dope fiends, they knew a lot of the same people and respected one another in spite of their race.

If a friend of Weldon's was in trouble or about to be killed, Big Mac would let him know. If Weldon knew of a black getting on thin ice, he would tell Big Mac. Often they could make these problems go away without violence.

In prison, relationships like this were called *working the corners* or being *plugged* in. Weldon worked the corners as well or better than anyone.

Big Mac came out the hallway door just as they closed it for end of hourly movement.

"Turn around, man, and walk with me. We got some talkin' to do," the huge man told Weldon. Weldon turned around and followed him back to the running track.

"I gave Yay-Yay a shot for you," he said as they reached the yard.

"I know, man. I saw him in the hallway and thanks, but, bubba, you got some real problems."

"I do?" Weldon asked, and felt a cold chill down his back. Big Mac didn't bullshit about things of this nature.

"Yeah, man, but look, I really love and trust you, brother, but I'm jumpin' way out on a limb with this one so you got to play it real close or they be some serious killin', it get out I let you know some shit like this. I'm sure you understand, but just remindin' you how touchy it be."

They were walking nonchalantly as if they were exchanging greetings, but Greg, an acquaintance of Weldon's, joined them and they both fell silent. In prison that's his cue to leave so he headed on around the track alone and they resumed the conversation.

"Hey, Mac, you know you can trust me, man. Let's get on with it."

"Okay, man. Don't get edgy. I do love your white ass to death or I wouldn't involve myself in this one. I got a man in the Dirty White Boys' gang likes that crack cocaine, so ever now and then he gets to talkin' about secret moves they got. He likes to impress me with his status in the gang and the more he impresses me the more crack cocaine I lay on him. You know, just like you do to me with that dog food you gives me from time to time like today," Big Mac said and flashed his gold-tooth smile on Weldon.

"Hey, man, I don't—" Weldon began, but Big Mac cut him off.

"Just jivin', man. Don't interrupt. They had a big meeting yesterday and they done put your brother Vern in the hat," he continued.

Weldon was so stunned he thought he misheard Big Mac.

"I don't think I heard you right, Mac. Run that by me again," he said.

"You heard me, man. Vern is in the hat and it's one a them top-priority moves," Big Mac told him.

"Why in the fuck would they want to kill Vern?" Weldon asked. It sounded too bizarre and incredible to be true.

In the old days when convicts wanted to kill someone, usually a stool pigeon, they would make five or six pieces of paper. Only one paper would have his name on it and each convict would draw a piece of paper from a hat or cap. If he got the paper with the name on it, he had to kill the victim. The mystery of it was that no one but the one who drew it knew who got the job. It was called *putting him in the hat,* and the saying had survived and made a strong comeback with prison gangs.

"I don't know any details, man. I just know who got put in the hat and I didn't even know you had a brother named Vern until this dude told me. That's why I came out here end of movement. I wanted to make sure him or his dogs don't see us talking. Let's kind of stay away from socializing until the smoke clears on this.

"I don't know what you gonna do, but I know you won't stand by and let it happen. So whatever moves you make, try and not let suspicion of who told you lead back to me. I ain't afraid of the motherfuckers, but I don't need a war with them right now. And I be jeopardizing my own road dogs!"

"I'll keep you covered, Mac. But, man, try and get some detail or maybe a time frame or something!" Weldon told him.

"Do what I can, homes, and thanks again for the gow. Later on," Big Mac said, and turned around to walk the opposite direction on the track, leaving Weldon with an almost physical burden of alarm. He went for the phones, thanking God the phone lines were short for this time of day.

Big Mac knew he wasn't in much danger of being exposed. Whichever gang member told him that would be killed by his own gang if it got out that he'd talked about a hit. That's why Weldon didn't ask the man's name. Big Mac wouldn't have told him anyway. That was his ace in the hole. The dude would never suspect him because Weldon wouldn't change attitude on him, not knowing who he was. Big Mac was no fool by a long shot.

But today he had carried his friendship with Weldon to a new level, past the point of no return and Weldon knew it as well as he did. Their relationship had switched to totally convict values, no longer the hybrid friendship blacks and whites enjoy. They were now into serious, no-bullshit trust, loyalty, and respect. The bottom line is they would stand, and if necessary die, together against anyone, blacks or whites, if their commitment to one another or their personal honor was challenged. That was a very big step to take with a white boy and Mac had to know that Weldon felt that as strong or stronger than he did.

Suddenly they were much more valuable and important to one another as human beings. Big Mac had no qualms about it, it was just so bizarre that things happen like that.

"Lord, I can't get a handle on this life and how to live it, but it sho be a lot of fun working the kinks out. Thank you for another day, and give me a bunch more!" he muttered to himself when he entered the cellblock. Yay-Yay was waiting on the second tier, smiling and waving him to come on up to his cell.

No one was home, but Weldon left a message for Vern. His tone of voice would let them know how important it was. Vern was going to have to take some precautions soon. He went in on the next movement still wondering why anyone would want to kill Vern. It didn't make sense. Weldon had never been involved with prison gangs and Vern didn't even fully understand what they were and how they operated.

CHAPTER 4

Vern pulled off the ditch bank into a clearing between the orchard and a farmhouse where about fifty other vehicles were parked and got that old feeling. There was something about a chicken fight that did to him what dope must do to a dope fiend. His blood began to flow more forcefully and he could feel it pound in his ears like a wave breaking on the seashore.

Several cars and pickups were pulled into a tight circle with trunks open and tailgates down selling fried chicken, beer, fried clams, hot dogs, and an assortment of cold drinks and chips. But most of those present were gathered farther on in a rough circle, some of them waving money and making bets with a little Filipino who walked among them with a small notebook in his hand. The fights had started already.

It was a peach farm fallen on hard times and rented out for chicken fights on weekends. There were only two roads out, one down the ditch bank, and the peach trees gave perfect cover from passersby.

"We're late," Melvin said as they disembarked from the pickup.

"Yeah, but not too late," Vern told him.

"I don't see how in the hell anyone can eat fried chicken at a chicken fight. Yuk!" Curly said, looking with disgust at the big tub of fried chicken sitting on the tailgate of an old red pickup.

"Let's get some clams," Paula said, walking toward the clam vendor's car. Vern lifted Gatorbait's carrying cage out of the pickup and walked around the cars toward the chicken fight. Melvin ambled along behind him carrying a leather case that contained his knives.

Old Pokini saw them coming and left the crowd to meet them. Pokini was half-Japanese, half–Filipino-Hawaiian. He had somehow taken over most of the chicken fights and labor camp gambling in the San Joaquin Valley. His control had improved things considerably in the world of local chicken fights and gambling. Everyone got paid off immediately and the games and fights were honest.

Pokini was a serious gambler who would take any edge he could get to win your money, but he wouldn't cheat. Rumor had it that he'd killed three men in Hawaii with a hatchet over cheating in one of his dice games. Vern figured that reputation was what had enabled him to take over around Fresno so easily. He was a small man and always went barefoot and wore a big straw hat to chicken fights. He looked like he'd be at home pulling a rickshaw in China. He still wore overalls and plaid shirts. For some reason he strove to look destitute.

"Hey, Vern, you got one chicken dere; I thot you finish wid da chicken," Pokini said in his singsong hybrid of Hawaiian, Tagalog, and English as they drew near.

"Yeah, Poky, I got one left so I thought I'd fight him today. If he gets killed, I don't have to worry about it anymore," Vern told him.

"Hey, Melvin, you maybe tie me some knife today? I pay good as anybody," Pokini asked Melvin.

"I'm tyin' Vern's chicken, but if it's another fight, I'll tie yours," Melvin replied.

"How much you gonna fight him for, Vern?"

Vern reached in his pocket and took out a wad of one-hundred-dollar bills.

"There's forty-eight hundred here. I'll fight him for that," Vern said.

"Well, I don' tink you fight him today; only one chicken left to fight because all booked up. You fight dis chicken he got to fight da Tasmanian Devil. Nobody else want dat chicken," Pokini said with a big smile as Vern stood holding the wad of bills out.

Vern wasn't showing the money to prove he had it but to prove he was betting his own personal money on his own chicken. It was sort of a game they played. Usually to old Pokini's advantage, somehow.

The Tasmanian Devil was Pokini's chicken and he had won seven fights in a row. Pokini was grooming him for the tournaments in Arizona and it was almost impossible to get anyone around the Valley to put a chicken against him. Chicken fighting is legal in Arizona and only the best chickens win there. The Devil was a roller. When chickens fight they usually run together and fly straight up and flail at each other with their spurs until one is mortally wounded. They can only stay up in the air for a few seconds before bouncing to the ground and flying up again.

But when The Devil flew up, he would roll back on his wings until only his spurs with their razor-sharp knives were toward the other chicken. As they sank toward the ground, the opposing chicken would be coming down on the spurs. It was like settling on a buzz saw. No chicken had yet survived the tactic. But Vern kept holding out the money.

"I'll fight him," he said.

"Put da money up, I collect afta da fight," Pokini said, and Vern put the money back into his pocket.

"We fight last," Pokini said and turned to go back to the crowd around the fights.

Vern handed the carrying cage to Melvin.

"Tie them knives good, Melvin. If he loses, I don't want it to be because a knife was loose."

Melvin took the cage and went off without replying. Vern was obviously too keyed up to hold a decent conversation with anyone. He wandered on up to the fighting circle where two men held their chickens as a little Filipino wandered around gathering the last of the bets. One chicken was red and the other cream-colored with rusty spots.

"Two hundred on the red chicken," the man next to Vern told the Filipino as he approached with his notebook.

"Two hundred red chicken," the little man said and made a notation in his notebook. No money ever changed hands until after the fight.

The bets were in and the two men squatting in the dirt holding their chickens moved in and let the chickens peck one another. They went into a frenzy of pecking because they couldn't get their spurs in action and the excitement of the crowd began to mount. The emotion was enhanced because many of the bettors were drunk or well on their way. Vern spotted two of the Mayhew brothers in the crowd. They were Vern's cousins and rawjaw hillbilly pimps. Vern despised both of them. They were famous for ganging up on people in fights and beating their women.

The crowd quieted some as the men backed off a few feet and let the chickens go. Pokini had stepped into the circle now and was acting as referee. The chickens ran straight at each other and flew up as they met, their spurs with the razor-sharp knives flailing furiously at one another. Caught up in the excitement, Vern found himself yelling for the white chicken, who was smaller but had plenty of fight in him.

They settled to the ground from the first pass with no mortal damage done to either chicken. The white had a patch of blood where he'd been nicked on one wing, but he ran at the red chicken and flew up again. This time the red chicken was slow on the rise and the knife on the white chicken's spur caught him flush on the neck, almost severing his head from his body. The red chicken hit the ground like a punctured balloon. He lay on his side as his spurs kept working by reflex, but they only dug at the ground and turned him around in a circle as the white chicken pecked at him victoriously.

"Get him up! Get him up!" Claude Mayhew screamed in a drunken rage. But the red chicken's owner saw it was no use and signaled the other man to pick up his chicken. The white chicken's owner grabbed his chicken and kissed him as the red pumped his life out into the dirt. The spurs now slowed to an intermittent spasmodic jerk.

Two helpers raked over the blood where the red chicken had fallen before his owner removed him. The little bet taker went around the circle paying off and collecting. Vern had always been amazed that they didn't collect the money up front. But he'd never seen anyone welsh on a bet. It just wasn't done.

Vern was too nervous about his own upcoming fight to watch another, so he turned away and met Curly walking up to the circle. He put his arm around her and turned back toward the pickup.

"You look lonely, girl," he said.

"Nah, just wanted to ask you something," she replied.

"Where's Paula?" he asked.

"She's in that dice game over there," Curly said, pointing to where a bunch of people were gathered. Paula was down on her knees right in the middle of them, waving a handful of money. Someone had a ten for a point and she was yelling, "Two to one he don't make it."

"Where in the hell did she get that money?"

"I gave her our party money to play on. She feels lucky," Curly told him.

"Curly, you're so fucking generous that you might starve us all to death one of these days. God help us if you decide to start giving pussy away instead of selling it," Vern told her as he reached into the cooler in back of the pickup and got a beer.

"Never happen, sport, but that's what I wanted to ask you. Do you think I should turn a couple of tricks here? I've had two good offers and if Gatorbait did lose and Paula lost, well . . . !"

"Forget it, girl," he said, putting his arm around her again. "Money ain't everything. You're going with me to watch Gatorbait send The Tasmanian Devil back to hell, where he belongs. Bring me some luck. The working day is over as of right now."

As they walked back by the dice game in the hot afternoon sunshine, they heard a roar of raucous argument and Paula's strident voice yelling, "Fuck you, Oren. That money was on the big eight!" The Filipino who ran the game was struggling to position himself between the plaintiffs and settle things down. Curly tried to stop, but Vern pulled her on.

"Let her handle it. She ain't gonna have me over there fighting a bunch of fucking drunks while my chicken is fighting," he told her.

Melvin was waiting near the circle holding Gatorbait under one arm like a mother would hold a baby. The knives were tied on him with little leather sheaths over them. Gatorbait was alternately gazing calmly then anxiously around.

"How's he look?" Vern asked.

"This sumbitch is itchin' for some action. I can feel his heart speed up every time we get near that ring. If I thought you was going to pay me, I'd bet on him myself."

"Shit, Melvin. You know I'll pay you!"

"Just joking, man. Don't be so fucking uptight. Only two things can happen now and we're up next. Tell you what I'll do. I'll take them empty cages for my pay. The ones at your place."

"You got 'em," Vern said as they walked back to the ring.

Melvin took the sheaths off the rooster's spurs and Vern took Gatorbait and held him tightly with both hands over the wings. He didn't have that expert touch with chickens that Melvin had. The chicken's heart did get to racing when they entered the killing ring, but so did his own. Pokini squatted, holding The Devil, a fierce-looking green-and-black chicken. Vern was relieved to see their sizes were dead even. He squatted down and put Gatorbait on the ground facing Pokini and The Devil.

"Les hook 'em up, brother," Pokini said and began walking toward Vern. Vern moved in and The Devil was already bobbing his head, trying to peck before they were close enough. Gatorbait's head was still and gently moving like a cobra watching a flute player. But Vern could tell by the chicken's temperature and heartbeat that its attention was focused on The Devil.

"God, don't let him run," Vern said to himself. It was his first fight, and now and then a fighting rooster would turn tail and run on his maiden outing. When a chicken ran, the spectators would hem it in, catch it, then present it to the owner, who would immediately wring its neck and concede the fight. It filled Vern with dread to think about having to wring Gatorbait's neck. But he would do it if he had to. Yet it wasn't a real fear. If he wouldn't run from a gator, he wouldn't run from a tiny dinosaur.

The roosters pecked and clucked at one another for a few seconds and Vern and Pokini backed up. Gatorbait was hard to hold now. He was digging at the ground and straining to get at The Devil. Vern looked up at Curly who gave him a thumbs-up. He looked at Pokini, who nodded, and they let the roosters go.

Vern had a hard time registering what happened next. For one reason his view from Gatorbait's rear wasn't quite as good as the yelling spectators had from the sidelines. The betting had been extremely heavy in favor of The Devil and the crowd roared when Pokini let him go.

Gatorbait's feet left the ground by the time he'd taken two steps and he covered half the distance to The Devil in the air and seemed to be gaining altitude all the way. He flew so fast and furiously that his wings sounded like a deck of cards being shuffled.

The odd move startled The Devil, who altered his own rush trying to meet Gatorbait. He didn't start up himself until Gatorbait was right on him and his feet only got about three or four inches off the ground. One of Gatorbait's thrusting spurs, armed with a knife as sharp as a single-edge razor blade, hit The Devil in the center of his beak where it joined his head. Curly and Melvin saw a bright gout of blood spurt in the sunshine.

Gatorbait landed on the other side of the fallen Devil near Pokini. He turned to make another pass, saw The Devil down, and ran over to peck at the dying chicken. Vern initially thought The Devil just rolled early and was taking the low ground. But Curly and Melvin jumping up and down, slapping each other's backs, and the stunned silence of the crowd cleared his vision somewhat. The Devil had done his last roll. Vern picked Gatorbait up and began stroking and calming him.

Pokini walked over shaking his head. He glanced at The

Devil, who was dead as a doornail. Vern felt elated that Gatorbait hadn't received a scratch. He stood there stroking and calming Gatorbait until Pokini finished counting out forty-eight hundred dollars and handing the bills to him.

Then he looked up the road and saw trouble coming. Oren Mayhew was walking fast toward the chicken ring. Actually he was lurching along under the influence of a river of booze. Paula was walking fast right behind him and Vern knew immediately what the trouble was. He handed Gatorbait to Melvin.

"Take him to the cage and, Curly, you go with him and I mean right now. I don't want you to contribute anything to this bullshit headed down the road."

She didn't argue and she and Melvin passed by Mayhew just as he reached the chicken ring. Paula tried to engage Curly in conversation as they passed, but Curly just mumbled "Later" and kept walking.

Vern was so mad at Paula he had knots in both jaws, but he wouldn't be able to show the anger at her until they got home or somewhere private. She had obviously mouthed off at this big stupid asshole and the idiot was now seeking justice from Vern. He looked at Mayhew's fat, sweating red face. The man had dirty-blond uncut hair that really looked greasy and sideburns that came all the way down his fat jaws and flared out along the jawbone. The only place Vern had seen sideburns like that was on a vaquero in a forty-year-old Mexican movie.

"Vern, you got to straighten this bitch out," Mayhew grunted.

"You're the bitch, you motherfucker," Paula told him.

"See there, man!" Mayhew yelled, pointing indignantly at her.

"Paula, shut up. Don't say anything else," Vern told her as calmly as he could manage. Over her shoulder he saw Oren's brother, Claude, walking toward them.

"Man, she called me a punk and a gimp and everything else in front of all them people. She's your old lady so you got to smack her for that. Either you smack her ass or I'm going to do it myself," Oren said with his fat chest heaving, staring defiantly at Vern.

"Well, Oren, I guess you are right about that, so you go ahead and smack her," Vern said. "But you'd better be careful not to touch her while you are doing it, because if you ever touch her in any way, I will cut your fucking head off."

"What the fuck is that supposed to mean?" Oren blustered, still trying to hold on to his bluff.

"Let's do it this way. Just walk over there and touch her. Put one finger on her and I'll show you exactly what I mean," Vern said, and put his hand in his pocket on the hawkbill pocketknife he always carried, as Claude came up alongside his brother.

"Oren, let's go. Just dummy up and let's get out of here. We can think about it later," Claude said to his brother. Out of the corner of his eye, Vern saw Melvin enter the crowd again and felt relieved about that. The chicken fights were over, but most of the spectators were hanging on, probably hoping to see a human knife fight.

Oren stood there for a moment, then he went on out of the crowd mumbling.

Vern put his arm around Paula's shoulders and she put hers around his waist. Melvin followed them to the pickup.

"I'm sorry, Vern. I know I shouldn't put you in that position, but I can't stand that fat bastard," Paula said.

"How'd you do in the game?" Vern asked her.

"I won nine hundred dollars. That's what the prick was really mad about. I made a four and broke him."

"Man, we had a good day here," Vern said as they approached

the pickup. He looked at Gatorbait in his cage still dancing around and excited and all the anger at Paula drained out of him. Curly was sitting in the pickup fiddling with the radio.

"Get the camera out, Curly," Vern yelled and took Gatorbait out of his cage and brought him to the back of the pickup. The smile came easy for the pictures. Curly never had to tell him to say cheese once.

CHAPTER 5

On the ride back to Fresno, Curly broke out the bottle of downers Melvin had brought and she and Paula ate two each.

"Don't get carried away on those things," Vern warned them.

Paula and Curly loved to get stoned on downers. The pills Melvin sold were Tuinal, a very strong sleep-inducing sedative. Vern let them take pills only on their days off, and so far they had never broken his rule.

"Are you mad at me, Vern?" Paula asked as the pills began to mellow her out.

"I don't think so. I mean, he said all you called him was a punk and a gimp and I don't see where you lied about either one."

"What's a gimp?" Melvin asked from behind Curly.

"A pimp without a whore," Curly told him.

"Oren don't have a whore right now, does he?" Vern asked.

"No, June left him before he could beat her to death," Paula replied.

"Then he's a gimp and for sure a punk," Vern told her. "I don't see how I can get mad at you for telling the truth."

"Man, I don't think there could be a sorrier son of a bitch in the world than a pimp without a whore," Melvin reasoned, and they all laughed.

As they rode along in the late-afternoon sunshine, Vern looked at the passing landscape of the 99 highway. Old grain mills and cotton gins now standing fallow and forlorn as housing developments sprang up around them. He felt nostalgic for the fields he and Paula once worked. But having a good chicken helped his melancholy feeling.

They were in a serious party mood by the time they got back to Fresno. Everyone wanted to stop by the Sagebrush Club next to the fairgrounds, but they had to take Gatorbait home first. Vern put him out with food and water in one of the cages he had sold to Melvin.

"You know, that fucker took off flying like a quail when you let him go, Vern," Melvin remarked. "I never saw a chicken get up that fast."

"I didn't either, but I hope he can do it again," Vern said as they got ready to load up in his town car and head for the Sagebrush Club. On his way out, Vern saw that his answering machine was flashing. When he checked, there was a message from Weldon, who almost never left a message if no one was home. Vern played it twice before erasing it: "Vern, be very careful and get someone up here soon. I have to see you. It's urgent!" was all Weldon said, but Vern could hear something almost like fear in his voice. It wasn't like Weldon to worry about anything. As Vern climbed into the car, he told everybody that Weldon had called. He kept the message to himself.

Dannie Martin

Curly had been thinking about Weldon all day. She liked to go visit him at least once a month on Sunday. She loved him to death, but their relationship was strange. All she'd ever wanted to be was a prostitute and that's all he didn't want her to be. Not while she was with him, anyway.

He'd made her stay home and keep house while he went around smuggling and selling dope, then pulling robberies when things got bad. She had been with him over a year before she found out he was a serious heroin addict. By that time she was hopelessly attached to him. After his arrest she moved in with Vern and Paula and started hustling again and Weldon never complained about that.

She thought about the lieutenant she'd met at the prison while visiting Weldon. The majority of prison guards are young men fresh from the military or criminal justice classes. The one thing they all have in common is an overriding desire for pussy. And they are not choosy.

When prisons are built, convict wives move nearby to be close to their husbands. Pretty soon after that, a bar or nightclub springs up in the neighborhood where the wives and the guards hang out. Quid pro quo is the name of the game. Sancho's Place was the Soledad version and that's where Curly had met the lieutenant. After the first time it was always the same with him. He would come to her motel room on Saturday night. When she opened the door to his knock, he would be saying in a frantic, breathless voice, "Get your clothes off; get your clothes off."

She would disrobe quickly and he would push her back on the bed. Then he'd get down on his knees beside the bed and eat her pussy while he jacked off onto the side of the bed. Soon as he was done, he'd get up, arrange his clothes, pick up the heroin from a nightstand, and leave without a word. He did the exact same thing every time and it never took over three minutes.

He had been so easy to corrupt that she was almost ashamed of herself, but it saved her a lot of trouble trying to sneak the drugs to Weldon in the visiting room. She only took him two grams a month, so he never had enough to get hooked inside prison. He seemed satisfied with that arrangement.

Although Vern would let her keep money to do things for Weldon, he would have no part of the heroin. The first time she told him Weldon wanted some, he had said, "You do what you have to do. I hate that shit. I don't want anything to do with it."

Weldon would only have to do half his sentence if he stayed out of trouble. The seven years he had left to do seemed like a long time, but it would go by. She wondered how she would feel by then. Life with Vern and Paula was about as good as it had ever been for her.

Her reverie was broken when Vern pulled into the parking lot of the Sagebrush. She and Paula took another of the pretty little blue-and-white Tuinals. Once again she wondered why people called them rainbows. When she got out of the car, she was stumbling a little already and took Paula's arm. She loved the rubbery, devil-may-care feeling that the pills gave her. Paula had to be watched closely while she was under the influence. Rainbows tended to make her argumentative and ready for a fight.

Paula and Curly grabbed a table near the dance floor while Vern and Melvin went to the bar for drinks. Tom Jernigan, a local country singer, was performing and the band was just warming up.

The Sagebrush was the hangout for many of the thieves, pimps, whores, and assorted dope dealers and hustlers in Fresno. There had been some monumental fights and a shoot-out or two in the bar and parking lot. The police were continually agitating to close the place but so far had been unsuccessful. The owners didn't really welcome this crowd—they were just stuck with it.

When Vern and Melvin walked back to their table carrying the drinks, a man was with them. He looked to be about twenty-five and was short and lean with a good build. He had wavy black hair and was wearing Levi's and a tank top. His upper arms and chest were adorned with an assortment of tattoos.

"This is Little Joe, a friend of Weldon's who just got out," Vern announced when they reached the table with the drinks.

Curly and Paula shook hands with the man and Curly felt Paula's knee hit hers under the table. The man was good-looking, with big green eyes that contrasted nicely with his black hair. But Curly got an uneasy feeling about him. He never actually smiled as he was being introduced.

The band kicked off with a fast tune and Vern and Paula made for the dance floor. They were two of the best dancers in Fresno. When they really got wound up, people sometimes just stopped and watched them.

"Care to dance?" Little Joe asked Curly, holding out his hands.

"Why not?" She smiled, taking his hand, and followed him to the crowded dance floor.

He danced away from her for a moment, then pulled her to him and began grinding against her. She felt uncomfortable with the move but tried to go along with it.

"I just got out after six years," he said.

"That's awful," she replied and tried to get some distance between them. He seemed more intent on rubbing bellies than dancing. He pulled her back against him forcefully.

"I haven't fucked yet. I thought you might take care of me," he breathed in her ear.

"That's your problem, not mine," she answered, still trying to get some distance between them.

"Well, you turn tricks, baby, and I got the money," he said, pulling her back against him.

"This is my day off, and even if it wasn't, I don't turn tricks with friends of Weldon or Vern, so if you're wanting to fuck, man, you're sitting at the wrong table," she told him just as the song ended. He tried to argue, but she ignored him as they walked back to their table.

"Care to dance?" he asked Paula as she and Vern got back.

"Sure," she said, and they took off for the dance floor.

Vern downed a double shot of Wild Turkey and told Curly "C'mon!" She went back to the dance floor and settled in his arms for a slow one. As they danced she glanced over at Paula and saw that Paula was having the same type of conversation with Little Joe that she had just had. She hoped that Vern wouldn't notice what was going on. Curly hated arguments and fighting and there had already been enough of that for one day.

When they all got back to the table, Little Joe grabbed his drink.

"I'm going back to the bar. See you all later," he said.

"Fucking creep," Paula whispered in Curly's ear as they sat down.

"What's wrong with him?" Melvin asked as Little Joe departed.

"I believe it has to do with an unrequited hard-on," Paula replied, but Melvin was no longer listening. He'd just spotted what looked like a lonely housewife sitting down at the bar.

"Uh oh," he said, and got up quickly, grabbing his drink and heading for the bar. Melvin could spot a lonely housewife a mile away.

"I don't believe that asshole is a friend of Weldon's," Paula told Curly as another woman took Vern back to the dance floor.

"I don't either," Curly responded.

Curly and Paula weren't the only ones eyeing Little Joe. Bill Jefferson and Robert White had been assigned from the Los Angeles station to watch Little Joe's every move, and they had been with him ever since he left the prison gate. Little Joe had known he would probably be followed and had spent a minimal amount of time trying to figure out who might be on his tail.

He had noticed the two black men a couple of times but hadn't really thought that they might be heat. Now even as he spent all his energy trying to fuck either Paula or Curly, Little Joe did have enough sense left to finally get a make on his tail when the two black men took a table near them and tried to act as if they were having fun.

Only a few minutes later, it seemed that everyone in the bar was dog-eyeing the two men. The Sagebrush was obviously not a place that welcomed blacks and some of these drunken city cowboys looked to have murder in their eye. A man at a nearby table asked loudly enough to be heard over the band, "What are these niggers doing in here?"

Jefferson and White acted as if they didn't hear the remark, but Robert leaned over to Bill and said quietly, "Man, we fucked up coming in here. Even the bartender is burning us, and I'm pretty sure the little slimeball just knocked us off as his tail."

"Yeah. Go call the boss and tell him we got to back off and get a change up. But get it done and let's get the hell out of here. This shit could turn into a rodeo real quick and if it does, I'm gonna be the most serious clown that ever stepped in horseshit!"

"I'll be right back," Bill replied and hurriedly went for the phone.

The force he worked for was so secretive they didn't even have a building or suite of rooms to work out of. Right now, headquarters was a trailer parked at the Orange County police department.

"Back up, but try and keep him in some kind of visual contact. I'll have someone there by morning. But get the hell out of that place right now," their supervisor told Bill.

They gulped their drinks and tried to find a decent place to observe Li'l Joe from. They parked down the street near a closed auto-parts store, but by 2:30 A.M. they realized they had lost him.

For Vern the night degenerated into an orgy of drinking, dancing, falling down on the dance floor, and laughing. It was just what Curly and Paula needed after a hard week's work. They paid no more attention to Little Joe or anyone else unless it was a dancing or drinking partner.

At two o'clock, when the bar closed, Vern somehow got them loaded up in the backseat of the Town Car, where Paula and Curly fell asleep in each other's arms. Melvin was long gone with his lonely housewife and Vern slowly but surely drove them home, only to find the unwelcome sight of a dirty blue '78 Dodge van with sliding doors sitting in the driveway. Curly's brother, Sam Perry, came climbing out of it just as they drove up.

"Hey, Vern, I'm broke, man, and need to stay with you all for a few days," he told Vern.

Vern then made what he would remember as one of the worst mistakes in his life. But at least he could say he was drunk when he did it.

"Take the extra bedroom, man. Stay as long as you like," he told Sam. Then one at a time he carried Curly and Paula into the house and laid them on the bed. After he put Paula down, he fell in with them. He didn't even have enough sense left to take off his boots. The extra bedroom was just off the living room and was equipped with a TV, VCR, and a nice small bed. Melvin was about the only one who ever used it.

CHAPTER 6

Vern was going to come up with Curly on the weekend, but meantime Weldon was going crazy trying to figure out what the hell could be going on. If he couldn't discover the why of the matter, he wasn't sure that he could persuade Vern to take proper precautions. Vern liked to believe that everyone had a reason for their actions. He was totally unaware of the irrationality of gang members.

To top it all off, Brian Ward had come around and told Weldon that Vern and the girls had disrespected Little Joe in a bar in Fresno. Weldon had already talked with Curly on the phone and on a visit about that night. She said Joe had called and apologized and took her, Paula, and Vern out to dinner and acted very nice. He said all that time had made him crazy for sex and that it wouldn't happen again. She said Vern had thought that pretty good of Little Joe. He said not many men were willing to admit being an ass and apologize to women.

Weldon saw it another way. Little Joe had probably been assigned to kill Vern but didn't know it until after that night. He'd been getting back in their good graces so that he could get a better shot at him.

Big Mac finally cleared things up for Weldon on Thursday. "Man, some bikers think he snitched on a crank lab they had up there by Mariposa. A Dirty White Boy named Tank that dealt a lot of their stuff used to trick Paula. Some biker broad heard him braggin' to Paula about how good the product they makin' was. They think Vern got their lab took down by the narcs and they leanin' on the DWB to take him out. I ain't askin' the dude no more. That's all I get for you there," Big Mac told him.

The whole deal came clear to Weldon. He remembered Tank Crowell well. Tank was a main trick of Paula's and had lavished gifts of jewelry and money on her. Even Vern was impressed at the amount of money she got off the guy. He would sometimes pay her two thousand dollars to spend the weekend with him.

He was getting rich dealing crank that a crew of Gypsy Jokers was making near Fresno. They had a good-sized operation, turning out twenty to thirty pounds a week. Tank was in love with Paula and wanted to impress her as being a high-rolling gangster so he told her everything about the operation, but she wrote most of it off as bullshit.

Only after the lab was busted did she realize he was telling the truth. The DWB murdered Tank not long after the bust came down when they realized from news accounts how much crank he was moving and how much money he'd been holding out on them. Many of them disliked Paula because they figured all the cash she took off of Tank rightfully belonged to them.

What really made Vern look bad now was that just before the bust on the lab, Paula had got loaded on downers, tricked a vice squad cop, then got so mad that he'd fucked her before he arrested her that she'd cut him with a little pearl-handled knife that Vern had given her for her birthday. The cut was superficial, but the *Fresno Bee* newspaper made it look bad: "Prostitute stabs, assaults vice cop!"

She'd had to fuck two high-powered attorneys, the DA, and a judge to get the charges dropped. The DA had recommended in open court that the case be dismissed and the judge had agreed. To the bikers busted with the lab that looked sort of strange. They figured Vern had cut a deal on them to get her charges dropped. The reason they suspected Vern was that the transcripts referred to the confidential informant as a male. It wouldn't be anything new for a pimp to rat on someone to get his whore out of trouble. Anyone who knew Vern well would know better. That wasn't his style at all.

Weldon knew Little Joe would do Vern if they told him to. He'd killed two convicts already for them. He loved the killer respect he got from everyone in the gang and from many more convicts who weren't in the gang. Vern was in grave danger. Weldon hoped that when he laid things out in detail that Vern would take notice and get busy putting some protection on himself. Vern couldn't just sit around and wait for something to happen. Weldon believed they should make a move before the gang did and hoped he could convince Vern that he knew what he was talking about.

The Stepper was in the hole again for one of his stunts. But that was okay with Weldon. He had decided not to tell the old man about the contract on Vern. Not that he didn't trust him, but why burden him with the problem and cause him to be uneasy around the gang members? The cell was quiet now and Weldon needed time to think.

The following Sunday Vern and Paula came to visit. Weldon's heart beat faster when he saw them and he hugged Paula close.

"Vern, you've got to do something. There's a hit out on you for sure, man. They plan to knock you out of the box and I'm sure Little Joe is the one who is going to do it," Weldon told him as soon as they sat down.

"Weldon, why in the hell would they want to kill me? I've never done anything to them." Vern sounded totally exasperated.

"Well, they think you did. They think Tank told Paula all about their lab and that you gave it up to get her out of that assault on a vice cop."

"That's bullshit!" Vern exploded. "She fucked every fucking judge in Fresno to get out of that fucking case!"

"*Shhh,* hold your voice down," Weldon told him, looking around to see if any gang members were near. He was glad they had come on a Sunday, when the visiting room was full and noisy.

"Weldon, I think you're just paranoid. You sure you haven't been using any crank or anything?" Vern said in a lower voice.

"I mean, what we don't understand here is how would a nigger know what the DWB gang is up to? It don't make enough sense," Paula put in.

Weldon was getting mad and had to take a few deep breaths before he replied.

"No, I'm not paranoid and I believe what that 'nigger,' as you call him, says as much as I would believe God if he told me personally. One thing I know for sure, there's no way to straighten out this shit because their indictment listed a 'confidential informant,' and there's no way to find out for sure who it was. The judge can't even find out.

"Vern, listen to me. You've got to kill Little Joe before he kills you. That's all there is to it. We've got to let them know they aren't playing any kids' games here. You knock Little Joe off and I'll stab a couple of them in here. We got to move before they do. Don't you understand me, Brother?" Weldon almost pleaded.

Vern still wasn't convinced. "Maybe I should just talk to Little Joe, you know, confront him about it," Vern said.

"Goddamn, no, Brother!" Weldon exploded this time. "We can't tip our hand. It's the only edge we have. You confront the little snaky bastard and they know we know. Then they'd get paranoid. I'd have to start watching my back in here and they would put another member on you that we didn't know about. You only have two choices: either kill Little Joe or wait around until he kills you. That's the bottom line. It's that serious, man." Weldon spoke as forcefully as he could.

"Well, shit, Weldon, if Vern kills Little Joe, then wouldn't we all be in a war with the DWB? Wouldn't they just send someone else to do the job anyway? If this is true, isn't all this bullshit a dead end anyway?" Paula asked.

"No, because as soon as Vern takes out Little Joe, I'll hit Brian and Jack, the two who probably ordered it. These gangs operate on paranoia and that will get them so paranoid they will think someone in the clique is telling us everything. Pretty soon, they will get to speculating and probably killing each other just like they are speculating on you. That's another reason people fear them so much. The crazy fucks are liable to do anything," Weldon insisted.

There was no way for Weldon to figure how the DWB would move because they didn't operate like the old gangs. Things had just changed too much.

"Okay. I'm going to think it over, and meanwhile keep a good eye on things," Vern said. He was very torn about the whole deal. Part of him wanted to heed Weldon's advice, but another part of him wanted to think it was bullshit. He had to do some serious thinking before he just up and killed someone.

"Don't think about it long, Brother. Just do it, and as soon as you make your move have Curly call the lieutenant and let me know so I can move on Brian and Jack before they know what's going on," Weldon said as they got up to leave.

"What do you think, hon?" Paula asked Vern as they drove home.

"I don't know, babe. I've never dealt in paranoid shit like this before. It's all prison gang stuff and I can't sort it out. I do know it has me awful worried and I may just take Little Joe out to be safe. Meanwhile, you keep that pistol in your purse loaded and cocked and take it everywhere you go," he replied.

"I will, hon, but I just can't believe this fucking bullshit. We've never snitched on anyone in our lives. One of them fucking gang members will turn snitch before we do," she said.

Vern knew she was right, but dealing with these assholes, right wasn't always right and wrong was sometimes the right thing to do. This was the most frustrating, worrisome shit he'd ever been involved in.

But as he drove away from the prison, looking out at the fields of sugar beets and other verdant growth that stretched for miles, it made him feel better. The condo folks hadn't made it to Salinas yet.

CHAPTER 7

Curly's brother, Sam, was driving Vern nuts. He'd been in the house now over a month and a half and Vern had only seen him two or three times. Many nights around two in the morning, Vern would hear the old Dodge van start up and take off. He would often come back a day or two later and lock himself in his room and watch TV for hours on end before he took off again. He was a crank freak and kept very odd hours.

It was getting over into October now. Vern had known about the hit on him for a month now and he didn't like Sam being in the way.

Sometimes at three or four in the morning, they would hear him in the kitchen fixing himself a sandwich. What bothered him was that Sam had never said how long he planned to stay and never bought any groceries or even offered any help at all to the household. Vern tolerated it because he was Curly's brother and he knew Curly loved him, but his patience was wearing thin.

The blatant disrespect was the problem. Yet this stuff with the gang had him distracted now to the point he couldn't deal with anything. It kept him confused and disoriented. He got to thinking he should just kill Little Joe, but he still wasn't convinced and it was hard to kill someone over a rumor. The guy seemed genuinely nice.

But the rest of his life was going so good that it was hard to believe. Gatorbait had won three more fights since his first outing. He was the most beautiful fighting machine Vern had ever seen. The last chicken he'd fought had been a good flyer also and he and Gatorbait had looked like two hummingbirds in the air. Gatorbait had finally flown to one side, then came in at an angle and cut the chicken's throat with his spurs. Vern had fought him for six thousand, ten thousand, and fifteen thousand. His bankroll now stood at close to fifty thousand, including the money that Paula and Curly had made. Things were looking up.

Paula and Curly had pretty well worked their way out of the labor camps and Vern was proud of them. They still had one Filipino camp that they worked twice a week, more from sentimental purposes than anything. But mainly these days they worked calls only.

They had a big book of numbers of individual tricks. Either Curly or Paula would get up early and call the numbers in their book until noon, making appointments for the afternoon.

They were averaging two thousand a week each, and Vern told them that's all they had to make each week. Paula was beginning to make noise about filing some kind of income tax and Vern knew she was right about that. He made plans to see a tax man before the year was over.

On a Wednesday night, as Vern went in to bed late, he met Sam coming out of the guest room. Curly's brother had her hair and eye color, but the resemblance ended there. He had a nasty red scar that went from his forehead through his left eyelid and down to his chin, the result of a head-on collision where he went through his own windshield. The scar lent him a sinister appearance. He'd never worked, and as far as Vern could see, he was just a crank freak, petty thief, and professional houseguest.

"You've been here quite a while now, Sam," Vern said to him when they met in front of the extra bedroom.

"Oh, yeah, and thanks, man. I'll be movin' on this weekend," Sam replied and Vern let it go at that.

On that Saturday Vern was fighting Gatorbait again, but they had to drive all the way to Stockton. Curly and Paula were still asleep when Melvin showed up around six in the morning. Vern made them some coffee, and locked up the house, then loaded Gatorbait up in Melvin's pickup and they took off.

"Have you been feeding that alligator?" Melvin asked Vern when they were under way.

"Oh, that son of a bitch," Vern replied. "I bought him some chickens from Safeway and threw them in there and he wouldn't eat them. They laid there till they were full of maggots. Ugh, it was gross. So now I've been paying a couple of kids for carp they catch out of the canal. I give them two bucks apiece for big carp and they bring me about ten a week. I put them in there live and the gator eats them."

"Maybe you ought to buy him some live chickens," Melvin said.

"Fuck that. He can eat fish," Vern declared.

Melvin fiddled with the radio until he homed in on a good country station and settled back in the driver's seat. Like Vern, he never fastened his seat belt unless he was drunk. Twice he'd passed out before he got it fastened or had the car started, so it seemed like a good idea.

Vern sat there watching Melvin as they drove along toward

Stockton. Really looking at him for the first time in a good while. It was easy to be around Melvin and not pay much attention to him. That was the attitude Melvin seemed to encourage. In social situations he just sort of hovered around the fringe and never made a play for attention.

Vern had heard Paula and Curly both talk about what a good-looking man Melvin was. He was short, about five foot, six or seven, with dark brown hair and eyes that were the light blue you sometimes see in blocks of ice. He was stockily built and looked good in his clothes. His teeth were beautiful and he had a ready smile that showed them frequently.

"Baby Face," Curly sometimes called him. She and Paula loved to tease Melvin. But as sweet and gentle as he looked, Vern knew he was as tough as a corncob. He'd done his share of fighting with some good-sized opponents and Vern didn't remember any he had lost. Red and Casper, the two oldest Mayhew brothers, had pulled knives on Melvin one night in the parking lot of the Sagebrush. They both now had identical little bowl-like depressions in their foreheads where Melvin dented their skulls with a ball peen hammer. Melvin told Vern it was better than buying advertising on a billboard saying "Leave me alone."

Riding down the road this morning, Vern suddenly realized that everything he knew about Melvin was only what he'd observed. Melvin had never told him much about his private life. It seemed odd, because they had been good friends for close to a dozen years. Vern knew Melvin was a thief and must be a good one. He'd never been arrested.

When Paula first began hustling, she'd been seventeen and Vern was sixteen. When they left home they spent the first couple of weeks with a second cousin of Vern's in Parlier named Nelljo. She was Melvin's aunt, and after they had been there a week, Melvin showed up. He'd left his folks in Oklahoma and never went back. He was two years younger than Vern and all he ever said about Oklahoma was "I had a little problem back there."

Vern finally managed to buy an old '56 Chevy and he and Paula moved to Fresno and began staying in motels in order to be closer to the labor camps she worked. When they left Nelljo's Melvin had found work in a fruit-packing shed. He worked there for three years until Nelljo died, and that was the only job Vern ever knew of him having besides tying knives on fighting chickens. Nelljo's son Onnie had taught Melvin how to tie knives before he got himself stabbed to death in a barroom brawl. Vern didn't know who had taught Melvin to steal drugs, but they taught him well.

A few years ago Melvin had bought the house and ten acres near Parlier that Nelljo had lived on from her two daughters. One of them told Paula that Melvin paid for the land in cash but had asked them to work out a payment plan to where it looked like he was making monthly mortgage payments. Although it was fertile land, Melvin never grew anything there. Not even a garden. He'd torn down the old house Nelljo lived in and moved a double-wide mobile home onto the property. Onto that he'd built a shed for a washer and dryer and another room that contained weight-lifting equipment and a hot tub.

Vern never knew of him having a woman there over two days, and four fierce mongrel dogs seemed to be his only constant company. There was not much mystery about the pills he sold. They were all pharmaceutical drugs with the labels neatly scraped off. He was very careful and particular about who he sold drugs to but always seemed to have whatever any customer asked for. As far as Vern knew, Melvin never took any drugs other than a few uppers if he had to drive a long way. Vern had to respect the fact that Melvin had never spent a day in jail, or even been accused of anything.

One thing was obvious. Melvin idolized Vern for some reason or other. Vern had always known that. He had sometimes suspected also that Melvin was secretly in love with Paula. Like this morning, Melvin had probably gotten up as early as 4:30 to be at Vern's by 6:00, but made no complaint when Vern asked him to do it. Vern sometimes felt embarrassed at the devotion Melvin showed him, but at the same time he understood it was something he needed. He was trying to get up the nerve to ask Melvin some personal questions when Melvin looked over at him and said, "What are you lookin at, Vern?"

"I don't know. I ain't figured out what it is yet," Vern replied.

"Well, maybe if you got over here and drove, it would clear your head some."

"Hell, pull over. I'll drive awhile."

Melvin pulled to the side and got out. Vern slid over under the wheel, and when Melvin got back in, he set Gatorbait's cage between them on the seat.

"This may be the last time I see this old boy and I'm getting a little bit attached to him," Melvin said when he put Gatorbait down.

"I guess he's got a tough fight today, but I think he will win," Vern said.

"I must think so too because I brought four thousand to bet on him myself and you know I don't ever bet on no chicken. But a tough fight? Vern, I swear, for a chicken owner, you are unclear on the fucking concept."

"How's that?" Vern asked.

"Man, Pokini is gonna run a chicken at you today that an ostrich might not be able to beat. Don't think he ain't still stung about The Devil going down. But there's only three fights out here today and these are the toughest roosters in the country. I'm pretty sure you're matched up with old Rojo, and he killed ten chickens in a tournament in Arizona last year."

"Then why don't you put that four grand on Old Rojo?" Vern asked.

"'Cause I never heard of him whipping no alligator in that tournament," Melvin said, and they whooped and slapped a high five like a quarterback and an end who had just hooked up for a touchdown.

They pulled off the road in Stockton at a place called French Camp. The house they pulled up in front of had a huge backyard that ended at the river. It was a small place for a chicken fight, but there were very few people here. This one was by invitation only. Melvin whistled and glanced over at Vern when they saw a shiny herd of Cadillacs, Lincolns, and Mercedes parked around the house.

"Neighbors will probably think we're the hired help here," Melvin told Vern as he lifted Gatorbait out of the truck.

Their host was a huge Samoan from Hawaii who drove a new Lincoln. Vern had met him at a few chicken fights and knew he was Pokini's partner in some way or other. His name was Tai. He was well over six feet tall and weighed around three hundred pounds, and none of it looked like fat. He was one of the most formidable-looking men Vern had ever seen. He came walking across the yard with Pokini to meet them.

"Hey, Vern, Melvin, we hope you hungry. We make da kine luau. Pork sweet to da bone," he said while a Filipino houseboy took Gatorbait from Melvin and went around the house.

They all walked around back where the household help were unearthing a pig that had been roasting underground. It had been wrapped in what looked like burlap and banana leaves.

Two tables near the pit were laden with an assortment of delicious-looking fruits and vegetables. The houseboy came back and handed Vern and Melvin each a tall glass containing what tasted like a piña colada. Pokini never introduced them individually to the crowd of mostly old Oriental men. They just smiled and nodded at everyone present. They were the only non-Orientals there and there were no women at all in the crowd. Not even among the help.

"Goddamn, man. This might be worth four thousand dollars," Melvin said after biting into a big steaming slab of pork the houseboy had handed him on a wooden plate.

Vern thought the meat was about the best he'd ever tasted. It was tender and juicy and their big host kept urging more on them.

There were to be only three fights and Gatorbait was fighting Rojo in the second bout. When they were done eating, the old men began walking from cage to cage looking at the chickens and talking among themselves. This went on for a good thirty minutes as Melvin and Vern drank piña coladas in a balmy noonday breeze and watched them.

"How much you fight him for?" Pokini asked Vern before the first fight was to begin.

"I'll fight him for nineteen thousand," Vern told him, including Melvin's four thousand with his fifteen.

"You got the bet. Abel over there he bet fifty thousand on your chicken." Pokini pointed to an old, stooped Filipino man who looked their way and smiled, flashing a mouth full of gold teeth.

"We're rubbin' elbows with heavyweights here," Melvin whispered to Vern.

"Damn sure looks like it."

The first fight took a while. The two roosters were smart and cagey. They stayed just out of reach of each other like sparring boxers, then closed when they saw an opening. On their fourth pass the chicken Vern had been rooting for got hit in the head and the fight was over.

Melvin had Gatorbait tied and ready to go, but as Vern and Tai brought their birds to the ring, Melvin did something unusual. He walked over to Pokini, who was to act as referee, and said, "Hold it up, Poky, let me tie your chicken before this fight." He had agreed to tie a chicken for Pokini but would have usually waited until the second fight was over.

"I guess so," Pokini replied and walked Melvin over to a cage while Tai and Vern held their roosters at the edge of the ring. Vern could feel Gatorbait's heart racing. Rojo was a bigger chicken. He was red as his name implied and a formidable-looking beast who in a strange way resembled his owner.

Pokini and Melvin came back to the ring.

"Bring 'em in," Pokini said, and Vern and Tai closed with their birds, letting them peck and cluck at one another for a few seconds, then they backed up a ways and let them go.

It was obvious that Gatorbait had met his match. He went up early, but so did Rojo. No matter how high Gatorbait flew, the big chicken stayed with him. They came together once with not much damage done to either. When they flew up again they came straight at each other and their spurs sounded like typewriters as they connected with the opposing bird's chest.

When they came down from that pass, there was blood everywhere and big splotches of it on each chicken's breast.

They went up for the third time and when they came down Gatorbait had blood on his head and neck. Vern thought he was a goner, but as he prepared to fly up again, Rojo's legs went out from under him and he sank to the ground. He obviously had a deep internal wound, as blood was now dripping from his beak.

A second later Gatorbait went down also about a foot and a

half from where Rojo lay scratching at the dirt. Vern eased up closer. Tai was down on his hands and knees blowing on the head of Rojo, who was obviously expiring very rapidly. Gatorbait kept trying to get back up, but it looked like one of his legs was cut badly and blood was dripping from his beak to the ground.

So far neither one of them had pecked at the other. If they both died and neither tried to peck the other, the fight would be called a draw. But if one pecked last, he would be the winner. Rojo's head now settled to the earth in spite of Tai's prodding. He was dead or very close to it.

Gently Vern reached down and picked up Gatorbait.

"Hold it. You can't pick him up," Tai yelled. The blood veins were standing out on his neck like ropes.

"Yes, he can," Pokini and Melvin said at the same time.

Vern put Gatorbait down next to Rojo and Gatorbait pecked twice at the inert chicken. Rojo was dead. Tai picked up his chicken and Vern saw tears in the big man's eyes as he walked with the chicken hanging limply in his arms down toward the river, the excited hum and babble of their voices stalking him.

Gatorbait had won the fight, but Vern was sure he had lost him. A bad internal wound is certain death for a chicken and the blood dripping from his beak was a bad sign. Yet as Pokini counted out the nineteen thousand dollars, Vern kept looking at Gatorbait, who kept trying to get back to his feet. Just as Poky finished counting out the money, something possessed Vern. He ran to Gatorbait and scooped him up.

"C'mon, Melvin, let's go!" he yelled over his shoulder as he ran for the truck. When he got to the pickup, he grabbed a blanket from the bed and threw it across the front seat. Melvin arrived just as he put Gatorbait down and started the truck.

"What's up?" Melvin asked as Vern burned rubber out of the residential area.

"I'm taking him to a vet. Get those fucking knives off of him," Vern said.

Melvin had just got the knives off when Vern slid up in front of a bank of pay phones at a shopping mall. He leaped out of the truck and grabbed a phone book that was hanging from one of the phones. He riffled the Yellow Pages and took the number of the first veterinarian he saw.

"Laurel Street Clinic," a female voice said when he dialed the number.

"Listen, I have an emergency. A dog got hold of my parrot and it's hurt pretty bad. I need to bring it in right away," he said.

"Oh, my. Well, bring it in. We'll have an emergency room ready for you," she told him. Vern threw the phone down and ran for the truck, then had to run back to get the address out of the book. A woman using a nearby phone told him where the address on Laurel Street would be. When he got to the pickup, Melvin had Gatorbait's whole head in his mouth.

"What the fuck are you doing, Melvin?" Vern asked as he started the truck.

Melvin spat blood on the blanket before he replied.

"I'm cleaning the blood out of his mouth. He's choking on his own blood."

Vern kept glancing at Gatorbait as he drove. The rooster tried to get up and kept falling back down on the seat. Melvin kept his hand on the chicken to steady him. Blood spots were all over the blanket now as well as on Vern's and Melvin's hands and clothes. Vern parked in front of the clinic and jumped out and grabbed Gatorbait.

When he went in with the bloody rooster in his arms, a woman came around the desk to meet him.

"This is my parrot I called about," he said.

"Oh, my, that's the strangest-looking parrot I've ever seen.

Bring him right in here," she said, holding a door open that led into a room with a small table and medical instruments.

A young-looking man wearing Levi's and cowboy boots rushed in and began turning Gatorbait on the table, lifting wings and feathers and looking him over carefully.

"I think he has a deep internal wound," Vern said.

"Well, he may have one, but his tongue is cut. That's where the blood in his beak is coming from," the man replied and went on examining Gatorbait.

"If you can save him, I'll pay whatever it takes. I'll pay cash in advance today," Vern said.

"You can deal with my receptionist on that, but his leg is cut badly. If the nerve is severed, he's done for. A chicken can't make it on one leg."

"Do whatever you can," Vern told him. The man looked up directly into Vern's eyes.

"I'm going to have to report this, you know. There's a state law that says if I get a game chicken that looks like it was injured in a fight, I have to report it."

"Does that law say when you have to report it?" Melvin asked from just behind Vern. Vern hadn't seen him come into the room. The doctor scratched at his head for a minute.

"No, I don't recall it saying when. That's a good question. I'd have to look that up," he said. From his smile and expression they could tell he was sympathetic.

"Well, it's Saturday now. Fish and Game won't be open till Monday, anyway. How about reporting it Monday afternoon?" Melvin asked.

"That sounds reasonable. Make arrangements with my receptionist. I've got to get to work on his fella. What's his name, anyway?"

"Gatorbait," Vern said as the doctor carried the rooster into another room and closed the door.

Vern told the woman at the desk that his name was Oscar Splivens and gave a San Francisco address. He left her five hundred dollars and told her they could settle one way or the other when he came back on Monday.

"Where in the world did you get the name Oscar Splivens?" Melvin asked him when they got back in the truck.

"Hell, it's all I could think of," Vern told him.

"You know something, Melvin, I don't think I would have sold Gatorbait for nineteen thousand dollars."

"That's about as crazy as you can get over a chicken, but I kinda know how you feel about that bird. I was getting to like him a lot myself. Just something about his personality, I guess. I bet he ain't never had any pussy, either. It would really be obscene if a bad-ass rooster like him died without ever having a piece of ass. If he does live, you should get him a hen. That's what he fights so hard about anyway, you know."

"If that fucker makes it, he will get all he wants. I'm gonna put him out to stud. I don't plan on fighting him again. He's done made me close to fifty thousand dollars. I won't be able to match him with anything but the meanest chickens around. That is, unless I sneak him in under a bogus name, and that's not my style."

"Maybe you can fight him under the name Oscar Splivens, Jr.," Melvin said.

"You like my alias, huh?" Vern grinned.

"It is original. Hey, man, make sure there's no hole in your pocket. You still got my four thousand dollars!"

As they drove down the road feeling good in the warm night air, drinking cold beer and listening to George Strait and Clint Black and Reba McEntire, life seemed about as good as it could be.

CHAPTER 8

Melvin dropped him off in the early evening, and when he walked into the house, he kind of wished he'd stayed in Stockton a while longer, or at least got drunk before he came home. He didn't know what it was yet, but he knew it was bad.

Curly was sitting on the couch in front of a silent TV. She had her legs pulled up under her and was wearing an old fluffy cotton bathrobe that had belonged to Vern before she bought him a new one and appropriated it.

The look on her face told him that she had been hurt some way, and when Curly was hurt, it seemed that everything around her was hurting also.

"Hi, babe," she said to him, and Vern saw the corners of her mouth tremble as if she were about to cry. But from the look of her she was cried out. Vern knew it must be really bad when she didn't even comment about his blood-soaked clothes or inquire about Gatorbait.

Paula came to the door that led into the kitchen, and when

Vern started toward her she motioned him to follow and walked out the back door. She looked pale and drawn also, but Vern could tell she was more mad than hurt. He pulled the door shut and followed her on out toward the gator's pond. He began hoping that the gator hadn't eaten one of their neighbors, but the beast was lying by the pool.

"Paula, what the fuck is going on?" Vern asked her and she turned around.

"That fucking Sam robbed us," she told him.

Vern was stunned and just stood there for a minute or two before he found his voice.

"What do you mean?" he asked her.

"The bastard cleaned us out, took all our jewelry, he even took that big fake whiskey jug you kept all those old silver dimes and quarters in. He also found that twelve thousand you had rolled up and stuck in the bedpost."

"How the fuck did he do that?" Vern asked, and his own heart began to thump as he felt rage taking hold in him.

"Curly and I worked the Filipino labor camp today. We left around ten and got back at four-thirty. When we came in, Sam was gone and so was our jewelry and money. Your other money stash is still here, but it's a good thing he didn't know where you hide that."

"That rotten little punk motherfucker. I can't believe this shit," he breathed.

"That isn't all, Vern. He took that old wedding ring that their mom gave Curly before she died."

"What!" Vern almost screamed.

Curly had loved her mother dearly, and before she died the woman had given Curly her wedding ring because she wanted her to always have something to remember her by. They had been very poor and the ring was a cheap one. It had one small diamond, and it was attached to a plain fourteen-karat gold band.

Several times during the past year when Curly's mood turned melancholy, Vern had watched her take out the ring and look at it for a long time, trying it on one finger, then another, or just holding it in her hand and staring off into space.

"I gave her a hot bath in the tub and washed her back and babied her some but, Vern, be careful with her. I mean, she's really deeply hurt right now. You've got to make her understand that we don't think it's her fault. She's blaming herself right now because he's her brother. On top of the hurt about the ring she's feeling like she caused us to get robbed."

"Shit!" Vern declared. "Shit, shit, sheeeeeeiiiiitt!"

He turned around and started for the house.

"Vern!" Paula called.

"Shut the fuck up, Paula," he said and opened the door and made for the couch where Curly was still sitting as if hypnotized. She looked up and her eyes widened as he sat down beside her and took her in his arms, holding her very tight.

"Oh, Vern," she mumbled and began crying with great wracking sobs. He held her there for a long time, gently rubbing her back as her tears mingled with Gatorbait's blood on his T-shirt. Paula went into the bedroom until Curly had finished her cry.

When she had wound down some and Paula was back sitting next to Vern, Curly said, "Vern, it's my fault for having you let him stay here."

"Curly, you listen to me real good because I'm only going to tell you this one time," Vern told her. "In the first place I call the shots about who stays here and who don't. So it don't make no difference that he's your brother. I let him stay because I was feeling good about Gatorbait winning and our luck changing. I knew Sam was sorry and I let him stay against my own better judgment, so this one's on me, girl.

"Now if I ever hear you say— I'll do better than that. If your sweet face ever indicates to me that you are even thinking this might be your fault, I'm going to spank your ass until it's redder than this blood on my shirt, then I'm going to take my belt to you. Do you understand me? Huh?"

Curly bobbed her head up and down on his chest.

"Let's hear some conversation here, girl. I asked you a question. Do you understand me? Huh?"

"Yes, Vern. I understand," Curly replied, and Vern saw Paula smile.

"Now," he said, taking his arms from around Curly. "I know you all had a lot of jewelry. I'm not sure what he could of took of mine besides that silver change."

"He got that Rolex watch," Paula said.

"Goddamn!" Vern moaned. He'd won the watch in a chicken fight and it was very expensive.

"Well, anyway, I'm going to take a shower, and by the time I get back, I want you both to have me a list made out of what you think he took and as much description as you can. You know like if it had initials or a scratch or anything I can identify it by." He knew almost every thief and fence in Fresno.

He didn't have much hope of recovering the jewelry, but he wanted to give Curly a chore right now to get her mind off the wedding ring for a few minutes. He did intend to recover that ring one way or the other.

"Curly, go in Paula's stationery drawer and get two pens and some paper for you and her to write on."

Curly jumped up and when she went into the bedroom Vern put his arms around Paula.

"I shouldn't have let that son of a bitch stay here, hon," he told her.

"It *is* your fucking fault, Vern. You've heard the same things about him that everyone else has," she said against his throat and he drew back and looked at her.

"You ain't supposed to agree with me so easy, bitch." He smiled at her. "We live and we learn, you know."

"Yeah, I know." She laid her head back on his chest. "But if you don't get our stuff back, me and Curly are going shopping, man. I hope your chicken didn't get killed today, but from the looks of you, I guess it did."

"No, he won, babe, but he might be dead. I left him with a vet in Stockton," he told her just as Curly returned with the paper and two ballpoint pens.

"Get to work, girls," he told them and went in to take a shower. Curly looked a little better, but not very much.

When he left the shower they were at the kitchen table working on their lists and talking. He went into the bedroom and dressed very carefully, then threw a small suitcase on the bed and put in some extra pants, shorts, and socks. He was fairly certain that Sam wouldn't be staying around Fresno for a while. He went on out to the kitchen and got on the phone.

Melvin agreed to pick up Gatorbait on Monday if Vern wasn't home yet. Vern didn't bother to tell Melvin what the trouble was and Melvin didn't ask. No one else Vern called had seen Sam or heard anything about where he was. Vern decided his first stop would be Chester the Molester because Chester didn't have a phone.

Paula looked at him when he left the phone and followed him back into the bedroom.

"Are you leaving right now, Vern?" she asked.

"Yep," he said, while counting money from the day's winnings out onto the bed.

"When will you be coming back?" she asked.

"Soon as I find him," he replied.

"That may take a while," she said.

"Yeah, it may," he replied, then looked her in the eye. "I'm not coming home until I find him, Paula."

"I figured that," she said and looked down at the money as if she wanted to say something else but knew it was no use. She knew Vern better than anyone ever had. Even though there was still a lot about him she didn't fully understand. One was these mysterious missions he departed on occasionally.

But she did understand as well as he did that with the gang having a contract on him, it wouldn't hurt for him to be gone from Fresno for a while. Hopefully they would come to their senses or find out who really had given up the lab. She didn't want Vern to kill Little Joe on such skimpy information. It just wouldn't be right. She hated violence, and purely detested senseless violence.

Curly walked in as Vern laid four thousand dollars out on the bed.

"You all take this along with what you made today and go shopping. Take a couple days off and if you want to go out, call Melvin and have him take you somewhere. But I don't want you going to the Sagebrush while I'm gone," Vern told them. "Keep Melvin close and don't let anyone in here at night until they identify themselves. I'm taking your Blazer, Paula, because it draws less attention. Be careful with my Lincoln," he said as they traded keys.

He felt better because Paula had an automatic pistol she kept in her purse now. She knew how to use it and was almost as good a marksman as he was, and he was damn good.

"Be careful, big boy," Curly told him as Vern picked up the little suitcase.

He hugged Curly and Paula both up in his arms at the same time, and held them for a long time until Curly began quietly crying and Paula began sniffling.

"There's going to be a couple kids. A white kid and a black kid coming by here. Give them two dollars apiece for the carp they catch and put the fish live in the gator pond," he said into Curly's hair and she began wailing.

"Goddammit, Vern. Is that all you can think of at a time like this is that fucking alligator?" Paula yelled at him as he disengaged and made for the door.

"Dammit, Paula. That's Weldon's gator and I promised him I'd take care of it," he told her as he threw the suitcase in the back of the Blazer.

"Well, if you're gone over one week, I'll blow the motherfucker's head off!" Paula yelled, as Vern got behind the wheel of the car.

"I mean it, Vern, on the eighth day I'll kill that son of a bitch!" she yelled as he backed out. Curly's loud sobs underscored Paula's yelling as if they were being conducted. Vern saw the lights go on on their new neighbor's porch as he drove away.

He drove over to Clovis Avenue and went toward Clovis, which is seven miles due north of Fresno. Clovis is a small town that never caught up with the urban sprawl of the seventies and eighties. Its population is made up of poor southerners mostly, farm workers, and Mexicans. It was as if the town circled their wagons and decided to stay small. The maneuver hadn't worked. Clovis did stay small, but inch by inch Fresno was creeping in around it with shopping malls, huge discount stores, mega–gas stations, and fast-food joints. The seven miles that had once separated the two towns was now about three blocks of diminishing residential area.

Vern pulled into a street of rundown homes where clothes still hung on clotheslines and people kept chickens in their backyards. He pulled into the empty driveway of his Aunt Maybelle's house. She was his mother's sister and either eighty-two or eighty-five years old, depending on who you asked. She didn't have a car or a TV. She had a telephone only because Vern and Paula insisted on it, and paid for it. She was sitting in a rocking chair on her screened-in porch listening to the radio when Vern pulled in. He opened the screen door and leaned down to kiss her cheek.

"Howdy, May," he said, and handed her a pint of Southern Comfort. She loved sweet whiskey and he had always brought her Four Roses whiskey until it became so hard to find. But she took to Southern Comfort with no complaint at all.

"Bless your heart, son," she murmured and tucked the bottle under the blanket over her lap.

"I need to go into the basement for a few minutes," he told her, having to speak loud over the radio talk show that sounded as if it was on full volume. Someone talking about massacre, rape, and pillage in Rwanda.

"Go on ahead, son. How is that sweet Paula getting along?" she asked.

"She's fine, May. Said to tell you hello," Vern said, and went on in the house.

He went into her small, neat kitchen, and taking a key from the ring his house and car keys were on, unlocked the door of a utility closet that led to her basement. He switched the light on and looked carefully for spiders before descending the four steps. Vern was scared to death of spiders, although he was careful not to let anyone become aware of that fact. Paula had found it out when she'd brought home a big hairy tarantula she'd bought in a pet store and planned to keep as a pet.

The house itself was old but very clean. Vern paid a cleaning woman to come in once a week. There were hundreds of small ceramic birds and other whatnots on shelves.

The reclining chair had crocheted doilies on the arms. Vern's, Weldon's, Paula's, and Curly's pictures hung on her walls in various stages of their lives. One was of Weldon at two years old. May was a sweet woman with a very romantic and melancholy soul. Her house reflected her personality.

May's basement held Vern's gun collection, and it was impressive. Three of the walls were covered with rifles and shotguns of every caliber and age. He had everything from an 1893 .50-caliber buffalo gun to a .458-caliber elephant rifle.

The remaining wall held his pistols and there were three large locked steamer trunks that held more pistols. He had been buying and selling and trading guns for over ten years. No one except Paula knew where he kept his collection, and he spent at least one day a month cleaning, oiling, and just admiring them. He still had the first cap gun his mother had bought him to play cowboys and Indians with.

He opened one of the trunks and took out a .380 automatic with a seven-shot clip and worked the action on it and checked the date on the box of shells. Then he removed a .44 Magnum revolver and put it on the table beside the .380. He debated whether to take a shotgun also but decided against it. He put both guns and the shells in the pockets of the leather jacket he was wearing and went back upstairs.

"How is Weldon doing?" Maybelle asked him over the sound of the talk show.

"Well, he's in slow motion again but he seems to do okay like that," Vern told her.

"He should have never got mixed up with them Porter Ricans and them damn dope pills," she said.

"I guess you're right, May," Vern said and leaned down to kiss her good-bye. She called any kind of drugs "dope pills," and Vern didn't know if Weldon had ever even seen a Puerto Rican outside of prison. He left her there mumbling at the radio.

Chester the Molester lived in an old run-down trailer in a trailer court near a truck stop on the old 99 highway. Vern pulled up beside his 1980 Buick Skylark in the driveway. Chester was an old thief close to sixty. He got the name The Molester when he was in his forties and having a good run at stealing.

Every time he made a good score, he would have a bunch of young girls over to his house showing them hundred-dollar bills. Usually the younger the girl the more of Chester's hundred-dollar bills she wound up with.

Now, at the age of sixty, Chester had very little besides pornographic memories of young dope fiend girls to show for his years of lucrative thieving. He was about the ugliest man Vern had ever seen. He also had a glass eye whose socket seemed to continually drip onto his cheek. Vern dreaded even talking to him, but if anyone in Fresno knew where Sam was, Chester would know.

Chester had seen Vern's headlights and opened the door before Vern could knock. He was tall and slim with just a fringe of gray hair around a shiny, bald head. His ears stuck out from his head like a bat's ears and the glass eye was dripping as usual. Once again Vern marveled at how sheer ugly Chester was.

"Have you seen Curly's brother, Sam?" Vern asked as Chester ushered him into the dim foyer of the trailer. The only light was from a flickering black-and-white TV and Vern could see a partially eaten bowl of cold cereal on the coffee table in front of an old ratty couch. The room smelled moldy. He lit up a Camel while Chester dabbed at his eye with a crumpled handkerchief before replying.

"Yeah, he came by while ago and bought a gram of crank from

me, but he told me not to tell anyone I'd seen him."

"What did he pay for it with?" Vern asked.

"He gave me a bunch of change," Chester replied, and Vern could tell by his voice that Chester was getting worried.

"Where did he go when he left?" Vern asked.

"Man, I ain't got no idea, Vern. He was driving that old van," Chester said.

"Well, look here, Chester. He robbed me. That was my change he gave you. But that's okay. You can keep that. I'm looking for him and if I find out later that you knew anything about where he was and didn't tell me, I'm going to come back here and put your other eye out," Vern told him.

"I swear, Vern, I don't know. He made a call from that pay phone out there to a guy named Blake Ethridge in Oakland. I know Blake Ethridge cooks crank and hangs with the Hells Angels. I don't know if he's going up there or not, man. That's all I know."

"Okay, Chester, I'll take your word on that," Vern told him, and walked back to his car. Oakland is 180 miles from Fresno. Vern figured he could drive it easy before he needed to sleep.

He took the old 99 highway, intending to take a shortcut down around Modesto and hit 152 to 580 near Oakland. Vern liked the old roads and traveled on them whenever possible. The big new interstates were too boring and impersonal for his taste. The huge automated gas stations with cashiers behind windows that looked like drive-up banking reminded him of fast-food joints.

Now and then he would find decent conversation at a small filling station that progress had left barely alive. He could have used some old country small talk right about now but realized when he drove on through Madera that it wouldn't be available any time soon. The few small places were closed. He pulled over to the side of the road to check his equipment once more. He didn't even know this guy Blake Ethridge, but as slim as it was, it was the only piece of information he had to travel on. He put his leather jacket on because the night seemed chilly.

There was a small briefcase in the luggage compartment with a padlock on it. Vern had put the key to the padlock on a magnetic key holder in the bowels of the Blazer's motor under the hood. He got the key out now and opened the case. It held about a half ounce of weed, some Dexedrine pills he used for driving long distances, five hundred-dollar bills he kept for an emergency, a can of Mace, and a .45 automatic along with a box of shells that he carried for protection.

He wiped the .380 and the Magnum free of prints with the T-shirt and placed them in the briefcase along with the other items, locked it back up, and put the key under the hood.

All three of the guns in the case were stolen and untraceable. Most of the guns Vern owned were legitimate, but he kept up to ten that were untraceable. If any one of them had to be used, he could leave it at the scene if he needed to.

There was a name tag on the briefcase with the name and address of a man who had been killed during a robbery in Fresno the year before. If the items were ever found in the car, Vern planned to say that the man had left the case in his care and that he didn't know the gentleman was dead.

The story was a bit weak in spots, but Vern figured with a decent lawyer it was enough to create a reasonable doubt. It was better than having no story at all. He had no police record and figured his word should be as good as anyone's in a court of law.

CHAPTER 9

After Vern left, the house seemed to be too quiet. There was only the hum of the big cooler for company. Curly continued sitting in front of the silent TV, staring off into space. Paula walked silently from room to room as if she were busy at small chores but didn't have a clue as to what she was doing or what the hell she was going to do. Her main feeling was dread because she was certain that however this state of affairs was concluded, it was not going to have a happy ending.

She went into the kitchen and made a pot of ginger tea, and while it steeped walked to the bedroom and got out a joint of good Humboldt weed and the bottle of Tuinal. She put it all on a tray and sat the tray down on the coffee table in front of Curly.

"Let's get good and fucked up, Blondie," she said to her disconsolate companion.

"Sounds like a plan, Comadre," Curly replied and twisted the top of the pill bottle while Paula poured their tea and lit the joint. They ate two apiece to begin with and took long, deep drags of the killer weed.

Paula had given Curly the pet name of Blondie because like the woman in the comic strip, Curly never seemed to age any and was about as dumb as a bucket of rocks. Curly had responded by asking a Mexican trick of hers how to say "partner" in Spanish. He told her a male partner was *compadre* and a female partner was a *comadre*. They addressed each other this way only in private. Vern didn't even know about their pet names.

"God, I needed that!" Curly exclaimed, as the weed began to take hold. It was the kind of weed that would turn the corners of your mouth up and make you smile whether you wanted to or not.

"So did I," Paula agreed.

"I wish Sam wouldn't have took Mother's ring. It wasn't worth fifty dollars, I guess, but I would have given him a thousand dollars not to take it," Curly said.

Paula had been hoping to change the subject and get Curly's mind off the theft, but it was obvious now that Curly wouldn't, or couldn't, let go.

"You don't pay thieves not to steal from you, Blondie," she replied.

"I know that, but all my life he's been charging me not to hurt me, so a thousand bucks wouldn't have made any difference," Curly told her.

"What do you mean by that?" Paula asked.

"Oh, hell, he'd take my toys when we were kids, then make me rent them from him. If I told Mom, then he'd destroy whatever he'd taken. He took my lunch money at school. After I turned out he made me pay him not to tell Mom, then he wound up telling her anyway before she died."

"That fucking creep," Paula exclaimed. The pills were taking effect now and her anger was rising along with the rubbery feeling.

"He was eight and I was five when Dad run off and left us. I don't know why, but he's just been rotten since then. It seems to me that he was nice before that," Curly told her.

"Who turned you out to hustling?" Paula asked. It was something she had always been curious about but had never wanted to ask until now. Curly took a sip of the tea and settled back on the couch before replying.

"I turned myself out. I mean, I never thought it out and it didn't happen suddenly. I just sort of drifted into it. I remember right after Dad left, I thought maybe he left us because I was ugly or something. So I'd really doll myself up as much as I could, then, any man who came to our house, I'd climb right up in his lap. Even to this day I love to sit in a man's lap.

"When I was eleven I began to notice some changes in a few of their laps when I sat in them. This old horny preacher came by to bring us some food and got a big hard-on when I climbed up in his lap. Mom would say, 'Curly, you get down off of him! You're way too big to be up in people's laps.' And he'd say, 'Now, Dora, it's no bother at all. She's such a sweet child and I don't mind a bit.' His old dick would be jumping around like a fish out of the water."

They both laughed and Curly continued.

"One day I asked him for a dollar while Mom was in the kitchen making him some coffee. He kind of hum-hawed and I put my hand on his dick just sort of accidentally, and he gave me two dollars. That's all him and I ever done, but I'd get a dollar or two a week out of him just by putting my hand on him.

"Right about then I began to realize men would be a lot more generous if you touched the right buttons. I was touching one of my uncles and he told me he would give me five dollars to kiss it. Next thing I knew, he had it all the way down my throat and I've been hustling ever since.

"I really got burned and lied to a lot at first because I didn't know what I was doing. It's hard trying to learn something when you've got a bunch of horny, lying, scheming hard-ons for teachers."

"Tell me about it!" Paula exclaimed, and suddenly they were laughing, almost out of control. Paula got up and walked unsteadily into the kitchen, removed a quart bottle of beer from the fridge and sat it on the coffee table between them. Curly unscrewed the lid and took a long, gurgling drink right from the bottle.

"I'm getting good and loaded, Comadre," she said, looking blearily around the room.

"Don't feel lonesome, Blondie," Paula replied and handed her another Tuinal before she took another herself and downed it with a long pull on the beer.

"You know, Comadre, I really feel relieved in a way. When Sam stayed here I never said ten words to him. I think he realized that I'm not afraid of him anymore. Vern let him stay because he's my brother, but I planned on telling Vern what a sorry asshole he is and I think he was getting the idea. He took that ring because he knew it was all over and that's the last way he could ever hurt me. I'm sure of that," Curly said, having a hard time talking now without slurring her words.

Paula's head was now drooping toward her chest, and she kept jerking her head back up as if startled every time her chin got near her bosom. Curly watched her and wondered how Paula had kept that fresh look of youth and such a trim figure after all the years of hard and fast living. She was, by anyone's definition, a beautiful woman.

Her auburn hair was thick and shiny and more like a pelt than a head of hair. Her big hazel-green eyes were almond-shaped almost to the point of being Oriental and they peered out from a delicate oval face with high cheekbones. She had a striking resemblance to a young Ava Gardner, who Curly had seen in old movies.

Curly didn't really know how to feel jealous. It was something that had just never happened with her. That was one of the things that made her love Vern and Paula so much. They were as free of jealousy as she was. But Paula's bosom came very close to making Curly jealous.

They were ripe, firm gourds just above a slim waist. They tilted slightly upward where two rosebud nipples were planted in tan aureoles the size of silver dollars. When Paula walked around without a bra, they took on a life of their own. They looked like two puppies playing around under her shirt. Curly had seen men's jaws drop open in mid-sentence and stay that way when Paula walked by.

"How long will Vern be gone?" Curly asked, timing her words to catch Paula's head on the upswing.

"He'll be gone until he finds Sam," Paula replied.

"Well, what if he don't find him? I mean, Sam is about as slick as they come and he's got to know Vern will be looking for him!" Curly said.

"He will find him. He's like one of them bloodhounds when he gets like this," Paula replied, then said softly, "Curly?"

"What?" Curly asked, startled a little bit more awake when Paula called her by name instead of Blondie.

"This could get real bad, hon. I mean, someone could be hurt bad. I know Sam is your family, your own blood and all . . ."

Paula's voice kept slowing and restarting as if she were having a hard time finding the right words. A tear sprang to the corner of Curly's eye before Paula got all her words out. She got up and came around the coffee table and seated herself on Paula's lap, put her arms around her, and hugged her tightly.

"Comadre," she whispered in Paula's ear. "I think I know what's bothering you, so forget about it. You and Vern and Weldon are my family. You're my blood, and you will be always."

"God, I hoped you would feel that way about things," Paula said, and the relief in her voice was obvious. Curly kissed her on the cheek and stood up.

"I've got to have a man tonight and we're both too fucked up to drive. Is it all right if I call up one of these tricks and bring him here to that extra bedroom?" she asked.

Paula gazed blearily at her watch before replying.

"Go ahead, but be sure and tell him not to ever come again unless you call him, because Vern would go crazy if a trick showed up here knocking on the door."

"I'll make sure of that," Curly said, and went out into the kitchen. When she came back she put an old Louis Armstrong record on the stereo and they finished the beer to the lyrics of "Mack the Knife."

They had finished another half quart before the knock came at the door and Curly got up to let him in. Paula wasn't a bit surprised to see Pete of the long dick that she'd refused to trick at the motel.

He seemed overjoyed to see them, and they sat on either side of him on the couch as Curly rolled him a fat joint of the Humboldt weed and explained that this would be the only time he could ever come to the house.

He was a tall, lanky man and to Paula's eyes one of those strange male specimens that were so ugly as to be almost handsome in the sheer inconsistency of features. He had a strong resemblance to Lyle Lovett, the country singer who Julia Roberts had recently married.

He was nervous at first, fidgeting around on the couch next to Curly while she and Paula made small talk to put him at ease.

Paula kept looking at his hands and saw that Curly was doing the same thing. When they realized what they were doing, they both began laughing hysterically while Pete just sat there grinning at them.

"We're not laughing at you, Pete. It's just this weed," Curly told him.

"Hell, I wouldn't care if you was. You are both beautiful when you laugh." He grinned.

"Why, thank you, Pete," Paula said. She adored compliments, even from a trick.

Paula had come up with a theory lately that a man's dick when hard was exactly as long as the distance from the end of his middle finger to the base of his palm just before it joined the wrist. She and Curly had been surreptitiously measuring tricks in order to prove or disprove the theory.

So far they had found it to be true over 90 percent of the time. There were aberrations, of course. One of Paula's tricks had a dick that was no bigger around than a pencil and about an inch and a half long. Nature did have aberrations, but the theory was so consistently borne out that they were about to declare it a universal truth.

Pete was obviously an aberration. But not that much of one. His hands were as enormous as one of those basketball players who can hold a ball in each hand. He had very long fingers and palms, but they both knew that his dick dwarfed the distance from fingertip to wrist. For the life of her, Paula couldn't figure why Curly liked to trick him. To her, it would be like being fucked by a fence post.

After a few jokes and a swig on their beer, he took three hundred-dollar bills from his wallet and laid them on the coffee table.

"I really like a man who doesn't have to be told what to do," Paula said, smiling and eyeing the money.

"Well, looky here, let's do a threesome. You all take that and let's all get in the same bed. Maybe have a little show," Pete said hopefully.

Paula reached down and took the bills from the table. She carefully folded one and stuck it in Pete's shirt pocket. She folded the two remaining bills and shoved them down the neck of Curly's T-shirt as she got to her feet and patted Pete on the head as she would have petted a puppy.

"Not tonight, dear. I have a headache," she said and weaved and wobbled to her bedroom.

"I'll make you think there's two of me anyway, sugar," she heard Curly tell him as she closed the door.

Paula felt as if she had no more than lain down when Curly was shaking her awake. She rolled over and looked at the bedside clock and groaned when she saw it was only 7:30.

"Let's go surprise Weldon with a visit," Curly urged. "You can sleep on the way. I'll drive."

"Oh, God," Paula said as she strove to get up. Her head was pounding like a base drum. This was the only thing she hated about Vern and Curly. Both of them loved to wake her at some ungodly hour on a grand whim. She always went along, though she dearly loved her sleep.

By the time they got out to Vern's Lincoln, she noticed that Curly was walking very slow and got in the car gingerly.

"What's the matter, Blondie?" Paula asked.

"I feel like I've been fucked by a parking meter," Curly told her.

"At least you didn't have to feed it," Paula said, and was asleep before Curly could reply. She didn't even stir when Curly jumped out at the connection's house and bought two grams of tar heroin for Weldon.

CHAPTER 10

On the ride over to Salinas, Paula came half awake and sat back in the seat daydreaming and drifting back and forth into sleep as Curly drove and sang along with the songs from a country-and-western station on the radio. The way she herself had turned out hadn't been that much different from Curly.

She and Vern had become sweethearts when she was thirteen and he was twelve and had been together ever since. She even had her hand on him when he had his first orgasm. He didn't think the memory was all that romantic and still got pissed off when she reminded him of it.

Paula had three brothers and four sisters, and the summer she turned thirteen they moved into a shack in west Fresno next door to Vern's family. Vern and Weldon lived with Vern's mother and stepfather, a very mean drunk that everyone called Snake.

Her father had moved them down from Modesto in the late summer to pick cotton in Fresno. Vern and his family were working the same field and the man they rented the shacks from owned the farm where the cotton grew. Less than a week after they began picking, Weldon left home and Paula didn't see him again until after she and Vern made their own getaway.

Snake made Vern pull a twelve-foot cotton sack that was about three times as long as he was and very difficult to handle. Grown-ups pulled twelve-foot sacks and women and children usually pulled nine-footers on down to four-foot sacks, depending on their size and strength. But Snake wanted Vern pulling a twelve-footer because he said he didn't want him to lose valuable picking time weighing up.

Paula always picked the row next to Vern and would help him pull the sack when it began to fill and help him climb the ladder of the trailer to empty it after he weighed up. Snake constantly razzed him about having to get a girl's help to pull his sack.

Cotton picking began in late August—the hottest part of the hottest month of the year—and carried over into October. But Paula always like picking cotton better than the figs or peaches or grapes because school always began right after cotton, and she loved going to school.

Ironically, it was falling in love with Vern that made a whore out of her. She had always understood that and always thought it a fair price to pay. Of course Vern never had a clue and Paula had never seen any reason to enlighten him.

Vern never complained about the twelve-foot sack or anything else, and though she could tell he hated Snake, he worked hard, hoping to make life a little bit more comfortable for his mother, a very nice Christian woman who had made a serious mistake in marrying Snake.

Paula saw right away that beneath the iron-willed effort this fragile boy put out every day, he was operating on sheer willpower. His heart just wasn't in it. He hated work, and especially fieldwork, with a passion. He never told her as much, but she knew.

She also knew that no matter how much he loved her, she could never ask him to work like that to take care of her. About the time she was becoming aware of these thoughts and feelings, he told her that Weldon was in reform school for burglary. His attitude about it alarmed her because he figured Weldon got caught because he was careless.

"If I steal or rob something, I'm going to do it right. I'll get away with it," he declared.

She told him he was talking nonsense, but as they moved from cotton to figs and peaches, he kept coming back to the subject and Paula figured it was just a matter of time before he tried his luck at being an outlaw. She didn't have near the faith that he did that he would be good at it.

By the time she was sixteen, Snake and her father had become drinking buddies and the two families followed the fieldwork together. That was the year her father and mother told her she couldn't go back to school anymore. She had had her heart set on going to college and made good-enough grades to earn a partial scholarship. It broke her heart when they told her she couldn't even attend her last year of high school. By this time she could see that Vern was on the edge of chaos, so it was while they worked their last cotton field that she decided to take control of both their lives until Vern could take over.

She had no idea of how it would turn out, but she knew if she failed, no one would go to jail. The most she had to lose was her good reputation and possibly Vern if he couldn't live with what she was doing. But she figured she'd lose him anyway if she didn't do something. Her initial foray into whoredom was still vivid in her mind.

The field boss in the cotton field they worked every year had been lusting after her since he first laid eyes on her when she was thirteen. He was a large, potbellied redneck who wore overalls and chewed Redman tobacco. As unattractive as he was, Paula had seen him many times sneaking a woman picker into his camper that he parked in the field. She'd figured he must be bribing them with money, as there was no way his looks would have done it.

In the beginning he helped her weigh her sack and used the opportunity to brush up against her or "accidentally" fondle her breast. The second time he made the same move she shoved him away and told him in no uncertain terms that she'd weigh her sack without his help.

But he was a congenial and well-mannered man. He apologized and then began talking with and teasing her until she became relaxed around him. She realized later that he had gentled her the same way a cowboy gentles an unbroken horse.

By the year she was sixteen, he was helping her weigh the sack again and copping a feel here and there. She would consent to these "accidents" as long as he added a few extra pounds to the weight of her sack. Cotton pickers are paid by the pound, and at each weighing Everett, the field boss, would sign a slip of paper attesting to the sack weight and put it in a box. At the end of the day, he tallied everyone's slips and paid them accordingly. Paula always got paid for thirty or forty pounds more than she had picked that day.

Everett, however, was getting very frustrated. He was tired of the clandestine touching and wanted her to join him in the camper for a siesta. Sex wasn't new to Paula. She'd had sex with a neighbor boy when she was ten years old. She had been doing it off and on ever since but hadn't really enjoyed it until Vern came along. Just as she had helped him to his first orgasm, she'd had her first one with him.

Vern was the most beautiful boy she'd ever seen with his clothes off. He was slim but firm, and his muscles were perfectly defined and reminded her of this statue she had fantasized over in a history book. Making love with him in her arms was ecstasy.

On that final day in the field, she and Vern had weighed up together just before noon. Everett was always careful with her when Vern was around. As young and innocent as he looked, there was a vaguely menacing air about Vern that intimidated even older men. He was polite enough and it was nothing that could be seen, but even Paula could feel it.

As they paid for sodas from the ice chest beside the trailer to drink with their lunch, Paula saw Everett looking at her with that hungry look in his eyes. It had lately become a beseeching look that told her he was desperate and consumed by his lust for her. She decided on the spot to explore the boundaries of his obsession.

They walked to a shade tree at the edge of the field where Vern's mother and Snake were eating, and put their lunch down on their sacks. Paula sat beside Vern and when they began eating, she looked toward the trailer where Everett was drinking a beer and looking her way. She got up and told Vern, "I'll be right back," and walked back to the trailer. No one thought anything about it as there was a portable toilet on the far side of the trailer next to Everett's pickup.

Everett's eyes were glued to her every step of the way. She stopped just out of reach and said to him, "Everett, if you want it, you can have it, but I want a hundred and fifty dollars."

His eyes grew wide and he swallowed his tobacco with a big, gulping swallow.

"Goddamn, Paula, a hundred and fifty dollars!" he exclaimed incredulously.

"Just forget it, then," she said and turned to walk back to her lunch. At that point she hoped he would let her go because she'd pretty much changed her mind again and wasn't at all sure she wanted to do this.

"Wait!" he exclaimed, and she turned back around and looked him defiantly in the eye.

"I'll pay it, Paula, I'll pay it," he repeated, and the resigned look on his big red face made her wish she'd asked for two hundred. She walked on around the trailer with him right behind her. When she drew near his pickup, she stopped and held out her hand.

"Look, let me just give you seventy-five now and the other half tomorrow so I'll have enough cash to pay everybody," he said as he pulled out a long leather wallet attached to a chain on his overalls.

"None of that shit, Everett. If you run short, write someone a check. I don't have all day. If you argue any more it's going to be two hundred," she replied.

He carefully counted out a hundred and fifty dollars, and as he handed the money to her, his hand was shaking badly and he was breathing hard as if he'd been running. She glanced down at the fly of his overalls. It looked like there was a tent pole beneath his pants. There wouldn't be any problem with getting him ready.

The interior of the camper was stifling hot. She quickly removed her jeans and panties and then deliberately slowly took off her T-shirt and bra as he stood there looking and blowing his warm breath on her. Sweat was already making the ends of her hair wet where it lay against her shoulders.

"Oh my God! Oh my God!" he kept repeating reverently when she was naked and reached out to fondle her breasts. He ran his thumb over her nipples and hefted the weight of them in his hand while his other hand wandered over her buttocks.

"Oh my God!" he said again as he pinched her nipples hard

and Paula felt herself becoming wet in spite of the sordid situation.

He gently pushed her back onto the narrow bed, pulled her legs apart and stood between them before dropping his overalls. He didn't even unbutton the straps, just slid them down over his shoulders and let the trousers fall around his knees. His big belly and chest were hairy as an ape and his dick was sticking out from his body like a tree limb. It was big and heavy like the rest of him.

He caught her legs at the back of her knees and pushed them up until her knees were near her chest. He entered her standing up and leaning forward. His breathing now sounded like a dog panting and he kept saying over and over, "Oh my God! Oh my God!" Paula wanted to giggle, but once he got inside her, it wasn't funny.

As he fucked her, sweat dripped from his red face onto her breasts. He pounded her hard enough that she was biting her lips to keep from crying out with pain. The look on his face was more violent than loving and she could feel his big, hairy balls slapping up against her ass.

Paula hoped no one was watching the pickup because it had to be rocking back and forth like it was in an earthquake. No sooner had Everett collapsed atop her than she pushed him off and quickly got her clothes on and stepped out into the sunshine.

When she found Vern still eating lunch, she said, "Get up and let's go back to work."

"Hey, let's rest awhile. I ain't even smoked yet," Vern replied.

"We're going now," she said, and when he saw the look in her eye, he got up and gathered up their empty sacks.

He followed her back to the trailer where Everett was dazedly emerging from his camper.

"Figure up our money, Everett, we're going home," she told him.

Everett silently tallied up the slips and paid them what they had coming.

"Give these sacks to Snake," she told Everett, taking the sacks from an astounded Vern's arms and throwing them at the field boss's feet. She took Vern by the hand and began walking toward the highway, going in a direction that they wouldn't pass by her family or his.

"Paula, what the fuck are you doing?" Vern asked before they had gone twenty steps.

"We're quitting, Vern. We aren't ever going to pick any more fucking cotton or figs or grapes or any fucking thing else," she told him and squeezed his hand and gave him a big smile.

He stopped there at the edge of the highway and looked at her closely like she had gone crazy or something.

"Come on, Paula, what the hell is going on?" he asked. She knew this had to be confusing, but she also knew they couldn't stop. She looked back at where Everett was standing by the cotton trailer looking at them, then she looked up the highway that went to Fresno and watched little heat waves rising like warm snakes from the asphalt. She looked back into Vern's questioning eyes.

"Vern, just trust me and I'll explain it all. You said you wanted to be an outlaw, didn't you?"

"Well, yeah, I said that," he replied.

"I love you, man," she murmured, running her hand through his soft damp hair. "I'm gonna be one with you. So let's go outlaw for a while. We can't do it in a cotton field."

He looked at her for a long moment.

"Let's go do it, girl," he said, taking her hand, and they started back up the road with their thumbs out.

A grungy hippie in a '69 Impala pulled over to give them a

ride. As they got in, they heard someone yelling and looked back to see Snake running up the road: "Vern! Vern! Get your damned ass back here, Vern!"

"That guy is yelling at you all, ain't he," the hippie said.

"Fuck him, drive," Paula replied.

"You didn't rob him or nothing, did you?" the hippie asked as he pulled back onto the road.

"Nah. He's been robbing us of our youth," Vern said, and Paula was filled with pride at the words and the way Vern said them.

"I can dig it," the hippie replied, and speeded up until Snake was just a speck in his rearview mirror.

CHAPTER 11

When Curly woke her up, they were sitting in front of a motel room in Salinas.

"I called home and Vern left a message on the machine. He's up in Oakland and wants us to ask Weldon if he knows anyone in there that knows Blake Ethridge, so I guess it's good we came."

"I've got to take a shower before we go visit," Paula replied. Her head was pounding.

"We got time, hon. This is our room right here," Curly told her. Curly felt ashamed of herself because she'd left Paula here sleeping in the hot sun while she'd tricked the lieutenant. But she hadn't known how else to handle things without renting two rooms. What Paula didn't know wouldn't hurt her anyway.

The prison visiting room was full of people and the noise level near unbearable. Weekends were the main visiting days and almost every chair in the room was taken. Kids ran around yelling, fighting, begging money for the vending machines and playing while their parents sat looking at one another, holding hands and wishing they could hear over the noise. Paula hated herself for thinking it, but she was thrilled that it was Weldon and not Vern they were coming to visit. She had the same thought every time she came with Curly to see Weldon.

A guard behind a desk at the front of the room took their driver's licenses and told them to have a seat. Weldon would be out soon. The last two chairs in the room were right beside the guard's desk, which is the last place any visitors wanted to be sitting.

"I knew this was what would happen. It's the price we pay for being late," Curly said.

"Well, what the hell, it's worth it to see old Weldon," Paula replied in a very loud voice and still Curly just barely made out what she said.

After what seemed a very long wait, the door at the rear of the room opened and Weldon came striding into the visiting area with a big grin on his face and his eyes searching for Curly. She jumped up waving and he headed in their direction. He hugged them both at the same time, burying his nose in their hair and taking long drafts of their scent.

"Jesus Christ! You two smell good," he exclaimed while squeezing them tightly.

"We showered up just for you, big boy," Paula told him.

Weldon wasn't big. He was about the same size as Melvin, with coal-black hair and dark brown eyes. He looked rugged and compact with a slim waist, wide shoulders, and muscular limbs. His high-cheekboned face held in place a fiercely hooked hatchet of a nose that made him look a lot more Indian than the nominal Cherokee that was in his blood. Paula could never get over how different he and Vern looked and how identical these two brothers sounded when they talked.

Over Paula's shoulder Weldon spotted a friend of his visiting with his brother at a table in the far corner of the room. He disengaged from Paula and Curly.

"I'll be back in just a minute," he said and walked off in that direction.

"Where's he going?" Paula asked Curly in a near shout.

"I'm not sure, but I think he's working on getting us a better spot," Curly shouted back over the adolescent chaos.

Max Brown looked up at Weldon as he approached the table.

"Hey, Weldon, meet my brother Robert. Robert, this is Weldon Coy, a good homeboy of ours from Fresno," he said, and Robert stood up to shake hands. There was one other guard in the visiting room besides the one behind the desk. This one ambled around the room keeping a close eye on the convicts and their visitors. Weldon noticed this one looking their way and knew he'd have to act fast. Once a convict is in the visiting room, he is supposed to talk only to his own visitors.

"Look here, Max, I've got these two broads visiting and we're stuck right on the cop's desk. I can't even cop a feel. I'm hoping you'll trade tables. I'll have a little something in a day or two and I'll send a slam down your way," Weldon told him in a fast monologue, trying to get it all in before the roving cop got there.

"You got it, man," Max said, getting up with his coffee while his brother gathered up a deck of cards they had been playing gin rummy with.

"Homey, that's two of the finest-looking heifers I've seen in many a day and that's counting the TV and everything," Max said.

"The blonde is my people and the other is my brother Vern's wife. I'll introduce you right now," Weldon replied just as the guard walked up.

"You're gonna have to get with your own visitors or I'll have to terminate your visit, Coy. That goes for you also, Brown," the guard told them, but Weldon could tell by the tone of his voice that he wasn't prepared to do anything that drastic yet. He was more or less just going through the motions and letting them know who the boss was.

"Yes, sir, we're just trading tables here, won't happen again," Weldon told him as they walked off toward Curly and Paula.

"Vern's in Oakland and I called home just before we left the motel. There's a message from him on the machine. He wants you to ask around in here if any of your friends from the Bay Area know of a guy named Blake Ethridge," Curly told him when they were seated at the new table. The noise was way down back here in the corner and she spoke in a near normal tone of voice.

"Blake Ethridge . . . Blake Ethridge . . . Hell, know him myself. Did time at Quentin with him. He's a biker from Oakland. Why does Vern want to find him?" Weldon asked.

"That's it!" Curly exclaimed. "He did tell me to mention the guy's a biker, but I zoned out on that. We really don't know why he wants to find the guy. But Vern ain't mad at him or anything. Just wants to talk about something," Curly told Weldon. She and Paula had agreed not to mention getting robbed. Vern could tell Weldon if he wanted to.

"Give me a day or so. I'll find out how to contact him," Weldon told them.

"Hey! What's your old cellie The Stepper doing? We've not heard from him or about him in a while now," Paula asked.

"Let's get some goodies and I'll try and get you all up-to-date on The Step," Weldon said.

They got up and went to the snack machines. Curly always brought three rolls of quarters and they sometimes spent the entire thirty dollars.

On a visit almost a year ago, Weldon had mentioned The Stepper to Curly and Paula and they had both become fascinated by the old man. Paula was almost obsessive about him. She had asked Weldon so much that he had finally given The Step Paula's phone number and told him to call her. Paula was thrilled to hear from him and told him to call her at least once a week. But she told Weldon that it was still better to hear things about The Step from Weldon because the man would talk about absolutely everything except himself. He didn't think there was anything special about his exploits.

Weldon opened a microwave chili and a Pepsi and began telling them about The Stepper's latest adventures while they nibbled on a pepperoni pizza and slipped quarters to passing kids to keep them quiet. Curly liked to tell Paula that the only thing Weldon did better than eating pussy was telling stories, and that much was true.

He had that slow country way of telling a story and somehow primed the punch line as he went along until it sort of exploded on its own.

But there is another angle to the funny things that happen in a prison. There are times when a humorous event also evokes a sad commentary on the human condition. In there, "laughing until you cry" is no cliché but a reality. Although The Stepper was very agile in those muddy areas, he sometimes left people doing both.

Weldon told them that a few days before in the afternoon, a scream came out of isolation that was heard way down the hallway. It sounded sort of like a panther and was terrifying in a way because O-Wing, or isolation, is semisoundproof. It takes a heap of pain to send that type of yell past those barricades, Weldon told them.

The men in isolation are let out of their cells thirty minutes a day for exercise. California law dictates the practice. There are twenty cells on a range or tier. They hold two men each. Beginning at 8:00 A.M. the first cell will be racked open so that the two men may walk up and down for thirty minutes in front of the other cells. After which time they go back in and the next cell is racked open.

Although designated as exercise time, convicts usually have to use that time to shower also or they don't get to shower. Some people do push-ups and jumping jacks. Others run errands, taking books and magazines back and forth for friends on the tier. A guard stands outside a grille gate watching everyone and racking doors when their time is up.

A convicted child molester was placed in a cell alone on the same tier The Stepper was on. The molester was given a cell to himself to keep him from being attacked by other convicts, who despise child molesters. But having a cell to oneself is a luxury. So as far as convicts are concerned, prison officials were actually rewarding the creep for being a child molester by giving him a single cell. They can call it "protective custody," but it's still a reward.

This particular fellow had "turned the corner" on being a degenerate pervert. He was a real sicko. All day long he stood naked in his cell looking at underwear ads in teen magazines and playing with himself.

He was a big, fat, hairy slob, but his head was bald except for a fringe above his ears that he used to comb strands of across his bald dome. He had a fat underbelly that hung in folds around his dick and balls. He was grotesquely ugly and thought he was God's gift to prepubescent girls.

He would stand there at times when the magazines or his fantasy excited him, holding his dick in his hand and propositioning convicts who were out for exercise.

"Hey, man, suck my dick for me, just reach through here and touch it," he would breathe frantically at passersby. A couple of cons who got mad and tried to snatch him through the bars had been put in the back in strip cells with just a hole in the floor to shit in and no exercise. Prison officials were very serious about protecting this pervert.

One day as The Stepper walked by, the molester asked him to suck his dick.

"*Psst,* hey, pal, put your mouth on this through the bars, suck on it!" the man said, showing The Stepper his little crooked dick.

"Okay, I'll do it, but I want to hold your nuts in a spoon while I suck it. That's the only way I'll do it," The Stepper told him.

"Okay, okay!" the man whispered back through the bars.

"Well, look here, I've got to go find a spoon now. I notice you have a stool in there. So when I find the spoon and come back, I want you to stand up on that stool while I suck your dick. I don't want to kneel down because the cop down there will see me. If you stand on the stool, it will look like we are just standing here talking."

"No problem, but you better hurry. You only got thirty minutes and I want you to do it for a long time," the pervert said.

"I'll do it till you want me to stop," The Stepper promised and walked back to his cell. He had a large tablespoon in there that he'd stolen off his breakfast tray.

As his cellie watched, he rolled about half a roll of toilet paper around his fist, then tucked both ends in, forming what cons call a "bomb." When lit in the center it burns for over ten minutes. Cons use them to heat coffee and other liquids.

The Stepper used this one to heat the spoon until it was white-hot. He had to wrap a wet rag around the handle to keep from burning himself. His cellie couldn't figure out what the hell he was doing.

"I'm getting ready for some hot sex," The Stepper told him.

"Didn't you ever hear your grandma and grandpa talk about spoonin'?" he asked his perplexed cell mate as he left again.

A young black gang banger who celled next to the pervert had heard the entire conversation between The Stepper and the child molester, and by the time The Step got back, spoon in hand, the youngster had decided he wanted some also.

"Hey, man, I want you to do me too. I don't care you hold my nuts in the spoon long as you get down on my joint," he said.

"Okay, I do you next. Get it good and hard for me while I take care of him," The Stepper said.

"Awwright!!" the gang banger said.

The molester was up on the stool, dick in hand, and frantic with lust for The Stepper's lips. "Get on it, man. Get on it," he panted.

"Here we go, baby," The Stepper said, putting the white-hot spoon under the molester's scrotum and pressing firmly upward.

The fat pervert left the stool like a rocket taking off and some argued that scream could be heard in downtown Salinas. He fractured his skull on the roof of his cell and broke four ribs when he bounced off the edge of his bunk before hitting the cement floor out cold. The Stepper left the spoon in his cell and walked off nonchalantly. As he passed the young gang banger's cell, he stopped and said, "Your turn, baby."

The youngster, still in partial shock from the bloodcurdling yell, looked at The Stepper for a few seconds, rolled his eyes and said, "I think I go ahead and pass on that, man."

The cop at the end of the tier was yelling from behind the grille gate.

"Lock down! Lock down! Everybody in your cells! Lock down!"

The Stepper went to his own cell and watched like everyone

else as they carried the moaning, slobbering pervert out on a stretcher. The cop stopped on the way out and asked, "What happened down there, McCall? I saw you down by his cell when he screamed."

"I don't know. I think he was up on his stool playing with himself and fell off. Must of got good to him," The Stepper replied.

"I wonder what that fucking smell is?" the cop said as he went on out.

Curly and Paula were both horrified and amused by the story. Then Weldon decided it was time to get down to business. He'd already noticed a couple DWB gang members hard-eyeing Paula.

Weldon was glad that Vern was on an extended trip. He spent the rest of the visit enjoying Curly and trying to convince Paula that doing away with Little Joe was their best shot. He could tell he wasn't getting through to her, but hoped as time went on, she would wake up. He began to entertain the thought of stabbing Brian and Jack anyway. It could possibly stop the hit if he took out the gang leadership.

CHAPTER 12

Fresno is an agricultural city and county in the middle of the San Joaquin Valley. But Fresno is also halfway between San Francisco and Los Angeles. In the old days anyone who traveled from Los Angeles to San Francisco stopped there, and like a big net the city caught many of them.

The more colorful of the travelers it stopped were blues singers and thieves. In the forties and fifties several legends of the blues world moved to Fresno. Among them Mercy Dee Walton, Slim Green, and Sidney Maiden. Richard Riggins, known in the blues world as "Harmonica Slim," the brother-in-law of Muddy Waters, is a resident of Fresno.

The thieves who made Fresno their home wouldn't be as recognizable to the public as the blues men, but they stand tall in legends of the underworld. Chief among them would be men like Slim Gaylord, a pimp who ran whorehouses in Fresno in the forties and fifties. Melvin liked to tell Slim's story. He'd heard it from older thieves and dope fiends.

Slim made a ton of money. He liked top sirloin steaks and he liked to bury his money in the ground in his basement. He had a habit of wrapping the cash he buried in the butcher paper that his steaks came wrapped in.

One of the most popular stories told among the underworld in Fresno is about what happened when Slim had to call a plumber over a problem with his water pipes. The plumber went into Slim's basement, came back carrying his toolbox and told Slim the problem was complicated and that he would have to come back the following day.

After three days of this Slim became suspicious and went down to the basement after the plumber had left. Pieces of butcher paper lay all over the basement and every one of Slim's stashes had been dug up. The plumber had been carrying the money out in his toolbox.

One of Slim's main whores had an insufferable little spoiled poodle dog that she would leave in Slim's care while she worked. Slim routinely locked the whining little critter in the basement until just before she returned home. The lonely dog smelled the meat on the butcher paper and the rest is plumber's history. The plumber is reputed to have built a huge plumbing-supply company using Slim's money.

Melvin Nix was another thief who stopped in Fresno and so far he'd been very successful. On Monday morning, as he drove away from Stockton after picking up Gatorbait, he was giving some thought to that success. Mainly because he now faced a proposition that has been the waterloo of many a thief. That last big score.

It pissed him off that he had to drive back to Fresno because as soon as he dropped Gatorbait off at home, he had to drive right back to Sacramento to meet Ralph Prest, who had a plumbing business in Rocklin, the town where the San Francisco 49ers have their training camp.

But as he looked at the box that contained the dead bird in the seat next to him, he felt better about doing this for Vern. Gatorbait was going to have a decent funeral at home. Vern would be happy about that.

Melvin had a caretaker, Paul, at his house, a cousin of his with a gimp leg from polio who was wonderful with animals. Too good, Melvin sometimes thought, because after two years around Paul, Melvin's own dogs had begun barking and growling at him. Paul would fix Gatorbait up and freeze him until Vern got home, which reminded Melvin he'd have to get a flatbed truck and collect the cages he'd got from Vern. His thoughts drifted back to his friend Ralph Prest.

Ralph was a short, rotund man and one of the best burglars in the United States. He was originally from Detroit and in years past his specialty had been jewelry stores. He was a wizard with electronics and there wasn't an alarm out there he couldn't circumvent somehow to get to the vault. When he burgled a jewelry store, he opened the vault and took the entire inventory. Ralph was also an avid fisherman.

Years ago, when he left Detroit, he loaded up a van with fly-fishing equipment and drove through the states by way of Los Angeles and on up into Vancouver, Canada, stopping everywhere he could find a good fishing hole.

An astute detective belatedly figured out that in every town where Ralph Prest stopped to fish, a jewelry store was burglarized. The coincidence severely grated on the man's nerves, especially since he knew Ralph was a jewel thief and had been trying to gain enough evidence to arrest him for ten years.

On his way back to Detroit, Ralph was pulled over in Sacramento, California, and arrested. Fly-fishing equipment was all they found on him. Using as evidence the fact that everywhere he stopped a jewelry company was knocked off, he was tried in Sacramento for a local burglary.

A jury acquitted him and during his trial in Sacramento he decided he liked the neighborhood, and a few months later set up a plumbing business in Rocklin with some of his ill-gotten gains.

Melvin met him at a chicken fight and they became good friends. They were five years into their friendship before they realized they were both in the same line of business. Like everyone else, Ralph thought Melvin was just a small-time drug dealer who bought wholesale and sold retail. After five years of drinking, partying, and chasing women together, Ralph realized that Melvin didn't buy anything. He stole everything he sold, which did wonders for his profit margin. Melvin had burgled a drugstore in Rocklin on a weekend that he was visiting and Ralph put two and two together finally. He began to get interested in Melvin's line of business.

Melvin owned up to Ralph that he stole his inventory and told him that he was about to go out of business. Drugstores nowadays were getting much more sophisticated alarm systems. The ones that didn't have top-of-the-line alarms were carrying very few hard drugs in their inventory. Melvin was beginning to have a hard time making expenses and the risks were no longer worth the payoff.

Ralph thought on a higher level and had lately found a drug-supply warehouse in Sacramento that he said they could knock off. Melvin had often dreamed of getting inside a drug warehouse and was amazed that it could be done in spite of some of the best alarm systems in the world. Those places had alarms that a marble rolling along the floor would set off.

Melvin initially felt funny because, as he explained to Ralph, he had never worked with anyone. Ralph told Melvin he hadn't either, but that this situation was unique. While he had the expertise to get into a drug warehouse, he didn't know anyone to sell to. Melvin had the outlets. So Melvin was on his way now to look the place over with Ralph.

They rode out together and looked at it. There was a big fence in back where a railroad spur came in for loading and unloading.

"Those are good alarms," Melvin commented.

"I can get us by those if you can find the dope. I don't know a codeine from a vitamin C," Ralph replied.

"You get us in, I'll get the dope," Melvin assured him.

He knew if they got it, it would be his last score. But he hated thinking like that because many thieves had gone down on what they said would be their last score.

He shook the thought from his mind as he neared his house and began thinking of his present situation. He hadn't done badly in life for a farmer's kid with a third-grade education. His home and everything else he had was paid for and he had over a hundred and fifty thousand dollars buried in plastic PVC pipes. He used plastic pipes to bury money in because they couldn't be detected with a metal detector.

The only discordant note in his life was Paula. He was hopelessly in love with her. Had been since he first laid eyes on her. Loving Paula was the most frustrating thing Melvin had ever experienced. It was torture with no end in sight. Not only because Vern was his best friend, although that was bad enough. The most hurtful part to him was knowing that several men fucked her every day and he couldn't lay a finger on her. The cardinal rule in the outlaw life they lived was that you do not fuck the wives of your friends whether they are whores or not. It just isn't done.

As far as money went, he'd have gladly dug up all his money and given it to Vern for Paula if that were possible. He couldn't even consider another woman as a soul mate and felt kind of fucked up about that. But, still, loving Paula was nice even from a cold distance. His reverie was interrupted when he pulled into his driveway and the pack of raging mutts came barking frantically at the pickup. Paul limped out onto the front porch to see who had arrived.

"Anyone call while I was gone?" Melvin asked as he carried the bird to the porch.

"Paula called wanting to know if you got Gatorbait, and some guy named Phil Fisherman called to confirm an appointment," Paul told him.

Phil Fisherman was Ralph. Melvin went to the phone and dialed Paula. His house was decorated in an old western motif. All his furniture was made from beautifully wrought redwood. Even the coffee table was a redwood bole. There were Navajo rugs on the floor. A poster of Paul Newman as Butch Cassidy hung near the giant TV screen. Melvin felt a great sense of pleasure from looking at his home. An even greater sense of pleasure infused him when Paula's voice said "Hello?" in his ear.

"Paula, I think I'm falling in love with you," he said.

"Oh, fuck you, Melvin. You've been in love with me forever, and besides that you ain't got nothing to think with and besides that you'll have to wait your turn. I'm a one-man woman," she replied.

"Where am I on the list?" he asked. His heart began beating fast. They had never teased each other like this, and even though they were playing around, her answer was very important to him.

"You're number one, Baby Face. There's none ahead of you," she said and laughed, then added, "Did you get Gatorbait without getting arrested?"

"Oh, yeah, the doc never even reported anything because the bird died. Vern lost him, but I brought him on home because I know Vern will want him buried proper."

"That could be a while. Vern's on one of his journeys. Do you want to take me and Curly out? Maybe dance a few slow ones, rub bellies and bite some earlobes?" she asked. She didn't seem at all perturbed at the loss of the chicken.

Melvin registered on "Vern's journeys." Vern often went on extended trips alone. Ordinarily no one knew where he went or why. He was usually gone a good while and in an upbeat mood when he returned. Not even Melvin had the nuts to ask where he'd been and why. It was obvious Vern wanted these excursions kept secret.

"Oh, hell, yes, but I got an appointment tonight. How about tomorrow?"

"That will be fine, little guy. Tell that lonely housewife I say hello and call me tomorrow," she said.

"Paula, I swear to God," he began, but she'd already hung up.

"Shit!" he said and stomped back out to his pickup. The dogs chased him, barking all the way to the gate. Her remark about the lonely housewife galled him. It was true that he pursued the wives of squares, some of them separated and others not yet separated and others who were just lonely or horny. He knew the practice was dangerous, but it had seemed to be a good idea when he began doing it and it was addictive.

As a committed outlaw Melvin viewed square johns with just a dash of contempt. The rules that kept him away from the wives of other outlaws didn't apply to squares. They were fair game and he loved the forbidden aspect of laying up on another man's nest.

But he had originally begun pursuing wives because of his love for Paula. These women weren't looking for a husband and weren't near as emotionally demanding as single women. Many of them were so frustrated and horny by the time they decided to break loose for a night on the town that making love with them was an adventure. Loving Paula had pushed him in that direction and she now razzed him more than anyone for doing it.

He was almost to Sacramento before he realized that by thinking about his own sexual preferences, his mind had led him right back to Paula, the way it always did. He shook his head, trying once again to clear it of her image, and was relieved to see the Denny's restaurant sign on the highway where he always met Ralph.

When he pulled into a parking space right up against the building, he could see Ralph through the window sitting on a stool at the counter. Ralph was shorter than Melvin by a couple of inches and weighed 250 pounds. In his early fifties, he was prematurely gray with a big distinguished shock of white hair that made him look like a talk show host. He was a well-educated man whose dress and manners were impeccable. Tonight he wore a pink golf shirt, white slacks, and a pink-and-white windbreaker and still managed to look elegant.

"You're forty-five minutes late, buckaroo, and you know I really don't play that shit," he said after Melvin had seated himself on the adjoining stool at the counter.

"I apologize, Ralph. I had a tough schedule and if I'd of stopped and called here I'd of been an hour late." He did feel bad because Ralph was a stickler for punctuality.

"Well, call next time," Ralph replied, and signaled the waitress to bring Melvin a cup of coffee.

"I promise," Melvin said. "How's the wife and kids?"

"The boys are fine and that nutty bitch is just as nutty as she ever was," Ralph said in a disgusted tone of voice. Ralph had two teenage sons that he doted on, but his wife was a nagging, screeching woman that Melvin had only met once and hoped not to meet again. They discussed the '49ers until Melvin finished his coffee.

"Let's go look at that milk cow," Ralph said, and dropped a five-dollar bill on the counter. It was just getting dark as Melvin followed him out to a white van that had R. P. PLUMBING AND SUPPLY—ROCKLIN, CALIF. painted on the side.

"I wanted to show you the joint in the daytime, but I guess we can look at it in the dark. I've looked it over real well anyway," Ralph said as they drove out to the highway.

"I just want to see the general layout, anyway," Melvin replied as Ralph turned on to highway 80, which led to Reno.

"The layout is pretty well perfect for a caper and that's because they probably think they can't be had. I figure we'll go in early on a Saturday evening, while there's still good traffic. Then, if we need to stay late or make two trips, we don't have to worry about any early workers coming in on us because they are closed on Sunday," Ralph said.

"How long you think it will take us to get in?" Melvin asked.

"I figure two hours, three at the outside, depending on what's in the wall. But I'm not going to be much help except as a donkey when we get in there."

"That won't be no problem," Melvin told him. "I've never been in a drug warehouse before, but I'd bet money they keep all the narcotics in the same place. They could even have a second perimeter with another alarm on that."

"Let me worry about the alarms, that's my end of the deal. There's the joint right up there. The big gray building with all the floodlights." Ralph pointed to the right.

Melvin could see right away that it was a good location for a burglary. The front and sides of the building were well lit, but the back was dark. A cyclone fence with barbed wire on top ran straight back from the sides of the building for a good ways.

"Must be ten acres or more back there," Melvin said.

"It's a big area. There's a railroad track comes right up to the back and a loading dock back there. That's where I figure we'll go in," Ralph said. He had pulled to the shoulder of the highway and they now sat looking at the warehouse. It looked awesome, and Melvin could feel little ripples of chills running up and down his back just at the thought of getting in there.

"We're going to have to get it soon, son. My lawyer called and the Ninth Circuit is hearing my appeal four weeks from now and he says I got a dead-bang loser. He figures I got five weeks from right now before I have to go in."

"That's the shits," Melvin replied. "Hell, we can get it this coming weekend if you want."

"Yeah, that or the one after. I've put up enough for my boys to go to college on and enough for that cunt to live on and I'm low on cash. I should just have the bitch killed, but I can't very well kill the mother of my kids. I'm not that cold."

"Nah, you can't do that, man," Melvin said.

"I'm going to trust you to keep my end of the money, and if I need some, I'll just call you from the joint. Is that okay?" Ralph said.

"That's fine, but, hey, if you need some now, I can let you have thirty or forty thousand. All you got to do is drive down and pick it up," Melvin said.

"Thanks, Melvin, but I don't borrow money. I'm too good a thief to have to do that. But I really do appreciate the offer."

"I'll take care of your end as long as I'm alive," Melvin declared.

"I know you will. My lawyer says I'm going to Lompoc Prison

down by Santa Barbara. Not the camp. The max joint. Do you know anyone there? I need to get introduced to the right people in there and I've never done any time. I don't want to get off on the wrong foot."

"I know one old thief from Fresno down there, Chuck Broussard. I'll cut you in to him. But let me talk to Weldon, Vern's brother. Hell, he probably knows twenty or thirty people there. I'll get some names for you before you go in."

"I would appreciate that," Ralph said.

"No problem," Melvin told him.

Ralph had been sentenced to five years in a federal prison on the Dyer Act. Transporting a stolen car across state lines. His lawyer had managed to keep him on bail until his appeal was heard. Mainly because it was a petty crime that contained no violence. The charge itself was a pure frame-up.

A couple years back a thief friend of Ralph's had stopped by his home in Rocklin and asked Ralph to help him burgle a post office. He told Ralph they could get the cash and all the money orders. The man told Ralph that he would cash all the money orders and bring Ralph his end. But Ralph had declined. He wanted nothing to do with a job that left a paper trail.

The man then asked Ralph if he could leave his car at Ralph's house for a few days as he had to fly out of state on some business. Ralph said okay and drove the friend to the airport in San Francisco. That was the last he'd seen of him.

The car sat in front of his house for almost ninety days. Ralph's wife began yelling about it being an eyesore, which by then it was, having been shit on by several pigeons. It had also attracted a few graffiti artists. She demanded that Ralph drive it around back of their house so it would at least be out of sight. Ralph wanted to leave it where it was, but he finally acceded to her carping, as he usually did. This time it was a major mistake.

He had to jump-start it with battery cables. After he got it running, he pulled out into the road and was immediately swooped on by three carloads of FBI agents and arrested on the Dyer Act. The car had been stolen in Detroit a few blocks from Ralph's old home place.

Ralph's buddy had obviously been caught by the feds on some other charge and they had made him an offer he didn't refuse. After they made a stool pigeon of him, they sent him to bust Ralph. A typical FBI operation.

About the only way they can catch a good thief is to have one of his friends set him up. Even a very cautious thief is defenseless in that situation because thieves trust their friends.

The agents testified at trial that the local police had located the car and called them. They said they then staked it out so they could find out for sure who had possession of it. Ralph was amazed that they had been able to maintain that kind of surveillance without him noticing them.

Ralph also knew the real story. The feds were very unhappy about him beating the jewelry-store case. So they sent a snitch to him. They hoped Ralph would bite on the post office deal but gave the stoolie a stolen vehicle to use as a backup. At least he hadn't bought in to the post office caper.

Post office burglary carries twenty years and he would surely have been caught in the act or shot, one or the other. The Dyer Act only carries five years maximum and that's what the judge gave him. The stoolie hadn't shown his face anywhere since. But Ralph and the feds were the only ones who knew about him. The jury wasn't told about his part. All they knew was that Ralph had been pulled over while driving a stolen car.

"Let's do it a week from next Saturday. I'm taking my boys to

Disneyland this weekend. You can come up that Friday and we will get everything ready and go in Saturday evening," Ralph told Melvin on the ride back to Denny's.

"Okay. What do I need to bring?"

"Just buy a good camper shell for your truck that people outside can't see in, and bring your police scanner. That's about it," Ralph said.

"I'll see you Saturday," Melvin said when Ralph dropped him off at Denny's.

CHAPTER 13

It was Wednesday evening now and Vern was getting very edgy. He was on his third night of watching the Hells Angels clubhouse near the corner of Foothill and High streets in Oakland, California. All the activity here was at the entrance to the motorcycle shop next to the clubhouse. Vern watched people going and coming there, hoping to spot Sam. If Sam remained in Oakland for a while, he could very well be hanging out and partying with these bikers. Especially if this Blake Ethridge was a Hells Angel.

The October weather was getting cold and Vern had to wear sweatshirts with thermals under them to keep out the cold coming at him from the bay.

Vern didn't mind waiting and watching, but his lack of information made him very jumpy. Sam could be in Alaska as far as he knew. This was also a very awkward spot for a stakeout. There was a taco joint near the clubhouse and Vern spent some time there drinking beer and watching. But it was on the same side of High Street as the clubhouse, which made it difficult to observe the goings and comings.

There was really no place to park on the busy street and be halfway cool about it. This was a poor neighborhood in a mainly black area and even the new Blazer stuck out like a sore thumb. He tried parking a mile or so away and just walking in the neighborhood, but already a couple of the bikers who were around the shop all day began giving him hostile stares. They probably thought he was some kind of cop. If he didn't hear something from Paula and Curly tonight about this Blake Ethridge, he planned to move on and try something else. Maybe shake up everyone who knew Sam. He walked on tired feet back to the little Mexican café and dialed home again.

"Hello?" Curly's voice said in his ear.

"Hi, sugar. You found out anything for me yet?" he asked.

"Oh, Vern! I'm so glad you called," Curly exclaimed. "I'll put Paula on to tell you everything because I get confused, but first you have to tell me anything that I need to know."

"Now what could that be?" he asked.

"I don't have the faintest, but I'm not putting Paula on until I find out," Curly said in a low and menacing voice.

"I love you very much, Curly, and it feels good," he told her.

"I love you too, Vern, and I miss you so fucking much; here's Paula," she replied, and he could tell she was close to crying again.

"Hey, big guy," Paula said softly.

"Hey, girl," he replied.

"Weldon called us today and told us how to find the guy, but you'll have to go through a few changes. He said he don't belong to the Hells Angels."

"Shit, I've wasted three days," he exclaimed.

"Not really. He does know a lot of them and he's a biker, so that's probably as good a place to look as any," she informed him.

"Tell me what Weldon said."

"Weldon knows him; he was in San Quentin with him a few years ago," she said, and went on. "He don't know his phone number but gave me the number of a woman in Rodeo, California, over by Oakland. Her name is Margie and she will put you in touch with the guy. Weldon has called her already. Have you got a pen?"

"Yeah, just a minute."

"Okay, her phone number is the five-ten area code, seven-nine-nine, oh-seven-oh-one. Her name is Margie. She's a good friend of Blake's and he takes messages over there. He lives somewhere in Oakland," she told him.

"All right, babe, I'll get on the phone with her. Maybe I'll get lucky here. Did you and Curly buy any of them things, them . . . what do you call them?"

"Teddies, Vern. My, my, what in the world could you be thinking about?"

"You know what I'm thinking about, girl," he said softly.

"I guess I do. Man, I wish you'd of been with us last night. Melvin took us out to Pierce's Park. They had a good hillbilly band and we got blowed out. Melvin passed out, so we had to hire a taxi and bring him home with us. He had to send Paul to get his truck this morning, but we had a hell of a good time. Me and Curly are back working now. Made close to a thousand from noon to five yesterday."

"Good for you, girl. How is Weldon doing?"

"Guess he's okay. You know how he is. You never really know what he's thinking. He sure told us some funny stories about The Stepper. They both said to tell you howdy. We didn't tell him about Sam or any of that. You can tell him when you get ready.

But he's going crazy over that gang deal. We are going to have to find a way to get that settled," she said.

"Okay, Paula. I love you, sweetheart. I'm getting off here and I'll get home soon as I can."

"Vern?" she said before he could hang up.

"Yeah, babe?" he asked.

"That gator has four more days to live. I'm killing the son of a bitch at six o'clock Sunday afternoon," she said.

"Dammit, Paula!" he exclaimed, but the phone went dead in his ear. He dialed Margie, while hoping for the gator's sake that he found Sam before Sunday. He realized he'd forgot to ask about Gatorbait and wondered why Paula never mentioned him.

He got a recording, but as he began leaving a message, she picked up the phone.

"Weldon already told me about you," she said. "I can't give out Blake's address or phone number without asking him first. I expect him to drop by here tonight, but I haven't been able to reach him by phone. Why don't you just drive on over here and wait until I get in touch or he comes by. You can stay the night if you need to," she told him.

"Well, thanks. I'd like to do that," he said, and she gave him directions to her home. He preferred to stay at her home and have someone to talk with than to sit in a motel waiting for a phone to ring.

He got back on the freeway and drove out past the racetrack at Albany. Rodeo was about twenty miles north of Oakland. When he left the freeway, he stopped at a liquor store and bought a quart of Wild Turkey and a half case of Budweiser. He wanted to be prepared for a long evening.

She lived in a spick-and-span residential neighborhood about a mile off the freeway. Vern pulled the Blazer to the curb and a big menacing-looking rottweiler dog sauntered across the yard to stand by the driver's side door of the Blazer. Vern decided to just sit in the car for a bit and admire the well-trimmed lawn.

A woman he presumed to be Margie was standing in front of a screened-in porch holding a four- or five-year-old girl in her arms. The little sprout was gazing at Vern also, much in the same way a baby raccoon would look from its mother's back. Vern couldn't help but smile—she was a beautiful little blond girl with a sprig of hair standing up in back as if it had been ironed in place. She was a miniature version of Margie, minus the centurion hairdo.

"Rusty! Get back here," the woman yelled at the dog, and as the creature moseyed back to the porch, Vern got out of the Blazer holding the half case of Bud under his arm, and put the car keys in his pocket.

"Hello, I'm Margie," she said, and gave him a big, friendly smile.

"I'm Vern and glad to meet you," he replied, returning the smile.

"That's a lot of Bud you're holding there, but bring it on in and I'll help you drink it," she said as she turned back toward the house.

Vern followed her in. The place was small but well turned out, with white leather furniture, a crystal coffee table, and vases of red and white roses on the dining room and coffee tables.

"This is Cindy," she said as she put the little girl down.

"She's a knockout. Is she your daughter?" Vern asked as he set the beer on the coffee table, took off his leather coat, and hung it over the back of a chair.

"She's my granddaughter. I'll hang that up for you," she replied, and took his jacket into another room.

"I'm cooking, so bring the beer on into the kitchen and we'll talk and drink while I cook," she said when she came back. Vern followed and looked at her more closely. There was no way she looked like anyone's grandma.

She was very blond and petite, with skin that seemed to glow. Her lips were full and stretched over white teeth when she smiled. She was very well put together and didn't look a day over thirty years old.

"You sure don't look like Weldon's brother," she told him as he sat down at the kitchen table and opened two bottles of beer.

"Yeah, seems like he got the Indian side of the family and I caught the Irish," he told her. For some reason he felt immediately at ease around her, and that wasn't usually the case when he met new people.

"He sure is good-looking. I mean, I only met him a couple of times in between jails, but I suppose I had a little yen for him." She spoke with complete candor as she opened the oven and poked at a dish with a long fork. "I was really surprised when he called me after so long."

"He's the kind of guy women either love or hate. Not much in between," he told her and took a long pull on the beer.

"How 'bout you?" she asked, giving him a big smile and looking him right in the eye as she drank from the bottle of Bud. He'd noticed that she didn't offer him a glass and took her own right from the bottle, and it dawned on him what had made him feel so comfortable in her presence.

Although she was very feminine, she had the confidence of a man. She was relating to him as an equal and obviously felt secure in doing so. Very few women could pull that off, and especially if she lived and socialized among the same types of outlaws that he did. Dopers, thieves, bikers, pimps, and other assorted hoodlums are notorious chauvinists.

"No in between with me either. They all hate me," he told her.

"I doubt that." She laughed, then went to the refrigerator, got two more bottles of Bud, and sat down at the table with him.

"I need to know a little more about why you want to find Blake," she said. "I trust Weldon and all that, but if you came up here to make a move on him or something like that, I'd be in a bad position. He's a very special friend of mine."

"Nothing like that, believe me," Vern assured her.

"Well, if it were something like that it's doubtful you'd get out of this town alive. Damn, that girl is being too quiet," she said, jumping up and going out into the living room. She came back smiling. "Playing with dolls," she told him.

"Look here, Margie, I'm looking for my brother-in-law, a biker named Sam, only he don't have a motorcycle. I don't know what you call a biker without a motorcycle."

"I don't either." She laughed.

"Anyway, before he headed up this way, someone overheard him talking to Blake on the phone. I'm hoping Blake will help me find him. I don't know Blake, so I asked Weldon if he knew him and he steered me to you. That's the only reason I've got for wanting to talk with the guy. I'll be forever in your debt if you help me, but I don't mean you or any of your friends any harm. You have my word on that."

"All right, I guess we understand each other, and I think you've told me all you want to tell me," she said, going to the stove and pulling a hot dish from the oven.

"Do you like lasagna?" she asked.

"Love it," Vern said.

"You're in business, then. Blake will be by here soon, so let's eat while it's hot."

After they ate the lasagna, which was very good, she put Cindy to bed and Vern went back to the Blazer and retrieved the quart of Wild Turkey. They sat at the table making small talk. She stayed with the beer while he sipped at the whiskey.

He remembered conversations he'd had with Weldon a few years ago when his brother had been paroled from San Quentin. They had a habit of drinking and talking together after the others had gone to bed. Vern enjoyed the closeness to Weldon those times offered. They had spent very little quality time together in their lives.

Weldon had told Vern a lot of prison war stories, and there were many wars in prisons, from minor skirmishes to full-scale race riots and gang wars. Weldon had been in his share of all kinds. To Vern, the tales represented a fascinating slice of life, morbid adventures with grisly forms of violence that he could experience through Weldon's eyes and yet not be touched by them. Sort of like reading a good Stephen King horror story with the added touch of knowing the events were real.

As he talked with Margie he realized that he'd already heard about Blake Ethridge, although Weldon had always called him Dad. The man didn't have a nickname, which was rare for a convict, but Weldon gave everyone nicknames. He'd called Ethridge "Dad" because the man had five or six kids by four or five different women. He was also a legend in the Bay Area underworld.

Vern had been feeling excited when he arrived here at Margie's. In a strange way he enjoyed hunting people, especially if the person knew Vern was hunting him, as Sam surely did. The best thrill came at the point where the hunt began to turn successful, and Vern felt things were breaking his way when he'd found Margie.

But if memory served him right, this could also be the end of the trail. Weldon had told him that "Dad" was a very quiet and secretive man. Said he could go days at a time without talking if no one asked him anything. Weldon had also told Vern that Dad loved the few friends he cultivated and was very protective of them. So if Sam was his friend, Vern could turn from the hunter to the hunted real quick. It wasn't a very pleasant thought, but he didn't have time to dwell on it. Vern wondered how they would see him being here, but worrying wouldn't help anything. He'd just play it by ear.

"He's here!" Margie exclaimed around midnight when two motorcycles with loud pipes turned the corner and came roaring up the street to her house. Vern walked with her to the screened-in porch. He wanted to make sure Sam wasn't one of the visitors.

Two men parked their bikes and took off their helmets and attached them to the bikes as Vern and Margie watched from the porch. She turned on an outside light as they came walking up the drive.

"Blake, this is Vern, Weldon Coy's brother," she said by way of introduction when the first of the riders reached the porch.

"Good to meet you. This is Gary, a friend of mine," the man said, and Vern shook hands with them both before they all went back into the kitchen. Margie brought the two men a beer and handed Vern his half-full water glass of whiskey.

Blake Ethridge had long brown hair shot with gray around the sideburns. His wavy hair fell about his shoulders and he wore a black leather vest over a black silk T-shirt. He had on bell-bottom Levi's and a pair of lizardskin cowboy boots. Close to six feet tall, he was medium-built with just the beginning of a pot-belly. He carried himself with an air of strength and assurance. An angry knife scar ran from his right earlobe toward the corner of his mouth. His high-cheekboned face with prominent nose and deep-set eyes carried the impression of Indian blood.

The big, well-built youngster with him had long hair too and wore a gray vest under a denim jacket. He wore Levi's and a pair of military-style combat boots. A Hells Angel motorcycle club patch adorned the back of his jacket. He took a chair across from Vern. Ethridge declined Margie's offer to sit down and instead squatted Indian-fashion beside Vern's chair and took a long pull on the beer.

"I remember your brother Weldon. I was in San Quentin with him a few years back. You don't look like him at all," Ethridge told Vern.

"People tell me I sound like him," Vern replied.

"You do," Ethridge said. "What is it you want to see me about?"

"I'm looking for my brother-in-law Sam," Vern said.

"What's it about?" Ethridge asked.

Vern looked around the room at Margie and the other biker.

"I'd rather talk to you alone about it," he said.

"Okay. I'm not sure I can help you out. I'm going back to my house in Oakland right now. You could follow me, but I think it would be better if I left my bike here and rode with you. Then we could talk on the way," he told Vern.

"Sure, that's okay, but if you want to, we can just walk out here in the yard and talk," Vern replied. He felt a bit apprehensive about going along with this guy. What if he was a good friend of Sam's?

Vern knew he was being paranoid. If the guy had little enough sense to be a good friend of Sam's then Vern could be assured he wouldn't have enough sense to do anything right. Even set up an ambush. Fuck all that paranoia, he thought, I'll just go along here and stay on my toes.

He suddenly remembered something Weldon had told him and looked at Ethridge's hands as the man lit a filter-tip cigarette. He wore big rings on four of the five fingers of each hand, from a big death's-head gold ring to another that looked like antique gold with about twelve large diamonds in a golden square.

But the hands themselves were misshapen and deformed if one looked very closely at them. Vern remembered a story that Weldon had told him about Blake Ethridge's hands.

A man known for robbing drug dealers had been paroled to the Bay Area and stopped by Ethridge's house with another man to visit. Ethridge's wife and two young daughters were there, but he wasn't home. His wife showed them in and they kicked back in his living room to wait.

When he finally showed up, the man and his friend pulled a .44 and .357 Magnum and told him it was a robbery. They figured he made speed and should have a lot of drugs and money on hand. When he told them he only had a quarter ounce and the five hundred in his pocket, they got mad and threatened him and his family. But he insisted that was all he had. By this time they had him lying facedown on the floor with his hands out in front of him.

Finally the robber accepted what he offered but shot Ethridge through both hands with the .44 Magnum before they left the house. Weldon said it terrified Ethridge's wife and children. When Ethridge went to the hospital, he told the doctor that he'd been hitchhiking and someone had picked him up and shot him. The doctor called the police and he told them the same story.

Three months later, on a Sunday morning, the man who robbed him had been out in his front yard in Oakland washing his car. A sedan pulled up and the driver said, "Hey, Robert!" When the man looked up, water hose in hand, he was shot thirty times with an Uzi. Only twenty-four of the shells hit him, but that was enough.

The main reason that Weldon liked to tell the story was that Ethridge had forty-five thousand dollars in a money belt around his waist at the time he was being robbed and shot and his family was being terrorized and he never gave it up.

That was just one of the stories about Blake Ethridge. Vern had heard several of them.

"I don't like talking about things that matter here at Margie's. This is the first place they would bug if they wanted to hear me. So we can talk in your car. Can I have some of that whiskey?" Ethridge asked.

"Sure," Vern said, but Margie was already on her way out to the kitchen to bring him some. Ethridge had a very low voice, but he had such a commanding presence that whenever he talked, others in the room seemed to disregard their own conversation and tune in on his. The man had an extremely magnetic personality. Vern assumed that when he said "they," he was talking about the FBI or some other law enforcement agency.

Margie brought Vern's bottle out and after she poured Ethridge a glass and topped Vern's off, the youngster pulled out a small glassine bag and a straw. He shoved the straw into the bag, catching a sparkling powder in the end of it, then brought it to his nose and snorted it. He offered the bag and straw to Margie, who repeated the procedure and handed the bag to Vern.

"I'll pass on that," Vern told her. He didn't know if it was cocaine or crank, as they look the same. She passed the bag to Ethridge, who took a deep snort and handed it back to the youngster, who got up and shook hands with Vern again.

"I'm breaking camp, man. It was good meeting you," he told Vern.

"Same here," Vern told him.

"Wait a minute, Gary. I want you to see what Blake gave me for my birthday," Margie said and went toward her bedroom. They all stood there and waited. She came back into the room with a heavy gold chain around her neck. The chain was woven in an intricate pattern and she was attaching heavy gold earrings that matched the necklace to her ears.

"Aren't they gorgeous?" she asked when she got them on. They all agreed with her that they were fantastic. Vern looked over at Blake and they locked eyeballs for a minute, and Blake sort of nodded to Vern with a disgusted look on his face. The necklace and earrings were Paula's. Vern had given them to her at Christmas the year before.

The youngster fired up his motorcycle and Blake pushed his on up in the drive and they said their good-byes to Margie. Vern promised her he would stop back by sometime.

"Do you mind if I drive? I've never drove a Blazer," Ethridge asked.

"Be my guest," Vern said, handing him the keys.

The freeway was deserted at this hour, and before Vern knew it, Ethridge was driving almost a hundred miles an hour. Vern just fastened his seat belt and didn't say anything. The most he'd ever had it up to was seventy-five. But the man seemed like a good driver. They were roaring down 580 toward Oakland with very little traffic in their way.

"That was your necklace, wasn't it?" Ethridge said as he flashed the high beams to move a car in front over from the fast lane so he could pass.

"Yeah, it was my wife's, or one just like it," Vern replied.

"I really appreciate you not saying anything to Margie. It would have hurt her feelings bad."

"Never entered my mind. I figured you and I could talk it over," Vern replied.

"Well, what's the story, anyway?" Ethridge asked. He talked with such a soft voice that Vern had to move over in the seat to hear him.

"I've got two women right now and Sam is the brother of one of them. I let him stay with us for a while. You know, fed him, let him have the run of the place. Last weekend we were all gone and he robbed us. Took his own sister's stuff as well as mine and my other old lady's. I need to find him, man. There's a couple of things I don't understand about a move like that and I want him to enlighten me in person."

"Next thing I'd ask is if you knew for sure he done it. But since I got the fucking loot from him, I don't need to ask that," Ethridge said.

"Look here, I'm not hung up about the jewelry, you know. The way I see it, if you bought the stuff from him, that makes it yours. I would just appreciate it if you would help me find him," Vern said.

"I'm glad you're not all pushed out of shape, but I will get my part of the play as straight as I can. I shouldn't have dealt with the fucking creep. I never liked the son of a bitch, anyway. He was at Quentin with me and Weldon. Weldon sort of took him under his wing because he was that lady's brother. I forget her name."

"Curly," Vern said.

"Yeah, that's her—Curly," Ethridge said, as he took a cutoff from the freeway. They wound around some back roads and up a hill until they had a panoramic view of Oakland lying spread out before them in the night.

They parked in front of a house with a high fence around it. Ethridge pushed a button on a remote control in his pocket and a gate slid open on rollers. There were two Corvettes parked in the driveway of the garage. One new and the other six or seven years old.

"Curly is Weldon's old lady. He got sixteen years on a robbery charge and she got with me until he gets home. But that right there tells you something about Sam. He not only rips off his sister but also a guy who looked out for him in prison and he probably needed someone in there, as phony as he is," Vern explained as they walked up the drive.

"No doubt about it. He'd of got hurt two or three times around there if he hadn't been hanging out with Weldon," Ethridge said. A woman opened the door for them. She was holding a baby in her arms.

"This is my woman, JoAnne, and our new addition to the family. We named her Julie. JoAnne, this is Vern Coy," Ethridge said.

She was a small girl with dark hair and eyes. Petite yet voluptuous. The baby resembled them both and lay in her arms gazing out at the world with an utterly enchanted look on her face. The woman took Vern's hand and smiled: "Pleased to meet you."

"My pleasure," Vern replied.

The living room was small, with leather furniture and a classy-looking rock fireplace. It led out onto a redwood deck that looked down on another part of Oakland.

"Come on downstairs," Ethridge told him, and Vern followed him through a door off the kitchen and down a flight of stairs. There was a garage and a workroom that were chock-full of motorcycle parts, lathes for working metal, and every kind of antique slot machine one could imagine.

"My hobby," Ethridge said, as Vern admired the slots. There was another long leather couch down there and they took a seat on it. Vern still had the bottle of Wild Turkey, which by now was less than half full. Ethridge picked up a phone and called JoAnne upstairs, telling her to bring down some glasses and ice and a bottle of schnapps for him.

"Bring that box of jewelry I bought from Sam with you," he told her before he hung up.

She brought the box down along with the glasses, ice and

schnapps. After she walked back up the stairs, Ethridge placed the box on a coffee table and opened it up.

"I guess everything in here is your stuff?" he said.

The first thing Vern saw was his Rolex watch. But he was impressed with the amount of glittering gold, silver, semiprecious stones, and diamonds, most of which were Paula's. Vern had never realized until now the volume of jewelry she had. Paula was very good at talking tricks into giving her presents, and over the years some of them had been generous.

"I didn't care much for most of it because it's mostly custom-made stuff. But most of the stones are first-rate. I was going to keep them and maybe melt the gold down later. That set I gave Margie for her birthday is all that's missing out of what I got from Sam. There could be more that he dumped somewhere else, I don't know," Ethridge told him.

"How much did you pay him for it?" Vern asked, and took a drink of the cold whiskey he'd poured over ice cubes. Ethridge was drinking his straight from a water glass and the bottle was getting close to empty. Vern made a mental note to slow down, as he was beginning to feel drunk. Ethridge still looked dead sober.

As they talked on and studied one another through the night, Ethridge would occasionally snort a white powder from a small glassine bag and offer it to Vern.

Although Vern declined, he realized why Ethridge wasn't getting drunk. It was the crank. The speed. It kept him up. As he crouched Indian-fashion before Vern, who sat on an opulent leather couch, Vern had a sure thought.

This man would burn himself out and die before he was fifty. He wasn't far from it now. Vern also kept noticing JoAnne, who appeared unobtrusively bringing drinks, ashtrays, ice, and other needs. It was so obvious how she loved this man and seemed to bloom when she came near him. Vern also noticed how she tended the baby continuously. She was obviously a good mother.

Ethridge seemed to hesitate and think a lot before he replied to Vern. Vern knew it was because the man was having a hard time trusting him. But he could see that Ethridge was starting to realize he was telling the truth.

"I traded him something for it. In fact, I still owe him something because I was short when he came by," Ethridge said.

"Well, transfer it into dollars for me and I'll pay you back whatever it was worth to you," Vern told him.

"You just take it on home. It's not worth anything to me anymore. Sam told me that his aunt died and left it all to him in her estate. I should have known better. I really don't like him making a chump out of me. I'll deal with him when he calls about the rest," Ethridge said.

"No, I'll deal with all that for you. No use in old Sam having to apologize twice," Vern said, and they looked each other in the eye for a long moment.

"It's just that I can't take this stuff back from you without paying something. It wouldn't be right," he added.

"Yes, it would. It teaches me a lesson about dealing with creeps like Sam. You see, I've got this weak spot for guys I've been in prison with. I always think that since they have been in prison that they must be okay, or that we have something in common and should stick together or some shit like that.

"There may have been a time when that was true. But nowadays it don't work so well. I've been burned and lied to and fucked around more by ex-cons than I have these so-called squares out here."

"Why do you think that is?" Vern asked. It seemed like an interesting line of thought.

"I know why it is. They're putting all kinds of people in prison now that don't belong there. They get twenty years for having some dope or something, but they're not criminals. They don't have the criminal values. Many of them start snitching right away and get rewarded for it. They don't know a value from a humpback whale.

"Look what this fool Sam is doing. He's out here in the hunt with us and we're all supposed to be preying on society. But he's preying on us. He's taking from his own tribe. So now he don't belong to society and he don't belong to us. I wonder what the fuck he thinks he is or where he fits in. With a character like that, he's bound to rat on someone. It's just a matter of time. He don't have ethics that tell him not to be a rat."

"I think I see what you mean," Vern said. The whiskey was gone now and Ethridge twisted the cap off a bottle of cinnamon schnapps.

"Here, try this," he said. Vern didn't like sweet whiskey, but he did like cinnamon so he took a swig. It had a heavy texture and was very hot. He felt it burning all the way to his guts. But it wasn't bad. His bones themselves began feeling warmer.

Ethridge pulled a clear bag from his vest pocket along with a short straw and took another big snort and offered Vern some before putting it back up.

"You know, I've never done any time in jail or prison. But what you were saying about values was interesting, although I'd never thought about it like that. When I was a kid I used to watch these James Cagney movies. I wanted to be a thief or robber like Dillinger or Jesse James or one of them. But then I noticed how people tell on each other and I backed off of that dream. I didn't know who to trust and who not to trust," Vern found himself saying.

"Honorable thieves did trust one another in Jesse James's day. But now there's so many laws and so many new kinds of criminals because of them laws that no one trusts anybody. But that's a direct reflection on how sick this government is getting."

"I don't follow that," Vern said, taking another drink of the schnapps. He figured a couple more drinks of this and he wouldn't be following his nose, much less anything else. But this guy Blake was an interesting fellow and Vern wanted to keep him talking.

Vern was getting very drunk, but obviously the crank Ethridge was snorting was keeping him relatively sober.

"I'm a little older than you and I remember my family talking about Communist Russians denouncing their relatives and neighbors to the KGB. Everyone agreed about how disgusting it was that Russia had built a criminal justice system based entirely on informing. People there were afraid to even talk to anyone. So now look what's happening in our justice system.

"Take that John Gotti trial in New York. That underboss of his, Sam Gravano, 'Sammy the Bull.' He turned over on Gotti and while testifying against Gotti he admitted to twenty murders himself. Some of them he chopped up the bodies and they never even found remains.

"After Gotti's trial a judge sentenced Sammy the Bull to five years. The U.S. attorney is up there arguing that he should get less than five because he helped the government so much. That puts a message out loud and clear that if you're willing to snitch for the government, you can even get away with murder. Shit, I can get ten years for this little bag of dope right here and he gets five for twenty murders. Is that sick or what?"

"That is obscene," Vern said.

"But on the bright side, man, there are still plenty of good people around and your brother Weldon is one of the best. You may not believe me, but jewelry buying is not my line of business. Sam told me he was going to use the money to help Weldon get a lawyer."

"No shit?" Vern exclaimed. He didn't think he could get any madder than he was, but cold chills raced up and down his back.

"Well, fuck that. Is there anything I can do for Weldon? Money? Dope? Any way I can help him out?"

Vern was truly humbled by this man's attitude. Here he had got involved in a deal and was losing what must have been a lot of money or drugs, or both. A loss he didn't have to take but was accepting on principle. Now he was asking Vern if he could help Weldon in any way. Vern was at a loss for words for a minute or two.

"Paula and I take good care of Weldon financially, and Curly visits him regularly. He's got everything he needs. But I'll let him know you asked," Vern replied, then added, "Do you belong to the Hells Angels?"

"No, why do you ask?" Ethridge replied.

"Seems like a lot of your friends do, and I spent a few days watching their clubhouse in Oakland hoping to locate you or Sam. They don't seem to be what I've heard and read about them. I recognized this guy Sonny Barger out in front there one day, and he didn't look like what I'd pictured him."

"You mean his knuckles don't drag the ground when he walks?" Ethridge smiled.

"You might put it that way."

"Most of what is written about them is propaganda put out by law enforcement agencies. But the truth is that they are about like anyone else. Some of them work for a living and some don't, but they all share a set of common values and ethics. They don't live by anyone else's standards but their own. That makes the government hate them. Sonny has been the leader and arbiter of their rules for a lot of years and that makes him especially feared by the government."

"I'm not sure I understand these ethics and rules you're talking about," Vern told him.

"It goes back to what we were talking about a while ago. They keep their word. They pay their debts. They don't inform on anyone. They stand up for their brothers, their family, and what they believe in. The government sees that cohesiveness as a criminal conspiracy. I see it as a damn good and honorable way to live. Most of us bikers I guess feel like cowboys. We don't like barbed wire and cement. And we don't like being told what to do, which is the main function of big government."

Vern lost the rest of what he said. When he stood up, the phone next to Ethridge had been ringing. Now the man had his finger to his lips signaling JoAnne to be quiet and was pointing out to Vern another phone across the room and gesturing for Vern to pick it up. Vern walked over and gingerly took the phone off the hook and placed it against his ear. Sam's voice was coming in loud and clear.

"Just thought I'd check in with you. I'm down in San Luis Obispo," he was saying.

"I'm glad you did. I picked up those odds and ends for you and I don't like owing anyone. When will you be up this way again?" Ethridge asked him.

"I don't know, but it won't be until after the weekend. I've got some money out in the street up here and I want to get it all before I come back up there. Will that be okay?" Sam replied.

"Uh, I guess so, but I'd planned to go to Vegas next week, so what are we talking here, Monday? Tuesday? What day?" Ethridge asked him.

"I don't know, man. I'll call you back on the weekend. Is that okay?"

"Well, look here. I may need to leave suddenly and I don't

want you making a trip for nothing. Give me a number where I can reach you in case I have to take off," Ethridge told him. Vern got the feeling that Ethridge was playing Sam like a fish, but there was a note of uncertainty or paranoia in Sam's voice and the next thing he said revealed those fears.

"Oh, yeah, uh, hey, Blake, I called this guy named Chester in Fresno and he told me Weldon's brother Vern was by there looking for me. Chester said he mentioned your name because he'd heard me talking to you. I was wondering—did Vern try and get hold of you?"

"Oh, that's who that was. I didn't even remember Weldon having a brother. Yeah, some guy named Vern called when I wasn't here. I don't know how he got my number. But JoAnne thought he might be a cop or something. She told him I hadn't seen you in years. He said you might be coming up and he'd call back, but he ain't yet. What the fuck does he want, anyway?"

"Ah, him and I had an argument about him beating up my sister. I think he's just drunk and wanting to start some shit or something," Sam said, and Ethridge looked over at Vern and winked. But Vern couldn't see any humor in this bullshit. Sam was totally fucking crazy or something.

"You want me to talk to him? Straighten him out?" Ethridge asked.

"Nah, man, forget that, but if he calls back, you'd better shine him on. I'm pretty sure he's a snitch."

"A what?" Ethridge asked, looking over at Vern with a look approaching real concern on his face.

"Well, keep this between you and me, but I think he gave up a crank lab the Jokers had down by Fresno. He did it to get his old lady Paula out of a bad case. I've already told them about it, and they will be dealing with him before long. The guy is really bad news, so be careful."

"Thanks for telling me, man, but damn, don't wait so long next time. Hell, I might have had some kind of dealing with him had he got hold of me."

"Yeah, I'm sorry about that, but I didn't think you and him would ever cross one another's trail," Sam replied.

"Okay, well, where can I get hold of you?" Ethridge asked, and motioned for JoAnne to give Vern a pencil and paper. She retrieved the pad and ballpoint pen by Ethridge's phone and handed them to Vern.

"I'm at the Orcas Motel, right down by the water. The number is two-three-seven, oh-four-four-one, and ask for extension two-oh-six. That's my room number. I'm paid up until Sunday, so if I don't hear from you by then, I'll call Sunday morning before I check out," Sam said.

"Okay, pardner. I'll call if I take off soon. If not, I'll see you early next week," Ethridge said, and hung up the phone.

Vern had a sick feeling in the pit of his stomach as if he'd been kicked in the nuts. Sam had schemed this whole thing out so that he could rob them and then have a gang of bikers rub him out before he could get back at him. It was such a low-down evil plot to run on his own sister and brother-in-law, who had treated him with respect, that it made Vern physically sick to the point he wanted to throw up. Weldon had been right all the time. He was in very serious jeopardy.

"I'm not a rat," he told Ethridge, looking him steadily in the eye.

"I know that, Vern. But you'd better get this straightened out before it goes any further. The trouble with that kind of talk is that it's hard to squash once it gets out there. It sort of takes on a life of its own once it gets around. I know a few of them Jokers in Portland, and I'll tell them what I think is going on. Man, that's one low-down little creep you got for a brother-in-law. I had no idea the fool was that sick," Ethridge told him.

"I appreciate your vote of confidence," Vern told him, and over Ethridge's shoulder he saw a portrait of Hitler. Beneath the portrait was written, "Old age and treachery will overcome youth and good looks."

It seemed appropriate somehow to their preceding conversation.

CHAPTER 14

The Stepper was out of the hole. Not only out of the hole, but going home in the morning. Weldon couldn't believe it, and neither could anyone else. When a convict leaves prison, he gets a slip of paper with every place in the prison on it: laundry, library, education, cellblock, recreation yard, etc.

Before release he must go around to all these places and have the paper signed by the supervisor in that department. This is to ensure that he hasn't checked out books, clothes, or other institution goods and not returned them.

The sheet of paper is called "The Merry Go Round," and convicts dream of the day they step on the Merry Go Round. The Stepper had been released from isolation that morning in order to complete the process and had the slip of paper in his pocket with all the names signed except the cellblock guard. He wanted to wait until Mickey Mouse came on and make him sign it personally. The Stepper knew that it would burn Mickey Mouse's ass to have to sign his release paper.

He'd been carrying a writ around in a folder and visiting the law library for the past six years.

"I'm gonna beat this case," he would declare to anyone who would listen.

"Yeah, sure, Step," they would reply. Modern-day convicts have pretty well lost faith in higher courts. A long succession of Republican presidents beginning with Richard Nixon has packed the courts with judges who will find any rationale to evade the law if it means letting a convict out of jail. Even when police or prosecutors bungle or intentionally trample a defendant's rights, the courts are likely to say the error is excusable because authorities were acting in "good faith."

The Stepper had been arrested in a town near Los Angeles for robbing a supermarket. He had sawed a hole in the roof and waited for the manager and two assistants. When they walked in, he'd thrown down on them with a .45 pistol and made them open the safe. He'd been apprehended following the robbery after a high-speed chase. The police had deposited him in the back seat of a prowl car and driven him back to the market, where the manager and his assistants positively identified him as the robber. The following day they formally identified him in a lineup at the jail.

During a jury trial The Stepper contended that the lineup had been poisoned by the police driving him alone in the prowl car back to the scene of the crime. The trial judge denied his motion and he then appealed it all the way to the California Supreme Court, where his appeal was denied at the highest state level.

He then appealed to the Ninth Circuit Federal Court in San Francisco. The Ninth Circuit reluctantly agreed with him and overturned the conviction. Their ruling stated that he should be retried, excluding the lineup evidence. Their ruling still left The Stepper out on a limb because he'd been caught with the gun and the money.

He appealed the Ninth Circuit's ruling to the U.S. Supreme Court. His contention was that the action of the police was a violation of his due process rights under the Fifth and Fourteenth amendments to the Constitution. His theory was that a violation of "due process" required a dismissal of the charges because a violation of that nature could not be made right by a new trial. The Supreme Court agreed with him and ordered that the charges be dismissed.

His homeboys gave him a going-home party. The card table in front of Weldon's cell had been laid out with an assortment of Cokes, cookies, chips, dips, cheese, and other goodies The Stepper's friends had donated for an impromptu affair. Convicts kept coming down to congratulate him. There was a special air of excitement, as most everyone had thought The Stepper would never see daylight again.

When the doors were finally racked shut for the night at ten o'clock, The Stepper told Weldon he didn't plan on getting much sleep. Weldon told him that was okay and that they could talk the night away if it became necessary.

"To tell the truth, man, I'm a little bit scared," The Stepper confessed.

"Scared of what?" Weldon asked.

"You know, man, what with this new three-strikes bullshit, I'm going to get life in this place even if I steal a fucking candy bar. I've never learned a trade or anything, so I don't know what the hell I'm gonna do out there. I don't want to come back again.

"It's not that I'm afraid of prison," he continued. "I've been in prisons all my life and I can adjust to confinement. But it's the kind of assholes they put in here nowadays. I don't want to spend the rest of my life among the fools we're doing time with and that makes me want to stay out there. I just don't know how I'm going to do it."

"Well, look here, man. I haven't talked to Vern, but I did call Melvin Nix today. He said he will give you a place to stay as long as you want it. Paula said they will help you any way they can, and I know Vern will go along with that. So you get your ass down to Fresno and stay with them until you figure out what it is you want to do," Weldon told him.

"Ah, man, I don't like to impose on anyone. I wouldn't feel right just laying up on somebody," The Stepper replied, looking at the floor.

"Man, fuck all that. Melvin will give you plenty to do. He's got a big place and the only help he's got there now is a crippled guy named Paul who can't do no heavy stuff. I know you'll hold up your end, so just go on down there, at least until you get your feet on the ground. You'd better not panic and pull some stupid-ass robbery."

"Okay. I'll go down there. See how it works out," The Stepper said.

Late in the night, with just the faint glow of a floodlight near the fence shining in the cell window, the room was illuminated at regular intervals by a roving spotlight from a gun tower. During one of these illuminations Weldon said in a soft voice, "Hey, Step?"

"Yeah," The Stepper replied.

"Man, I'm really worried bout Vern, Paula, and Curly. They are all the family I got left besides my old auntie Maybelle and I doubt she will last until I get out."

"That's the elderly lady you wrote and told her you'd met this nice Puerto Rican fellow and was hoping to bring him over to dinner at her house as soon as you got out?"

"You son of a bitch! You wrote that damn letter and signed my fucking name on it," Weldon said while throwing back his wool army blanket and jumping up. He was still mad and ready to fight, as if the incident had happened eighteen seconds instead of eighteen months ago. He had known The Step had done it, he just couldn't prove it.

"Easy, homeboy. Easy. I mean, I didn't do it. I apologize for even bringing it up." The Stepper was cursing himself for an idiot, bringing that letter up now of all times.

Weldon sat down in his boxer shorts on the stool. The Step could see him well by the security light outside the cellblock. Weldon began feeling around under the lower bunk for his shower shoes. The cement floor was ice-cold. His toe hurt like hell. He had a bad ingrown toenail.

"Come on, homeboy, let me in on what's been bothering you if you can. You know I'll help you any way that I can. I know something is straining you up real close, homey. This is your last chance right here because I know you won't talk on no phone even if you decided to tell me something."

"You know, Stepper, I've known you longer than anyone. You were being kicked out of reform school for being too old probably before I was born. You've never been much but a dumb crook like me, only you don't have the excuse of being a dope fiend. I remember in the old days when you liked and trusted a lot of the guys in the gangs because they were good men. Still are.

"Then I remember how you began to hate these new ones like I do because they run on ignorance. Well, I got a problem with them. It's serious. I may need some help but, whatever, it stays between you and me," Weldon said.

"Lay it on me, man," The Stepper said.

Weldon told The Stepper everything except who it was that told him Vern was in the hat.

"I don't know what to do, man. Vern is off on a trip right now, but I'm afraid Joe will be laying for him when he gets back."

The Stepper thought about it for a long time, lying there watching the roving light from the tower pass the cell window every thirty seconds or so. He despised the DWB even more than Weldon did, and this kind of bullshit was exactly the reason he disliked them so much. Real prison gangs had some class and used a dab of common sense with their violence. These little new-breed gangsters had shit for brains and no conscience whatsoever.

Weldon, Vern, and their old ladies had become like family to him. He finally came to the only logical conclusion he could arrive at.

"I'll take care of Little Joe, and soon as I do, you hit these two monkeys that run things in here. I believe you are right. Moving on them three will surely get their minds off Vern. I don't believe you should push him any further. He's not educated in this bullshit like we are."

"Grady, you don't need to get involved," Weldon said.

"I'm involved already. Lay down and get yourself some sleep and call Curly every day because I'll move on him as soon as I locate him. He's not paranoid right now, so it shouldn't take me long."

Weldon got up and shook the old man's hand before he went to bed. It was the first good night's sleep he had had since Big Mac first told him that Vern was in the hat. The old man's word was like a fence post, and Weldon knew he would get the job done, or die trying.

He slept so soundly that when he woke up, he had missed breakfast and The Stepper was long gone. He felt good except for the ingrown toenail that was throbbing every time his heart beat. The Stepper had advised him to wear two pair of socks.

When he jammed his foot into his shoe, a horribly painful jolt ran from his big toe directly to the base of his skull. The toe of his right shoe had been stuffed with little pieces of cut-up cardboard.

"You dirty son of a bitch!!" he screamed. But The Stepper was halfway to Fresno and didn't hear him.

CHAPTER 15

When Vern awoke in the early morning daylight on Blake Ethridge's downstairs couch, he had a hangover out of west hell. Someone had been kind enough to put a blanket over him during the night. As he stumbled around groping for a light switch, he vowed once again to quit mixing beer and whiskey on an empty stomach. His clothes were scattered all over the room. When he got them on, he noticed a small refrigerator sitting in an alcove that contained a washer and dryer.

He opened the door and there was a six-pack of Miller's beer. He twisted the top off one and chugalugged it. He drank the second more slowly, and by the third bottle the pounding in his head slowed down enough so that it didn't hurt to walk. He decided not to drink anymore at all until he dealt with Sam.

He eased up the stairs, wondering how he was going to get out of the place without waking anyone up. He didn't have the foggiest idea of how to open the electric gate. Even with the hangover he felt better having the box with Paula's and Curly's jewelry under his arm. But there was still an icy block of rage and disbelief enveloping his heart. For the life of him he could not understand how someone could do what Sam had done and live with himself afterward.

Ethridge was sitting on his couch upstairs talking on the phone. He didn't look as if he'd been to bed yet and still didn't look tired. Vern took a chair across the room until he finished his conversation and hung up the phone. A big smile came over his face.

"That was Roberta on there," he told Vern, indicating the phone. "She's still mad as hell. That was some funny shit you told her last night and she's wanting to know if you're crazy or something. I told her you was probably tipsy and besides that you had some very serious business to deal with."

"Ah, what did I tell her?" Vern asked, only vaguely remembering the conversation. He blearily remembered a tall, blonde, good-looking woman talking to him the night before. Just before the schnapps got him completely.

"She told you she wanted you to take her out and party some while you are up here, and she don't do that often. That broad has everyone in Oakland after her."

"How did I make her mad?" Vern asked.

"You told her you'd do it, but she would have to pay you," Blake said and began laughing.

"Man, do you have any tomato juice or cold water?" Vern asked. His head was still pounding.

"Sure," Ethridge said, and got him a tall glass of tomato juice. "There's beer if you want some."

"Nah. This is fine. I wish I hadn't been so blunt with that lady. She was nice, but I don't chippy around. I've got two women who sell their bodies and give me the money. It wouldn't be right for me to take their money and spend it on another woman. So the only way I could party with another woman is if she paid for everything. That's just the way it is. I guess I could have been more diplomatic, but it's hard to just come out and tell a woman you're a pimp."

"I never heard that one before, and I know damn well Roberta never did either. Well, she won't be forgetting you for a while," Ethridge told him.

"I hope I didn't hurt her feelings too bad. Have you got a road map of northern California?" Vern asked.

"Not handy, but I can tell you how to get to San Luis Obispo," Ethridge said, and gave Vern the roads to take as Vern jotted the directions down in a little notebook he carried. Then he stood up.

"Look here, man. I'm not going to try and thank you again because there's no way. When you get by Fresno you stop in and see me. I'll make you a key to my fucking house if you ever want one. I'm really grateful for the way I've been treated and I speak for Paula, Curly, and Weldon also."

"Hey, man, no problem. Just be sure and give ole Sam my regards," Ethridge told him.

"I'll do it, man," Vern said, and Ethridge pushed a button near the TV. Vern heard the hum of the electric gate opening. They shook hands once more and he went out into the cool morning and put the box of jewelry next to the briefcase in the Blazer's luggage compartment.

He was almost a hundred miles down the road before he stopped at a gas station with a restaurant next door. He didn't want to stop at all, but his gas was low and he was hungry. He'd been resisting the urge to drive fast and kept well within the speed limit. He didn't want to be getting a traffic ticket that would put him anywhere near San Luis Obispo today.

But he knew Sam well enough to know that the man was a little bit cagey, if not very smart. If he gave careful thought to the conversation with Ethridge, he might become paranoid again. Or at least realize how foolish he'd been by giving out his room number. But there was also the fact that Sam didn't seem at all afraid of him and that was the part Vern didn't understand at all. Everyone that knew him well knew he was capable of violence, but Sam must have been out of the loop when talk went around. There wasn't much doubt in anyone's mind in Fresno that Vern had killed Snake.

A month before Vern turned twenty-one, his mother had called from the hospital and told him Snake had thrown her off their porch and broken her hip and two of her ribs. When Vern got mad she tried to calm him.

"Oh, son, he was just drunk. He will be up here to apologize soon as he sobers up. I just hope the Lord will forgive him for all he's done to us. God knows Weldon would have been a better man if Snake hadn't beat on him like he did."

Vern hung up the phone and grabbed a stolen army .45 pistol he'd bought the day before. He told Paula to drive him to his mother's house because he didn't trust himself to drive in the rage he was in. It was near midnight when they pulled up at the old shack near Kerman, where his mother and Snake lived.

"Turn the lights out and leave the motor running," he told Paula as he jumped out of the car and headed for the house. She hadn't seen the gun, as he had it stuck down inside his waistband under his shirt.

The front door was open and he flipped a light switch as he went in. When he opened the door to his mother's bedroom, he could hear Snake snoring and just make out his prone form lying on the bed. He walked over to the bed and roughly shook Snake awake.

"What? Who?" Snake mumbled, sitting up in the bed.

"It's Vern, Snake," Vern told him.

"Vern? What the hell do you want here? What the hell you waking me for?" Snake asked, that menacing tone in his voice that used to terrify Vern.

"I've come to say good-bye, Snake," Vern told him.

"Good-bye?" Snake replied. "Are you going somewheres?"

"No, you are," Vern said and shot him in his left eye with a .45 hollow-point shell. In the semidark room Vern saw a large stain blossom on the wallpaper behind Snake's head before his body jerked and slid half off the far edge. The hands jerked a time or two as if they were trying to grip something, then became still.

As he got back in the car, he saw lights come on in the next house and told Paula to keep the lights off until they were down the road aways. But the neighbors must not have been alarmed because it was three days before Snake's body was discovered. The police questioned Vern and Paula once in a desultory fashion and that was that. But Vern noticed that the various underworld characters he dealt with often began treating him with much more deference and respect after Snake's demise. It was as if they knew.

Then a few years ago he'd killed an illegal alien in a labor camp near Salinas. The man had pulled a knife on Paula and demanded his money back after she'd tricked him. When Vern came in on him, the man had come at him with the knife and Vern shot him in the heart.

That killing had been unfortunate because they couldn't understand each other's language. All Vern wanted was to get Paula and leave. But the man hadn't understood what he was saying.

Word of the killing got all over Fresno but Vern was never arrested for it.

If Sam had heard these stories, it surely puzzled Vern how he could be so nonchalant about ripping him off. Maybe the fool thought being Curly's brother gave him some protection. As he got back behind the wheel of the Blazer, he made a mental note to ask Sam about that when he ran up on him.

Vern was driving down Highway 1 and it seemed to be taking forever to get to San Luis Obispo. The road twisted and turned following the coastline of the Pacific Ocean. Some of the panoramic views were breathtaking, but Vern wasn't exactly in the mood for sightseeing. He did think it would be nice to drive this road with Paula and Curly sometime.

San Luis Obispo is 228 miles from San Francisco. Highway 1 was packed with slow recreational vehicles and it was almost ten o'clock before Vern pulled into the town. After consulting a telephone directory that hung in a phone booth, he discovered that the Orcas Motel was a few more miles down Highway 101, near a place called Avila Beach.

He had a leisurely meal in an Italian restaurant before he got back in the Blazer and drove down 101. The Orcas Motel was easy to find. It was a medium-size two-story affair near the beach. Vern guessed from Sam's room number, 206, that he would be on the second floor. He drove once slowly through the parking lot and didn't spot the van. But that meant nothing. With his newfound wealth Sam could be driving anything.

There was a bar about fifty yards down the same road the motel was on. Vern decided to park down there and watch the entrance to the motel. The bar would close at 2:00 A.M., but he figured he could sit there until almost 3:00 without drawing attention. Sam could be somewhere in a bar himself and be coming home around closing time.

There were several cars and pickups in the bar parking lot. It looked like a busy place. Vern parked out near the street so he would have an unobstructed view of the motel. He got out and walked to the bar, intending to get some soda pop to sip on in the Blazer while he waited.

As he took hold of the door to the bar, he glanced to his right and there was Sam's van, bigger than shit, parked right up against the rail that separated the wall from the parking lot. Vern let go of the door and looked at his watch. It was nearly one A.M. If Sam was in there, he'd have to be coming out soon.

Vern walked hurriedly back to the Blazer and drove it around to the side of the building where it couldn't be seen from Sam's van. He opened the back, took out the briefcase, and selected the .380 automatic. Checking the clip, he jacked a shell into the chamber. After being careful to note that the safety was on, he stuck the gun down into the waistband of the Levi's. He didn't want to blow his nuts off. He was hoping that the idiot wouldn't have a girl or a male companion with him. If he did, Vern decided to just try and follow him until he was alone.

He stood between two cars a few yards from Sam's van, watching the front door. People were beginning to emerge now and walk to their cars.

Sam came out the front door accompanied by a man and a woman. They stopped at the rear of Sam's van and had a conversation. Vern saw Sam gesturing toward the motel. It looked as if they were agreeing to meet him there. Finally they walked toward Vern and Sam made for the driver's-side door of his van. Vern walked fast around the couple and didn't pull his gun until he went around the back of the van. He caught Sam just as he was about to step up into the driver's seat. Sam heard Vern's footsteps on the gravel and looked around. His jaw dropped open, and when he saw the gun he began trying to mumble something.

"Shut up, Sam. If you make a wrong move, I'll kill everybody in this fucking parking lot," Vern told him in a low tone of voice.

"Now shut that door and walk real slow around the front of the van and around the corner of the building to where Paula's Blazer is parked and stand by the passenger side door. If you yell or try to run, I'm going to blow your spine out. Now move!" Vern ordered.

From this point on, Vern wasn't doing much thinking. He knew approximately where he was going and what he was going to do. He focused directly on keeping Sam under control until he got where he was going. The time for rationalization and justification was over.

Sam did as he was told. Vern walked behind him with the gun back in his waistband. As they turned the corner Vern saw the man and woman Sam had been talking with drive out of the parking lot toward the motel. When he stood beside the passenger door, Vern said to him, "Now open that door and get in. But I want you on your knees on the floorboard with your face pressed against the seat. If you lift your head up off that fucking seat, I'm going to blow it off. So don't make me mess up the upholstery. Now get in."

Sam got in and Vern walked around the front of the Blazer. He hadn't shaken Sam down for a weapon, and if he had one, now was the time he would pull it. Vern half hoped he would try something. He very cautiously came up on the driver's side, gun in hand, but Sam was still kneeling there with his head on the seat. Vern got in behind the wheel.

"Now put both hands on the seat beside your head where I can see them," Vern ordered and Sam complied. Vern started the motor and, keeping the gun in his left hand, drove around the bar and out onto the highway.

"Vern, let me talk to you," Sam pleaded in a quavering voice.

"Shut up, Sam. I got some things I want to ask you when we get where we can talk. But until then, shut the fuck up. Don't say another word," Vern replied. "It seems like you already done plenty of talking about me to everyone but me. This is a hell of a time to ask if you can talk to me. You lived at my house for weeks and never said a fucking word to me!" Vern told him.

He took a turnoff past the motel that led to Avila Beach and came to a turnout that led down to a beach with a jumble of large rocks. He could see a lighthouse just offshore as he pulled into the turnout and parked. The area was deserted and all he could hear was the waves breaking on the rocks.

"Let's take a walk on the beach," he said to Sam as he turned off the lights and ignition.

"Please, Vern, just let me talk to you a minute," Sam spoke with his face still pressed against the seat.

"Shut up!" Vern told him. "You'll have plenty of chance to talk. I just don't want to do it in the car!" He thought that was probably the first time in the punk's life that he'd said "please" to anyone.

Vern walked around and opened the passenger door.

"Get out slow and keep those hands where I can see them. This gun has a hair trigger and if my heart gets to beating too fast, it could go off."

Sam got out slow and Vern tried to calm some of the rage he felt by breathing deeply. He didn't want Sam to be any more terrified than he was because he could panic and begin yelling or running. He decided to try and calm him some. It seemed okay to lie to a dead man. What difference did it make?

"I don't intend to kill you, Sam, but if you lie to me about a couple things I'm going to ask you, then I'll blow both your fucking kneecaps off. That's why we're going down to the beach. If you make me shoot your ass, I don't want no company."

"Vern, I won't lie, I swear to God I won't. I'll tell you anything you want to know, man. I'm sorry, I'm—"

"Okay." Vern interrupted him. "Just walk on down toward that lighthouse out there. I'll tell you when to stop. Just walk natural like we're out for a stroll."

"That fucking Blake Ethridge gave me up, didn't he? I should have known he couldn't be trusted," Sam said, as he eased into the sand leading down to the beach.

"You gave yourself up because you are fucking ignorant. Just shut the fuck up until I tell you to stop." Vern was amazed at this asshole's ability to make him even madder than he already was. Here he was saying Blake Ethridge couldn't be trusted and the man was obviously the most honorable and trustworthy person Vern had met in a long time. He was astounded that only a short time ago he'd given this creep the run of his home.

The path they were on wound by a jumble of huge boulders. They were about a sixth of a mile from the road and Vern figured this was as good a place as any. He didn't want to leave the Blazer unattended for too long this time of night.

"Stop right there and sit on that rock," Vern said. The waves sounded very strong now as they battered the shore and he figured they must be close to the cold ocean. Something about a lighthouse on one side of him, a busy highway on the other, and Sam gathering his thoughts on a rock gave Vern one of those feelings that he had been here before. Some vague notion of a journey at an end. It looked like not a bad place to die in.

"What did I do to you that would make you do what you done to me?" Vern asked. Sam put his head down and shook it back and forth. "I mean, I can see you wanting to rob me. I got no problem with that. But putting a bogus snitch jacket on me with a bunch of thugs and bikers and me with your sister. Man, she could get killed in a crossfire or something. Ain't you got no respect for anybody? How in the fuck could you do a thing like that?" Vern demanded.

"You treated me right, Vern. It wasn't nothing personal, it's the crank made me do it. I'm hooked on the shit and I've got to get some help. I'm sorry, Vern. I'll make it up to you. I give my word on that."

"You don't get hooked on speed, Sam," Vern replied.

"Not physically, but psychologically you do, and I'm going to get some help, man, I promise you that. Just give me a chance and I'll pay back every dime. I'll pay it within ninety days, man, and I'll straighten out all them lies I told them guys. No shit, I'll make it up to you. Give me a chance, man." As he talked, Vern could smell a strong odor of feces on the ocean breeze.

He's really layin' on this group therapy stuff, Vern thought to himself. He thinks in his mind he's going to talk his way out of this. But from that smell his gut is telling him he ain't going to make it. His bowels are smarter than his brain. He decided he had wasted enough time on this and he didn't want to torment Sam any more than was necessary.

"What did you do with the ring that your mother left Curly when she died?" Vern asked him, and Sam looked up at him, a startled look on his face. In the glow of the lighthouse, Vern could see the ugly scar. But the face showed much more. His look gave away the fact that he'd just realized the talk was almost over.

"I didn't even know it was in there or I wouldn't of took it. I threw it out right outside Fresno at a rest stop," he said.

"In a garbage can?" Vern asked.

"Nah, man, by some trees. I think I could find it again, Vern." He was grabbing at straws now, and his eyes were beginning to shift around. His panic was growing out of hand.

"Good-bye, Sam," Vern told him and shot him in the forehead with the .380 as he began to rise from the rock. His head snapped back as if he'd been kicked, and his body arched like a diver doing a backward swan dive. He came to rest beside the rock on his back with one arm raised against it as if to ward off another round.

Vern took hold of the arm near the elbow and turned Sam over. A big chunk of the back of his head was gone and sand and weeds were matted in the hair next to the hole.

Vern kicked at the sand where he'd been standing as he backed away. His ears were ringing from the sound of the .380 going off and he knew someone could have heard it. He walked down to the edge of the water and threw the pistol as far as he could in the direction of the lighthouse.

He walked a ways along the water, then turned and headed for the Blazer, up on the road. As he got in to drive away, he felt relieved that no other cars had stopped nearby.

He knew these highways pretty well because in long-ago times he had brought Paula over to Pismo Beach to work the artichoke and lettuce seasons. He intended to drive all the way to Bakersfield before he stopped to rest. It looked like Paula wouldn't get to kill the gator after all. There was no doubt in his mind she'd do it Sunday if he wasn't back by then. He couldn't believe he'd forgotten to ask anyone about Gatorbait.

Vern pulled into the parking lot of a Vagabond Inn just before eight o'clock on Friday morning. He had finally made Bakersfield, and only then did he feel secure in the distance he had between him and San Luis Obispo. The roundabout route was part of his design. He wanted a motel receipt showing he was in Bakersfield. Paula could get any one of a dozen respectable tricks who would swear he'd been in Los Angeles the night before if he ever needed an alibi.

He was also bone-tired and didn't think he could drive another mile. When he cut the ignition the radio also went dead. It was a five-minute hourly newscast that broke up the continuous country AM station he'd been listening to. A newswoman was talking about a Fresno woman blown up by a car bomb. There were no details or names yet, but news like that made him uneasy, and touched off the feelings of dread he'd been having lately. Yet he felt that he could now deal with the gang threat somehow since he'd found the source of the problem.

The desert air was warm and the day already becoming hot when he stepped out of the Blazer and stood inspecting what looked like a million little bugs, butterflies, and grasshoppers squashed on the windshield, grille, and headlights. He felt worse about these innocent little creatures than the evil, sick piece of humanity he'd just done away with. Someone surely had been saved a lot of future pain and anguish.

The calendar in the motel office said November 11. Curly had a birthday coming in less than a week. Paula's was the twenty-fifth of November. He was glad his bankroll was healthy. He planned on getting Curly a nice little car this year. He thought she would look classy in a red convertible. Maybe one of those little Chrysler Le Barons.

He tried to call home before he went to sleep in the cool, clean room with a magnificent king-size bed. The phone was busy, which only meant it was out of order because he had call waiting. One of them probably got drunk and hung one of the phones up halfway off the hook, a habit he couldn't break them of no matter how much he bitched and threatened. The phone was their main source of income, for Christ's sake. When his head hit the cool pillow, he didn't worry about the phone or anything else for over eleven hours. He woke up at eight o'clock on Friday evening. Home was 108 miles down the road and he was anxious to get there.

CHAPTER 16

Thursday evening Paula and Curly had put on cut-off Levi's and halter tops and washed the Lincoln out in the driveway. Washing Vern's car was one of their favorite chores on hot days. They had sponges and big buckets of soapy water and giggled as cars slowed down and men whistled as they bent over sloshing a hub-cap or stretched over the hood with one leg straight out. It had been a warm November day and was still balmy out.

They always wound up in a sponge fight that progressed into a wrestling match over the water hose. They even applied a coat of Turtle Wax this time and the Lincoln sparkled like a gem in the driveway between the house and the street when they finished.

They planned to take the entire weekend off beginning Thursday afternoon, which was downright sacrilegious, because week-ends were when they made the bulk of their money. With Vern gone and their pockets full of gold, it seemed the right time to do it. They planned to shop till they dropped every day and party until the bars closed every night until Sunday morning. Their guilt was lessened by the fact that both their birthdays were coming up soon.

They were going to get a good night's sleep tonight and an early run at the department stores and the mall on Friday morning. Weldon had called and said The Stepper would be there Friday afternoon. They planned to party him until Sunday, because Melvin was going to be out of town and the old man wouldn't want to go out to Melvin's and move in until Melvin got home, anyway. They wanted to put him at ease and make him feel at home.

Vern had a cousin named Larry Ashland who had three working girls. Peggy, an amazon over six feet tall and the prettiest of the three, owed them for some downers and weed so she'd promised to take care of The Stepper on Friday night.

"I'll fuck him till he thinks he's nineteen again" is how she not-so-delicately put it. They made her promise not to take any money from him, not even as a tip. Paula told her she would just make her even on the drug debt. Larry was tight with money and he hated downers and wouldn't give Peggy any cash for them. Although he would reluctantly spring for an ounce of weed now and then and gripe like hell if Peggy smoked more than one joint a day. She owed Paula and Curly close to three hundred dollars.

They went to bed early on Thursday evening and woke up before six on Friday morning, something they almost never did when Vern was home and they were working. The only time he ever rose early was for a chicken fight. But they both loved the cool fall mornings and enjoyed drinking coffee and talking while the sun woke up the dark earth, a practice that wasn't possible after entertaining tricks all night.

They were out of milk on Friday morning and Curly hadn't dressed yet. Paula had on her Levi's and a T-shirt.

"I'll run down to that Seven-Eleven and get some milk and gas up the Lincoln while I'm there," Paula said, grabbing the keys off a peg on the wall.

"Get me a package of those apricot Danish rolls," Curly told her as she started for the door.

"God, I wish I could eat like you do and never get fat," Paula said as she wistfully watched Curly loading a cup of steaming coffee with half-and-half and a whole tablespoonful of sugar. Then she turned and went for the door.

Curly was blowing the hot coffee when it hit. There was a terrible *whomp* sound accompanied by intense pressure on her eardrums as the kitchen window shattered in toward her and it seemed like a tight band around her chest yanked her and the chair back against the kitchen wall. Hot coffee flew in a spray as her shoulders and the back of her head slid into the wall. Glass shards from the windows fell around her.

"Earthquake!" was her first thought as she fought to keep conscious and regain her feet. After the initial blast there was a deadly silent stillness broken only by the ringing in her ears. Suddenly she became worried about Paula and made her way to the door. She had a hard time opening it, then wished she hadn't.

Vern's Lincoln Town Car was a ball of fire. The front end was so demolished that it looked as if there was nothing left to burn but the frame. She ran as close as she could get to the scorching flames and couldn't even see what was left of Paula. Neighbors were rushing out of their houses and it seemed every dog in the neighborhood was howling.

She turned on the water, grabbed the hose that still lay there from the car wash, and began spurting water into the driver's side window until the flames subsided enough for her to see the charred, smoking hulk of what had been Paula. She sank to the ground and began throwing up and screaming at the same time.

She could hear a siren in the distance as suddenly people's hands were touching her and someone's arms went around her. She felt her face press into another woman's bosom just as she lost consciousness.

Thereafter was a blur of images, voices, and darkness. She had the feeling of movement as if she were riding lying down and someone was talking soothingly to her with a siren in the background. A peaceful, warm feeling enveloped her in the darkness until the image of Paula came back. Paula in a sitting position. Bald and with the same color and texture of a burned match. Parts of her missing. Paula looking like a doll Curly had once seen that had been burned at the dump. There was a screaming, choking, fighting woman beside her that she realized was her just before the darkness mercifully enfolded her again.

The Stepper arrived at the Greyhound bus station in Fresno at five in the afternoon. He was amazed that there was no one there to pick him up. No only amazed but bent out of shape about it. He felt this was totally disrespecting him. But he decided to reserve judgment on that until someone explained why they left him here high and dry. From what he knew of Paula and Vern, it just wasn't their style to do this. He grabbed a taxi in front of the bus station and gave Vern's address.

When the taxi pulled up at Vern's house, The Stepper almost told him to keep driving but a couple of the cops in the front yard were eyeballing the cab intently. He wasn't on any kind of parole and hadn't done anything wrong, so he figured "What the hell" and got out.

The two cops were standing inside a yellow tape that ran down Vern's driveway and cross the front yard. Written on the tape was CRIME SCENE, DO NOT ENTER. Two men in coveralls were digging around in the remains of Vern's demolished Lincoln. He paid the taxi driver, and as he approached the cops behind the tape, a well-dressed, dark-complected man in a suit came out of the house with two plastic evidence bags in his hand.

"Do you mind me asking what happened here?" The Stepper asked the nearest uniformed cop as he walked up to them with his airline carry bag in his hand.

"There was a bombing here this morning. Do you live around here?" the cop asked him.

"No, I'm a friend of the family," The Stepper replied.

"Then Detective Torres will be wanting to talk to you. The neighbors haven't been very helpful."

"Hey, Martin!" the cop yelled over at the well-dressed man who was now conferring with the two men who were digging around in the Lincoln.

"Actually, I'm a friend of a brother of the family. I don't think I can be of all that much help," The Stepper said as the detective walked toward them.

"Anything you know at all will help. Martin, this guy is a friend of the family," the cop told the detective. The cop was a big, sandy-haired beer-bellied individual who stood in stark contrast to the suave, olive-skinned man who joined them. He carried his suit coat over his arm and the only flaws in his appearance were the sweat stains around his armpits.

"Did you know the people that lived here?" the detective asked The Stepper.

"What do you mean, did I know them? Are they all dead?" The Stepper responded, and his heart was beating a hundred miles an hour. News like that would completely destroy Weldon.

"I'm sorry. I didn't phrase that very well. A woman was killed by a car bomb here this morning. Her name was Paula, but we don't have a last name for her yet. Another woman named Angela Perry is in shock out at the county hospital, but she's physically okay. We believe Paula's husband lives here also, but no one knows where he might be. The neighbors don't seem to know them at all, or say they don't, anyway.

"We need to get a last name on this Paula, and if possible a reason why anyone would do a thing like this to her. There must have been four sticks of dynamite in that car," the detective summed up, then looked at The Stepper as if to say, "It's your turn."

"I worked with his brother up in Salinas, and he asked me to stop by. The woman in the hospital is his wife. The guy who owns the house is Vernon Coy and Paula was his wife. I know he's on a business trip of some kind, but he was supposed to be here today. Possibly he had to lay over somewhere. That's everything I know about these people," The Stepper told him, and saw the detective eyeballing the tattoos on his arms. He wished he had worn a long-sleeved shirt.

"What kind of work does this Vernon do?" the detective asked, taking his notebook from a shirt pocket.

"I think he's a salesman of some kind, but I'm not sure," The Stepper responded.

"Do you know of anyone who may have been this mad at him or her?"

"Not the faintest idea in the world," The Stepper replied.

"Well, my name is Martin Torres," the detective said while fishing out a business card and handing it to The Stepper. The card read MARTIN TORRES, HOMICIDE DIVISION, along with a phone and fax number.

"If you hear anything at all, I hope you will call me," Torres added.

"I'm Grady McCall, and I'd be glad to help if I knew anything," The Stepper replied, putting the card in his shirt pocket.

"Do you mind if I look in that bag you are carrying?" Torres asked.

"I suppose that's a fair request. But I don't want you pawing around in there, so I'll just show-and-tell here," The Stepper replied, while squatting Indian-fashion and zipping the bag open. He moved the prison-issue windbreaker, Levi's, shirt, and socks around, along with his shaving bag, so that the detective could see all the contents of the bag. Then he zipped it closed and stood up.

"Would it be okay if I wait here until Vernon gets back? I believe he will be needing some company when he returns and finds that his wife has been killed," The Stepper asked Torres.

"You're probably right about that, but we don't want you in the house. In fact, you can sort of keep an eye on the place until he gets back. We're about done here and will be pulling out soon.

"You'll find some good chairs around back. There's also some animal-control people back there trying to hog-tie a mean alligator, so don't get in their way. I want this Coy to call me soon as he gets back. Day or night. Among other things I'd like him to bring me up to snuff on that big gator and how it came to be hanging out in his backyard," Torres added.

"I'll let him know for sure, and thanks," The Stepper told him.

"Okay, boys," the detective said as he turned away from The Stepper. "We're out of here, but leave the tape up to keep any hot-nose neighbors out. Somebody can come by and remove it after Coy gets home."

"Okay, boss," the bigger of the two uniform cops said, and walked over to his car and got his two-way radio out through the driver's window. The other cop, a tall, slim black man, drifted over toward the two in coveralls who were picking up their equipment. The detective stood there looking at The Stepper.

"What joint did you just come out of?" he asked The Stepper when they were out of earshot.

"Soledad," The Stepper replied truthfully.

"There's a lot about this deal here that strikes me as very strange. I'm sure Coy knows a lot more than I do about it. He probably won't tell me much, but you tell him if he don't call me soon, I'll come find him. You know the drill and you know I made you. I don't want these locals on your ass till you show your hand."

"Thanks. I'll tell him," The Stepper responded.

"I'm going to work overtime until I find out who done this and why. That woman was a very nice whore, and even a few of the cops around here liked and respected her. We don't feel that she had this coming."

"I didn't know her," The Stepper told him.

"Well, all that don't matter. But if you guys start getting revenge in this town, I'll tie your nuts in a figure eight," Torres said, and walked off in the direction of a plain white Ford parked on the street in front of Vern's house.

CHAPTER 17

The Stepper waited there until Torres drove away, then started walking. He'd noticed a 7-Eleven food store a few blocks from Vern's house with a phone out front. He knew how to get a message to Weldon. He wanted him to know about this before Brian and Jack. Or at least before they knew he knew about it.

He got some quarters from the store and rang up Bill O'Hara, the Catholic priest at Soledad. They called him Father Bill. He was a very nice man that prison authorities didn't like much at all because he went out of his way to help convicts.

"Grady, me boy, you're not in jail already are ye?" Father Bill asked when The Stepper got him on the phone. It sounded as if he was in his evening cups pretty good.

"No, Father, but I need you to run over to the prison and tell Weldon Coy something tonight. His sister-in-law, Paula, was killed by a car bomb today. Curly is okay, but she's in a hospital in shock. Tell him to call Vern tomorrow at home."

"My dear God. I'll go soon as I get my clothes back on," Father Bill responded.

"Don't go to his cellblock. Have the guard send him down to the chapel. You know how shy he is and everybody will be asking him questions if they see you down there at his cell," The Stepper added.

"I'll do it, son. He'll know within the hour. Is there anything else I can do?"

"No, that's it, Father, and thanks," The Stepper told him.

"I'll pray for ye, son."

"You do that, Father," The Stepper said, and hung up. Brian and Jack were probably the ones who needed the prayers right now, he was thinking, as he walked back to Vern's house.

When he got back to the house, everyone was gone, including the gator. The Stepper pulled a lounge chair in closer to the back of the house, threw his windbreaker over himself, and was asleep in no time at all. He hoped Vern would arrive soon. The weather was becoming cold and all he had was the windbreaker.

Vern's heart sank when he pulled up in the Blazer and saw the yellow tape across his yard and the remains of his Lincoln Town Car. He'd almost expelled the feeling of dread by convincing himself that a creep like Little Joe wouldn't know how to make a bomb. But the evidence was right there before him.

The radio had said that only one woman was killed. He had to shut his feelings down to keep from hoping that it wasn't Paula. He got out of the Blazer and walked past the Lincoln to inspect the front of his home. A smell of burned oil lingered everywhere. The kitchen window was shattered and big chunks of plaster lay on the ground. His front door looked like a fried pork skin.

He walked on around the house and out to the gator's pond. The gator was gone. As he turned to go back to the house, a voice stopped him.

"Vern?"

A cold chill raced up his back. He felt like a fool. If the voice was Little Joe's, he was done for. He didn't even have a weapon on him.

"Vern, it's me, The Stepper. I'm over here in the lounge chair," the old man said to Vern and got up very slowly. He didn't want to startle Vern any more than he had already.

Air went out of Vern like a punctured tire and he vowed to be more careful from now on.

"We were expecting you today, Grady," Vern said, walking over and taking the old man's hand. "Good to see you on the outside, brother," Vern said and stood looking at The Stepper. They stood there in stone silence for a minute or two just looking at each other in the darkness until The Stepper sensed what was probably on Vern's mind.

"It was Paula," he said, in a near whisper.

Vern looked like he had been punched hard. He stumbled forward and Grady helped him sit down on the lounge chair he'd been sleeping in. Vern put his elbows on his knees and dropped his head into his hands.

"Where's Curly?" he asked in a barely audible tone.

"She's in shock. They took her to the county hospital and sedated her. At least I think they did. It all happened way before I got here," The Stepper told him.

"Leave me alone for a few minutes," Vern said.

"Okay. I'll be around front."

"No, just go in the house and see if you can get some lights on. I'll be there in a little bit," Vern told him.

The Stepper went around and jerked the mangled front door open. The lights still worked, and when he turned them on, there were pieces of plaster and glass all over the floors. He found a half-full quart of Wild Turkey whiskey in the kitchen, poured himself a water glass full, found a dustpan and broom and went to work.

He was feeling the whiskey pretty good when Vern walked in looking pale and drained, his cheeks still damp from the silent tears he had cried. The Stepper poured them both a glassful of the whiskey and they sat down on the couch.

"We'll go get Curly in the morning," Vern said after he drank about half the glass.

"Okay, but they will probably try and keep her a few days for observation," The Stepper told him.

"Yeah, but we'll pick her up anyway. I think she'll be a lot better off here at home. That fucking psych ward is just like a jail and I don't want her there. I'll hire a doctor and nurse to stay here with her if I have to."

"No doubt about that," The Stepper said and took another drink.

"Grady?"

"Yeah."

"I know you had planned to stay with Melvin for a while. I also know how much Weldon trusts you. So I'm going to tell you something I've made up my mind about, then we don't ever need to talk about it again."

"Go ahead, shoot," The Stepper responded.

"All I ever done or knew how to do was pimp. Paula made a pimp out of me."

"She done a good job," The Stepper replied.

"Yeah, but that's over now. I won't have any time for that because I'm going to kill every Duboce White Boy I can find. I'm going to change the name of that gang to the Dead White Boys if I can. I don't want no help on that because it's not your beef."

"Vern, I wish you'd think about this revenge thing. I'm going to take out Little Joe soon as I can find him and I'm sure Weldon will move on two of them in there. Man, you can't kill all the motherfuckers. Let's do them three and call it even," The Stepper almost pleaded. He liked this young man very much and didn't want to see him throw his life away.

"Here's to success," The Stepper said, holding up his glass.

"I'll drink to that," Vern told him.

CHAPTER 18

On his way down the hall to the chapel, Weldon knew that someone in his family was dead or very near to being so. He just didn't know which one. A convict didn't get sent to the chapel this time of evening unless it was bad news. As he walked, he took out the pass the guard had written and looked at it again. His hands were sweating so badly the little square of paper was wet.

He looked at his Timex watch as he entered the chapel. It was 8:20. A bit less than two hours to lockup. He was glad Father Bill had sent for him instead of coming to the cellblock. Whatever this was he would probably want to keep a lid on it until tomorrow.

The chapel was empty and Weldon walked on past the pews to where Father Bill had his office. He opened the door without knocking. The old man was sitting behind his big oak desk with a pair of reading glasses down on his nose, reading from the Bible. The overhead fluorescent light lit his bald dome like a cue ball. He looked up over the glasses when Weldon entered the room.

"Father Bill, you know I'm not religious. I don't mean any disrespect, but I just want the secular aspect of the bad news without any spiritual foreplay, if it's okay with you," Weldon told him.

"Of course, son, I understand." Father Bill looked at the man before him standing there with fists clenched, bracing himself for bad news, and knew it wouldn't do any good to commiserate or beat around the holy bush.

"Sit down, Weldon. It's your sister-in-law, Paula," he said.

"What about her? Is she dead?" Weldon asked as he took the chair in front of the desk.

"I'm afraid so. She was killed by a car bomb early this morning," Father Bill told him.

"Was anyone else hurt?" Weldon asked hesitantly and Father Bill could see that the man was losing some of his composure and assurance.

"I don't believe so. Your friend Grady McCall called me a little while ago and asked me to come over and tell you that Paula had been killed by a car bomb. God have mercy on her soul. He said that a woman called Curly, I believe, had been admitted to a hospital in shock. I suppose for observation.

"He asked me to have you call your brother, Vern, at home tomorrow, but I'll put you through right now if you'd care to try him tonight," Father Bill told him.

"No, thank you, Father. I don't feel much like talking right now, to anyone. I'm very grateful to you for coming over tonight," Weldon said as he stood up to go.

"That's my job, son. I'll pray for Paula and I'll pray for you and Grady as well."

"Thank you, Father Bill. Put in a word for Curly and Vern while you're at it."

"I'll do it, son," the priest said as Weldon went out the office door.

It was still an hour before lockdown when Weldon made it back to his cellblock, where convicts played cards out on the walkway, watched TV, and showered in the showers at the front end of each tier.

Everything looked different to him now. So did the cons. Some looked in his eyes and decided not to greet him. No "How you doin'?"s. It seemed it took him an hour to walk the forty or fifty yards back to his cell. Yay-Yay was sitting on the stool in the cell carving a monkey out of a peach pit with a tiny carving knife he'd made from a single-edge razor blade. He looked up when Weldon entered the cell. Weldon was looking at the floor and had been forcing himself not to look up toward where Brian and Jack lived at the end of the second tier.

"Hey, Cowboy, you don't look too happy," Yay-Yay said, halting his carving in midstroke. Weldon had put in a word with the lieutenant and Yay-Yay had moved in as soon as The Stepper left.

"Paula's dead," Weldon told him and sank down on his lower bunk.

"No, man! That sweet woman? How could this happen, brother?" Yay-Yay asked him.

"I don't know, but I think someone put a bomb in Vern's car and got her by mistake," Weldon told him.

"Hijo, ese chingado la penche madre," Yay-Yay exclaimed. *"¿Quien hombre?"*

"I'm pretty sure those gentlemen right up there," Weldon said, pointing at Brian and Jack's cell directly above them on the second tier.

"You want to do it right now, Cowboy?" Yay-Yay said, and began putting up his hobby kit.

"No, I don't think they know she's dead yet. Too many people out on the tier tonight. I want to hit them at early breakfast call in the morning and I'll need your help getting their door open. They deadlock early breakfast."

Friday and Saturday nights are late lockup nights in most prison cellblocks. Convicts are allowed to stay up later on nights before weekends and holidays.

There are only two full meals served on weekends and holidays. Brunch around 11:00 A.M. and dinner around 5:00 or 6:00. But there is also an early breakfast that consists of a piece of coffee cake and maybe a box of Rice Krispies for those who want to get up and get it. The cells are racked open one tier at a time and stay open for five minutes, then are locked again until everyone returns from the mess hall. Some convicts keep their cell on "deadlock" for the early breakfast call.

The early-morning guard has a deadlock list as he goes around the cellblock opening tiers for breakfast. If, for instance, cell A-10 is on the deadlock list, the officer pushes the appropriate buttons in the control box at the end of the tier and that cell doesn't open when the rest are racked open for breakfast.

But if the convicts in A-10 decide to eat that particular morning, they send someone down the tier to tell the guard, "Open A-ten," and he does.

Some convicts, especially if they are paranoid, keep their cells deadlocked because in the dim mornings, with all the confusion, they are vulnerable to being attacked. Especially if they are heavy sleepers. Jack and Brian kept their cell deadlocked for security purposes because they never went to early breakfast.

"I'm going with you, Cowboy, so I'll go down and get Cholito to be the can opener," Yay-Yay replied. Cholito was Yay-Yay's homeboy from El Paso. The name means something like "Little Thug" in slang Spanish. He was a little man who was totally loyal to Yay-Yay and Weldon. They shared their dope with him and he ran errands and held contraband for them. He always had a smile on his face and was about as dangerous as a coral snake.

"You know what you're getting involved in, Yay-Yay. These guys have a big clique and we're going to have a war on our hands with all of them. I can take them both by myself," Weldon told him.

"No, man, if the first one yells, you don't get the second. Besides that, I hate that fucking Brian. I want his ass. Fuck their clique, let's bite a chunk out of it and see how deep they go."

"You probably ain't too smart, brother, but I sure do like your style," Weldon said, and put his arms around Yay-Yay and hugged him.

Yay-Yay went off to tell Cholito what was going on and to collect his knife. Weldon had his own knife in the stool leg. Yay-Yay's knife was made of a stainless-steel ladle handle. Weldon's was made of a big screwdriver that had been sharpened down like an ice pick. Convicts call that type of knife a "bonecrusher," because it will go right through bones, whereas less sturdy knives would be deflected or bent by a bone.

Their knives each had a leather strap attached to the handle end. Before an attack the strap would be wound and tied around the wrist and hand so that the knife couldn't slip out of one's grasp or be wrestled away by an opponent. Convicts call it being "strapped down," when they have their knives tied and are ready for action. Yay-Yay kept his knife hidden in a plumbing door next to his cell that he had made a key to fit.

Saturday morning they were strapped down when their door on the first tier rolled open for breakfast. They wore knit caps pulled low on their foreheads and denim jackets. They each wore a pair of large pants over their regular jeans.

They walked fast for the front of the cellblock, hit the stairwell to the second tier, and walked on the opposite side of the tier from where Brian and Jack lived in the end cell. The timing was just about perfect. Just as they rounded the end of the tier Cholito walked up to the harassed guard who was opening the control box and told him, "Rack open D-seventeen," which was Brian and Jack's cell. The cop just nodded and hit the buttons.

When the door came open Yay-Yay went in first. Brian slept with his head toward the wall and Yay-Yay went as far in as he could to give Weldon all the elbowroom he would need.

Brian slept on his back and Weldon heard his skin pop like a balloon bursting as Yay-Yay's knife drove deep into his chest. Jack was sleeping the other way, which was good for Weldon, but he ran into two problems. Jack slept on his side, which didn't afford a good target, and the sound of the door sliding open woke him up so that he was trying to raise himself when Weldon hit him.

Weldon's knife went through his arm near the shoulder and into his chest and Jack screamed a bloodcurdling scream. Yay-Yay had already hit Brian three times deep in his chest and was backing out when Jack screamed. Weldon pulled out and stabbed him again and Yay-Yay leaned down and stabbed him in the neck while saying to Weldon, "Let's move, pardner."

Convicts were running out of their doors in their shorts and the cop was yelling, "Lockdown! Everybody in your cells! Lockdown!" as Weldon and Yay-Yay shed their jackets and pants in the shower at the end of the tier, handed their knives to Cholito, who took off with them while Weldon and Yay-Yay headed down the hall nonchalantly toward the mess hall.

Cops were running everywhere now. One of them looked hard at Weldon and Yay-Yay and yelled, "You two! Get on that fucking wall!"

As Yay-Yay put his hands up on the wall, he and Weldon saw

with dismay that his hand was cut and bleeding from a small wound where his knife had evidently slipped. Three hospital orderlies went running by with Jack on a gurney, a trail of blood left behind them.

There were about twenty cops around them now. Both men were handcuffed and frog-marched to isolation. Once there, they were stripped naked, skin-searched, and relieved of all their possessions. But they got to keep the satisfaction.

The Stepper and Vern never slept at all on Friday night. They just talked, drank, and dozed in the chairs they were sitting in. Vern called Melvin several times and finally Paul told him that Melvin would definitely be out of touch and out of town until Sunday.

Vern knew Melvin was up to something. When he left on a score, he told Paul to just tell whoever called that he'd run down to the grocery or the cleaners or some other local errand. That way, if the cops got to looking for him, they wouldn't be sitting on the main highway leading back into Fresno, which would be the worst place to get caught, as he would be apt to have the goods on him still. Vern had taught him that trick years ago, after he had learned it from Weldon.

He had learned a lot from Weldon over the years. Many good tricks about survival and evading the law. Weldon would have been an excellent thief had it not been for his drug habit. The drugs were always his undoing. But in everything else, he was a very astute thinker.

Vern now wished to God he had listened to Weldon about Little Joe and the Duboce White Boys. He had made a fatal mistake that cost Paula her life. Weldon would never say, "I told you so," but Vern would always know Weldon had told him so and every time he shaved he would be looking at a damn hardheaded fool that wouldn't listen.

The phone rang as they got up to leave the house.

"Hello, Coy residence," Vern said into the mouthpiece.

"Let me speak to Curly, please," a gruff voice said.

"She's not here. I'm her brother and I'm on my way to pick her up right now. You can call back in two hours or I'll give her any message you'd like me to," Vern said politely. He figured it was a trick calling, and the voice remained silent for a good interval. Vern could hear the man's heavy breathing, actually closer to wheezing. Then he spoke up: "Well, it's bad news. Tell her that her friend Weldon was picked up for murder along with another man early this morning and he's over in isolation, so he won't be able to call for a while," the voice said.

"Can he have visits? What kind of evidence do they have?" Vern asked rapidly. He didn't want the voice to get away.

"Oh, yeah, business as usual on visits, but he only gets one phone call a week. As for evidence, it looks a lot worse on the other guy than on him. I've got to go." The voice sounded nervous.

"Can you leave a number where Curly can call back?" Vern asked.

"She knows the number. Just tell her it's her friend in Salinas," the voice said and the line went dead. Vern realized it was probably the lieutenant.

"Weldon's in the hole for murder," he told The Stepper after hanging up the phone.

"Did they get him cold?" The Stepper asked.

"No, but I think the guy who helped him has a problem," Vern replied.

"We will have to get them a good lawyer," The Stepper said as they went out the door.

"We will," Vern assured him.

"Well, it's going to take a good bundle of money for good lawyers and we can't just get warm bodies with legal books for a deal like murder. We got to get them some ass-kickin' legal heroes."

"We'll get them took care of, Grady. Just keep your old ass alive awhile!"

"It's been here awhile, son," Grady told him as they got in the car.

CHAPTER 19

The psych ward at the Fresno County hospital looks a lot like the old county jail. Sections of it still have bars and part of it is dormitory style. It's used for criminally insane people awaiting trial, those picked up wandering the streets talking to themselves, and potential and failed suicides. Curly was being held as a possible suicide. The head nurse told Vern she was being sedated with Valium and seemed close to a nervous breakdown. She'd been admitted on a seventy-two-hour observation. But her admission was not mandatory. She had been brought here mainly because she wasn't coherent enough to tell the police if she had any other relatives or friends she could stay with. The head nurse told him that in lucid moments she would tell them, "Vern will be here to get me pretty soon."

"Well, I'm here, so wake her up and tell her we're going home," Vern told her.

"Come on down to her room and be there when she wakes up," the woman said, and Vern followed her down the hallway.

"Hey, big boy. You wants some a this pussy?" a black woman said to Vern as they passed a dormitory. Then she laughed a laugh that sounded like "Yuk yukka yukka yuk."

A man in a cell they passed said to the matron, "Hubba hubba ding ding, baby, you got everything!"

"I think that line is way older than I am." She smiled at Vern as she put the key in the lock on Curly's room door.

There were two beds in the room and both women slept soundly. Vern made Curly out in the dim light beneath a window. She slept on her back and he could see a wisp of her blond hair rising and falling with each breath. She looked pale and drawn; the lines between her eyebrows were pronounced, as they were when she was worried or in deep thought. He brushed the hair from her mouth and said her name softly. "Curly?"

She opened her eyes and looked at him for a long moment, then said, "Vern!" and threw her arms around him.

"It's okay, girl. We're going home," he whispered to her.

"Oh, Vern," she said, clutching him tighter. He had to almost pry her arms from around his neck.

"Up we go, hon," the matron said, helping her out of the bed as Vern walked over near the front door to let her get dressed.

When Vern walked into the hospital to get Curly, The Stepper had gone to a bank of pay phones and called a man named Spider Lowe in Sacramento. He paid for the call with a roll of quarters he'd bought for this purpose and kept in an aluminum tube that had once held a cigar.

"Hey, Spider, it's The Stepper," he said when Spider came on the line.

"Man, when did you get out?" Spider asked him.

"Just this morning. I'm still in Salinas," The Stepper lied.

Spider Lowe was a Duboce White Boys wannabe. He wasn't in the clique, but he hung around with them and tried to make people think he was. He wasn't too smart and they used him for a gofer and to hold their knives and stash contraband, such as dope and tattoo guns when he was in prison with them.

He lived in Sacramento and they used his house as a crash pad and safe house. If they ranked high enough in the gang, he would even share his wife occasionally.

"Well, what's happening, brother? How can I help you out?" Spider asked him.

"Man, I got a score going and I need to get in touch with Little Joe. He left a number for me in Fresno and they said he's up there in Sacramento somewhere. I got a line on a dope-dealin' wetback's stash pad, but we got to do it by tomorrow night or it will be gone. Maybe close to a half a million there."

"Man, can I help?" Spider asked.

"I done cut Little Joe in, man. You know how mad he'd get. If I don't find him, I'll have to take it alone, but I need some backup here."

The phone was silent for a long time, and The Stepper knew that one way or the other he would get the information.

"Well, look, man, I don't know what's goin' on, but Little Joe is laying low and I ain't supposed to hook him up with nobody but Brian or Jack."

"Fuck, Spider, this is a fucking emergency, man! You know I ain't no fucking cop or snitch. We need that money bad, man! I'll cut you in for fifteen percent of my end. Just tell me how to get in touch."

"I don't know what good it would do. There's no phone up where he's at, man," Spider said.

"That's okay. I got wheels. I'll go up and get him. He probably forgot. Man, I won't tell him you told me where he is. If you want to tell him after the score, you can. He'll probably kick you down something on his end too," The Stepper urged.

"Okay, man, but don't ever tell him I told you. Have I got your word on that?"

"You got my word, man. I'll never tell anyone," The Stepper assured him.

"He's up at that weed dealer's house in Coarsegold. Lester Gordon. They call him Fat Lester. He gets paranoid and turns his phone off. It's off right now. He's afraid someone will say something on there and the feds will have it tapped, so he just don't talk on the phone."

"Not a bad idea," The Stepper assured him.

"I think Little Joe just made some kinda move in Fresno, plus his parole officer is looking for him already. Fat Lester has this little egg-shaped trailer house, you know one of them real small ones. It's out back of his house. He's letting Little Joe lay up there for a few days till things cool down."

"Well, how in the hell do I find this fat guy? I don't know anyone in Fresno," The Stepper said.

"His name and address are in the phone book. It's a little tiny town about sixty miles from Fresno up in the foothills. Up toward Yosemite National Park," Spider said.

"Okay, man. I hope I can catch up with him by Sunday. I can't afford to lose an easy score like this," The Stepper said.

"Okay, but I should get twenty percent because I'm going out on a limb right here," Spider told him.

"Man, you got my word. There's no stronger limb to go out on than that. But if it goes real smooth and the numbers are large, yeah, you will get twenty. Otherwise, it's fifteen," The Stepper responded. He liked to think of that last line as "Putting a sucker to sleep."

"Okay, you got a deal, old man," Spider exulted as he hung up.

The Stepper hung up the phone mumbling to himself.

"Yeah, you got a deal, you little creepy, loudmouth, troglylip, liverbrain, cowardly punk. You will get one hundred percent if we ever can't find one of your joined-up brothers." His next thought was that he might as well admit it to himself. He had joined Vern's war. He was going to be here with Vern until the last one went down on one side or the other. Or he fell to an early skirmish. Either way, from now on, it looked to be pure violence.

Grady's personality had not been suited to prison or war. He had always resented laws. So he never observed many of them, and that fact kept him in jail for much of his life. Inside jails he had hustled his fellow man now and then, sometimes running crooked poker or crap games.

When gang members lost in his games, they felt shamed somehow. He always made them pay off and wouldn't listen to their stories the way others would. The Stepper would listen politely, perhaps while rolling a cigarette, but when the speaker was finally finished, he'd say, "I want my money," as if he had not heard their story.

Gang members pulled that trick a lot. The new-breed gangs, anyway. They figured because they had all the backup that cons would be intimidated into not pressing for payment. The Stepper wasn't intimidated by anyone; by older cons, especially.

The young ones knew they would have to fight him if they didn't pay him. A few who had tried him out had been thoroughly stepped on by the Stepper.

That was a bit ironic to a man like him who had always hated violence. It was the ugliest thing he could imagine human beings doing to one another. And he was a man who loved and cherished beauty. Paula, that huge passion flower of a fragrant woman, had taken an interest in him, acted fascinated with him, flirted with him—made him wake up happy even though he was doing life in a wire-and-concrete cage where such feelings are dangerous to have.

Like Sleeping Beauty, she woke something back up in me, he thought. Then some sleazy little punk takes an order from a sleazier punk and takes her life like she's a piece of shit. A nobody. Takes my only loving dream of meeting her and putting my arms around her on this side of that concrete box. You wanna play games, motherfuckers? We'll play. Welcome to Vern's war!

"I found the little bastard, Vern," were the first words Curly ever heard The Stepper say on this side of the double fences with the rolled razor wire in between. Somehow she had thought he would be much more romantic than that. But a lot had changed since he was in there yesterday.

As they walked down the hospital steps with her arms around both of them, an old song by Dinah Washington began playing in her mind: "Lord, what a difference a day makes . . ." Oh—dear God, Paula! How can I live without you?

Detective Lieutenant Martin Torres sat in his office on Saturday morning talking to Bob McDonald, the man who had taught forensic jurisprudence to him in college. McDonald now lived and worked in Washington, D.C., where he taught forensic investigation techniques to FBI classes. Over the years they had become friends and Torres called him at home.

"Martin, you truly amaze me at times," McDonald was telling him.

"I don't know how. I mean something is wrong here. This guy Coy is just your average hillbilly pimp. The deceased was just a better-than-average whore, both operating around average Fresno yokels. I don't see any part of their game that would cross them up with a crew sophisticated enough to build a car bomb. That's Mafia stuff. It's just not done in Fresno," Torres responded, attempting to quell the sarcasm he detected in McDonald's voice.

"There you go using that word again, Martin."

"What word? Mafia?" Torres asked.

"No, Martin, *sophisticated*," McDonald told him, then asked, "Would you call my eleven-year-old son sophisticated?"

"Depends on how many of your lectures he's had to listen to," Torres responded, while beginning to feel about eleven years old himself.

"Well, since you've evidently forgotten a lecture or two on explosive devices, unsophisticated devices at that, let me refresh your memory."

"Okay, I'm getting the idea," Torres said.

"I hope so. Two sticks of dynamite and one electric blasting cap with two wires. Lift the hood, wind one wire around the top of a spark plug. Wire the ground wire around any piece of metal such as the battery holder or frame, then lay the dynamite down in there somewhere, and attach the blasting cap. Soon as someone turns the ignition—boom! My eleven-year-old son could figure that out."

Torres began to feel like a real moron. He'd been thinking some real gangsters had come to Fresno. "Okay, Bob, I get your point." He sighed.

"That's a common mistake, Martin. There is something about explosive devices, an aura perhaps, that tends to point toward sophistication, and in many cases that logic is justified. I know a couple of bombers who could blow your mailbox up with a well-aimed linear shape charge and not disturb a splinter of the post it sits on. Now, that's sophisticated.

"There are several ways to determine the mental acumen of even the thug who places a crude device like the one that killed your victim. For instance, long wires can be used and the explosive placed on a little Plexiglas trough under the seat that would direct the blast upward for a sure kill.

"Or the explosive could be placed on top of the motor in such a fashion that the blast would blow nuts, bolts, and other little shards of metal back through the car, chest-high. Ugly but effective. It sounds like your perpetrator just wired it up and left it hanging under the motor.

"From what you say, I figure he got lucky or she got very unlucky. His charge ripped the gas tank and oil pan, turning the vehicle into a ball of fire. I believe she was literally burned to death. You'd be surprised how many people survive car bombs. I think your victim would have made it had it not been for the fire."

"Jesus! What a way to go!" Torres exclaimed.

"Probably no worse than any other. The shock of the blast shut down the cranial nerve to the point where she felt nothing," McDonald assured him.

"Cranial nerve?" Torres asked.

"Yes, a peripheral nerve attached to the stem of the brain. There are twelve pairs of such nerves in—"

"Okay, okay," Torres interrupted. "I get the idea."

"Bob! Quit picking on your little brother. You're supposed to protect him, not beat up on him," Torres heard McDonald say into the telephone. An exaggerated screaming could be heard in the background.

"I'll get off here and let you break up that riot. Thanks a lot, Bob. You saved me a lot of wasted energy and probably a pile of extra paperwork."

"My pleasure, Martin," McDonald replied.

Torres hung up, wishing he could spend all his Saturday and Sunday mornings with his kids. He decided to spend the rest of this weekend with them. He felt a lot better knowing he wasn't up against some diabolically intelligent mad bomber. Just another Fresno crook who lost his conscience in a dope house or prison somewhere. He could catch an asshole like that. All he needed was a tiny bit of luck. He damn sure didn't have any evidence that he could see.

He left a note for his secretary to call Coy Monday and get him down here. Also to run a make on everyone who lived at Coy's house. When he locked the office door, he locked the entire case out of his mind for the remainder of the weekend. It was playtime. Maybe shoot some hoops with Benjamin, his own twelve-year-old son, better known as "Crazy Horse."

CHAPTER 20

Curly couldn't believe what was happening to her now. Paula had been murdered yesterday morning. There was no doubt about that, although she was still conning herself into believing that this was a dream and she would wake up in a minute and say, "Comadre, listen to some of this fucking crazy dream I had. You won't believe this!"

But even when she got to the dream, she knew that Comadre was the dream, was the reason for her to be dreaming it over and over. Her death had scripted the dream, and Curly couldn't play the role. Paula, her Comadre, was gone.

But now it did seem like a dream. It was a beautiful, gorgeous day. A clear blue sky with white clouds hanging like fluffed-up pillows in three-dimensional sunshine.

Vern had finally come for her after what seemed an eternity. And now she was riding alone in the backseat with a blanket over her while Vern drove and talked with The Stepper in some kind of cryptic verbal shorthand she didn't understand. Stuff like:

Vern: "Man, it don't matter. I can't help it if some donkey is in the way!"

The Stepper: "It does matter, and we back off from a crowd."

Vern: "That's the problem. I get close it's comin' down. Wrong place, wrong time, I'm sorry. Some folks are just unlucky."

The Stepper, after what seemed like ten miles of driving in silence: "Fuck that, Vern; no fucking way!"

It was obvious they were arguing intensely, but Curly didn't have a real for-sure idea about what and they damn sure weren't heading home. She couldn't stand it anymore. They had been driving at least forty miles and their argument seemed to be strictly about revenge and how to do it. No one said a damn word about Paula.

We aren't even talking about burying her. We don't even know where the fuck she's at, she thought to herself, then remembered Paula saying that she wanted to be cremated when she died, and it all became too much for her. Throwing the blanket to the floor and sitting up, she yelled at Vern, "What in the fuck are you guys talking about and where in the hell are we going?"

"Take it easy, hon," Vern said soothingly.

"Yeah, Curly. You wouldn't want to be at home now, so we're going to rent a nice peaceful cottage up here. Maybe stay a day or two," The Stepper put in.

"You're both full of shit and you're talking pig latin, you assholes. I'm not a fucking moron. I'm either with you or I'm not. If you don't trust me, then stop this fucking car and let me out right this second!" She insisted, and Vern pulled over to the side of the road.

"Here, you drive awhile, Grady, and I'll sit back there with Curly."

"I'm sorry, hon," Vern said, as he started to get in the back with Curly. But she jumped out the other side of the Blazer.

"I mean it, Vern. I'm either all the way with you guys or I'm staying here and that's it," she said. Vern was shocked. He'd never seen this kind of iron in Curly's makeup. He had never dreamed she could get that kind of resolve to the surface. It almost put him at a loss for words, for once in his life. He looked over at The Stepper, whose jaw had been set but looked softer now. Vern was loosening up himself. After all, she was their partner.

"So you tell me, man. I've heard there's no way a convict will ever trust a woman," Vern said to The Stepper, and it sounded as much like a question as anything and things seemed awfully tense for a moment.

"That's bullshit, but does she need this kind of action? We're committed, but why jeopardize her? She don't need that kind of bullshit in her life. Talk to her, Vern," The Stepper responded. They were all out of the Blazer now. Grady and Curly on one side and Vern over by the road. They studied one another over the top of the hood.

"Well, man, I . . ."

"No, Vern, he's right. He's absolutely right, so let me answer him," she said.

"Okay, hon, you call it," Vern told her and she could hear a tone of relief in his voice. She didn't feel good about what was going to happen to his relief.

"You're right, Stepper, I don't need it at all. I'm way past needing it. I've got to have it and I'll get it by myself if I have to. But I'm with you on that crowd shit.

"We know about injustice, don't we?" she said, glaring at Vern. "We don't know much about justice, but we can keep from doing anyone an injustice. We don't have to be like them to get even. Let's do it by the book!"

They both walked over to her and put their arms around her. Grady got there first and was hugging her tight when Vern got his arms around her.

"Okay. I'll do it however you guys call it. If there's someone else around, we wait until we get him alone. But don't let the little fucker get away. I'll go crazy if that little bastard gets away," Vern insisted.

"Don't worry, hon, he won't get away," Curly said and kissed him on the lids of both his closed wet eyes. Only then did she realize she'd understood every nuance of their conversation and had had a pretty good idea all the time why they weren't going home. She knew Vern that well. This was far from a dream.

They rented one room with two double beds at a Motel Six in Coarsegold. Curly rented the room using the name Susan Gage, and wrote down the Blazer's license plate number with the digits altered. They agonized over renting a room up here, but Curly had no clothes and only the emergency makeup she kept in her purse.

She took off to look for a clothing store while Vern and The Stepper took the guns from Vern's briefcase and checked them out carefully.

"I'm never going to be packing one of these unless we're going after a DWB or robbing a bank. It's a felony and a life sentence if I get caught with a gun. For you or Curly, it's only a misdemeanor. So you two will have to carry all the guns," The Stepper told Vern as he inspected the .45 and shoved a clip home. "Nice piece here," he added.

"Yeah, that's an army forty-five. Knock a mule down. We will have Curly keep yours in her purse along with the one I give her. She gets caught with them, she can say a trick gave them to her as security on money he owed, and that you didn't know she was carrying them around," Vern assured him.

While Curly was gone, Vern found Fat Lester's address in a phone book. When she returned, he drove to a hardware store and bought a shovel, two pairs of gloves, a water hose, and some three-in-one oil. One of the guns needed oil on the trigger mechanism, and something The Stepper had said about the guns got Vern to thinking.

If they did kill Little Joe, they would have to drive over sixty miles back to Fresno. They would be vulnerable to being stopped and Vern decided to just leave the guns here and pick them up later if he needed them. When he got back to the motel, he had The Stepper siphon two gallons of gas out of the Blazer into a can he had in the back. He did it just at dark when he was pretty sure no one was looking.

Curly went for takeout and they ate hamburgers in the room. No one mentioned Paula or the reason they were up here. To their surprise they discovered they were all hungry.

Vern made them put everything in the Blazer and they all carefully wiped the room down, wiping anything they might have touched. About a half mile from Lester's turnoff they stopped, and Vern found a place off the road to dig a hole. The soil was sandy but hard, yet the hole didn't have to be deep. They dropped the pieces of hose in it that The Stepper had used to siphon the gas.

"What do we do if there's dogs?" Curly asked.

"Kill them if we have to," Vern replied.

As they turned up Fat Lester's driveway, they were relieved to see that his house was dark and no cars sat in the driveway. There was a motorcycle parked in an open garage and a big black Labrador dog came out of the garage barking and wagging his tail at the same time.

"He won't be a problem," Curly said. She dreaded killing an animal.

"We won't have any trouble with him," The Stepper remarked. He was very good at sensing what Curly was thinking about.

There were lights on in the little trailer house about a block from the main house. A brand-new, sleek Pontiac Trans Am was pulled up very close to the trailer door.

Vern parked the Blazer a good distance from the trailer and The Stepper eased out with the gas can and took off into the darkness to circle round the back of the trailer. Curly grabbed the Lab and began petting and talking to him so that he wouldn't attempt to follow The Stepper. There weren't any trees, but there were several large bushes that gave fair cover. To Curly they looked like manzanita.

With the Blazer's motor off, they could hear music and someone laughing coming from the little trailer house. Some kind of gangsta rap music that thumped like a crazy magnified heartbeat.

"Get behind the wheel and stay ready to get out of here fast, and keep an eye on the main house," Vern told Curly and began walking toward the trailer. He checked the .44 Magnum one more time to be sure it wasn't cocked. The Stepper had the .45. The Lab followed along behind him, sniffing at his boots and Levi's. It was a very small trailer, probably not over fourteen to sixteen feet long. He was only about eight long steps from the Trans Am.

"Hey, in the trailer!" he yelled, standing still beside a treelike bush with the Trans Am between him and the trailer door.

He saw movement behind a curtained window, and after a few seconds the music stopped and a woman opened the inner door of the trailer, leaving the screen locked, and peered out into the night.

She wore a tight top that ended a few inches above the waistband of the Levi's she wore. Vern could tell she was well built but that was about all he could see of her. The light framed her from behind.

"Who's out there and what do you want?" she yelled back.

"We need to speak with Little Joe for a minute. Tell him to come on out," Vern replied, loud enough for her to hear well. It took her a bit to reply, as if she were getting her lines from someone.

"I don't know any Little Joe. I'm here alone and if you don't leave right now, I'm calling the cops," she replied. Vern couldn't see any phone lines at all running to the trailer. But it was dark and he couldn't be sure.

"Okay. Tell him he's got two minutes to come out here. If he don't, we're coming in after him," Vern yelled. He saw a movement at the corner of the trailer. The dog yelped and started off and Vern grabbed him by the collar. The Stepper was pouring the gas. Vern moved back around the shrub and toward the left end of the trailer, dragging the dog along with him. The Stepper would be covering the other end after he lit the gas.

The woman, obviously very panicked now, reached for the latch on the screen door, then dropped her hand as if someone had told her not to touch it.

"Listen, I told you there's no one here but me," she yelled back, and her voice was breaking. Evidently Little Joe was going to make her stay there and use her as a shield when they came barging in. Vern waited to reply until he thought about two minutes had passed.

"Okay, pardner. Bring them out!" he yelled, letting go of the dog, and switching the pistol to his right hand.

A match lit up like a small firefly in the night, then turned into an inferno before their eyes. There was a whomping sound and a ball of fire engulfed three sides of the little trailer and underneath the back. Grady had poured the gas all the way around it, leaving the front the only place not consumed by the flames. The night lit up as if a Christmas decoration had suddenly been turned on.

The woman screamed and jerked the screen open. She tried to jump so far from the trailer that she fell down, and as she struggled to her feet, The Stepper yelled, "Run, bitch! Run for your life and keep on running." She did run and passed a few feet from Vern but was so obviously panicked she never even saw him.

Little Joe came out right behind her holding a rifle in front of him that looked like an AK-47. The Trans Am was still between Vern and him, but Vern heard the loud bam of the .45 as The Stepper got off three shots, which all missed their target.

Little Joe, thinking he'd located the source of his problem, turned and fired a burst in The Stepper's direction and came running around the front of the Trans Am, obviously trying to get the car between him and The Stepper. Vern gut-shot him twice with the .44 Magnum. The two shots sounded almost like one, they were so close together. The rifle went straight up in the air as Little Joe was hurled back onto the hood of the car, arms outflung.

"Are you okay, pardner?" Vern yelled as he looked into the night. The dog was nowhere in sight. The flames were dying down now, but it was obvious the trailer would burn. Dry grass beneath it was burning fiercely.

"Yeah, I'm pretty sure he missed, but I'm lucky I hit the dirt. I swear I heard them shots go over me," The Stepper said as he got back to his feet. Vern didn't see any need to even look at Little Joe. He was sure he had hit him good. Now he heard dogs barking not far away in the direction where the woman had run. Curly had the motor running when they got back to the Blazer.

"Keep the lights out until we get back to the road," Vern told her.

They found the hole easily and buried the guns. After Vern

had carefully covered them up, he got behind the wheel with Curly beside him. They made it almost to Pinedale, a little town seven miles north of Fresno, before the California Highway Patrol pulled them over.

Vern showed them his driver's license and they went over the car very carefully, making them all three stand beside the road while they searched. They took a good look at the shovel, but The Stepper had cleaned it and wiped it down with three-in-one oil.

"Sorry to inconvenience you," one cop said as he handed Vern back his driver's license and insurance form.

"No problem, Officer," Vern said as they got back in to go home. Right then, Vern began thinking that he just might let things go and try to get on with his life. Paula had been avenged and that's about all she would have expected or wanted. She wouldn't have wanted him to keep on killing until he destroyed his own life. When he pulled in at home, he was too tired to even think about it. Arrangements for Paula's cremation and funeral would have to be made now and after that he could talk with Curly and The Stepper about what they would do next. He found himself hoping that this old outlaw's character was as good as it appeared to be, because he was part of Vern's family now. For better or for worse.

The police had left a note on Vern's door telling him not to move the Lincoln, that they would be around Monday to get it. He was also instructed to call a Detective Martin Torres on Monday morning.

The bedrooms and bathrooms hadn't been altered by the blast. Vern told The Stepper to take the main bedroom and took Curly to the guest bedroom. He didn't want her looking at Paula's things right now and he didn't really want to look at them himself.

Dog-tired and overcome with loss and grief, Curly and Vern clung to each other, sleeping fitfully like recently orphaned children. It was going to take a long time getting used to living without her. It seemed to Vern that she'd been with him all his life.

He encouraged Curly to sleep late while he and The Stepper tried to make the house livable again. They ran around all day finding new window frames and other items. He bought a canvas tarp and covered the Lincoln with it so Curly wouldn't have to look at the charred mess from the kitchen window. Peggy called him on Sunday evening.

"Vern, I need to see you right away," she told him.

"Where's Larry?" he asked.

"He's gone for a while. Just come on over and I'll explain," she told him, and he could tell by the tone of her voice that she wouldn't say anything else on the phone.

"Can I bring Curly and The Stepper?" he asked.

"Oh, hell, yes, just get over here!" she said and hung up.

His cousin Larry Ashland lived about four miles from Vern. Larry had three girls working, including Peggy. Vern didn't care much for him because he occasionally beat his women. He got by on his looks rather than his brains and was one of those pimps who cover up their mental deficiencies with silent, arrogant vanity and overblown egos.

Vern sometimes wondered why Peggy stayed with Larry. She was a very smart woman and a top-notch whore. Larry treated her like shit to the extent she would let him. But Vern had noticed when she finally put her foot down, Larry would take his conceit and back up. That, more than anything, is what made Vern lose respect for him. There was a weakness at the foundation of Larry's personality that would never let Vern trust him.

"What's happening, Peggy?" Vern asked when they entered

the silent house and Peggy shut and locked the door behind them.

"Come on," she replied, and they followed her to the bedroom at the end of a hallway. Larry's house was laid out like a Spanish rancher's spread. A patio and courtyard with a pool were separated from the house by huge sliding glass doors. Two long hallways leading from the living room held bedrooms and bathrooms. *Ostentatious* was the word Paula had come up with to describe it, and that sounded about right to Vern, whatever it meant. The word itself was about as long as Larry's ego.

She opened the bedroom door onto a tableau that shocked the three visitors into a stunned and petrified silence. Melvin was lying on his back in a small trundle bed with bandages the length of his naked chest and an IV unit hooked into his arm. A small bald-headed man with just a ring of hair above his ears looked up at the visitors.

"Will he be okay without you for a while, Mosely?" Peggy asked the little man when they entered.

"Oh, yes, he's doing quite well," the stranger responded.

"Then wait in the living room while we talk to him, but don't leave the house under any circumstances," Peggy told him.

"Okay, but, uh, may I call my wife?" he asked her on his way out.

"No, wait on the couch until I get there and I'll dial her for you. I want to make sure you don't say anything foolish. Now get your ass out there!" she said forcefully, and the little man almost stumbled as he sped up. Peggy shut the door behind him as Vern walked to Melvin's bedside. Melvin looked at him and offered a halfhearted smile. He lifted his right hand to shake with The Stepper and a look of pure agony crossed his features.

"Goddammit, Melvin, you don't have to shake hands," Peggy

told him, then added, "He got shot in the chest last Friday night. He drove all the way to Madera and called me from a phone there. He said your line was busy, so I went and got him. My God, there was blood an inch deep in his truck. I don't see how he made it. Dr. Mosely is a trick of mine who likes punishment, but he's also one of the best internists in Fresno.

"I called him and he came over to his office and operated on Melvin right there, using me as a nurse. The bullet kind of bounced off a rib and tore him up pretty good, so Mosely had to do a lot of cutting. God, it was awful. We moved him over here this morning and Larry went fucking bananas. But we couldn't leave him at the clinic. It's open tomorrow.

"Look at this," she said, and pulled the sheet down to Melvin's pubic hair line. The bandage ran from there up to his breastbone. She peeled the bandage back to show an angry red ditch, stitched up like a zipper.

"He's got drains, about four, where it's not closed up, and Mosely says that the biggest worry now is a staph infection, but ironically there's less chance of him getting that at home than in the hospital. Some muscles got cut, so it hurts him to move, but the little fucker won't be still." She smiled.

"How in the hell did you get that doctor to do all that?" The Stepper asked.

"He likes to be ordered around and disciplined a bit. He's having the time of his life, but Larry has gone with Sandy and Gloria and he's calling every hour saying we got to get Melvin out of here. He's terrified because Melvin isn't the only one who got shot."

"That may be an understatement," The Stepper said, looking at Vern.

"Take me home, man," Melvin told Vern, who was already

wondering if the bed came apart or folded and how they were going to get him in the Blazer and keep him out of sight.

"Is there any of this stuff you want to tell us, Melvin?" Vern inquired. "If you don't want to, man, just let it go. I'm just fucking curious because you're usually so damn careful."

Melvin looked around to make sure Mosely wasn't in the room. "Ralph wanted to make one extra trip because we couldn't carry everything at once. I didn't see no problem, but they had us made when we got back.

"Some trigger-happy cop killed Ralph and I got the cop, but I don't think he died. News keeps saying he's critical. The motherfucker was a good shot and had balls. He popped me good on his way down. None of his buddies came within twenty feet of me. That's how I got away. They went so nuts they got to shooting at each other. Until the smoke cleared, no one knew who was who or where. I heeled-and-toed it almost a mile to my truck. That's what almost killed me," he explained. He fell silent and they all knew that would be his last word on the topic.

Everyone was aware of the felony murder rule in California. If two men are committing a crime and one of them dies or is killed, his partner in the crime can be held responsible for his death. Can indeed be tried for first-degree murder.

"It's probably going to hurt, man," Vern told him.

"I don't give a fuck. Get me out of this asshole's house," Melvin croaked. It was obvious that even talking hurt him.

"I'll have Mosely give him a good shot of morphine so you can move him," Peggy said and left to get the little man. The Stepper was already down on his knees looking at the underside of the bed.

"We can fold the legs," he told Vern.

"Hell, we're in business then. Curly, you take care of the drip bottle while we move him," Vern replied.

"Oh, I can remove that now. It's just sugar water, anyway," Mosely told Vern as he came back in with Peggy. He went to his bag and began preparing a syringe for Melvin.

"Can you give Curly here a shot of that also?" Vern asked him, nodding at Curly.

"Well, I suppose so, at a much smaller dose," Mosely said, looking at Curly.

"Then give her one," Vern said as he and The Stepper began to deal with the folding legs.

After the doctor administered their shots and removed the bottle, they carried Melvin to the Blazer and slid him in with very little difficulty.

"Where's Paula?" he asked as they carried him, and everyone acted as if they hadn't heard. Curly stayed in the back with Melvin and they loaded up to leave. Peggy walked to the passenger side, reached through the open window and grabbed The Stepper by the hair.

"Leave this gentleman here with me for a while. I need to talk to him for a few minutes."

"How are we going to unload Melvin?" Vern asked her.

"We'll be right along, just wait on us," she said and opened The Stepper's door.

"Yeah, probably about fifteen seconds," the old man said as he got out, and Vern was very pleased to see Curly smile in the rearview mirror. Her eyelids looked heavy now as the morphine took hold. Vern wished he could have a shot himself, but someone had to stay sane around here. This was one of those weekends that would be with him until the Grim Reaper came to collect.

"Where's Paula?" Melvin croaked again, but no one heard him this time either.

The third time he asked, Curly said to him, "Melvin, shut up. You sound like a fucking parrot."

The Blazer was suddenly entombed with a deadly silence, broken only by the sound of the motor. Curly and Vern both knew deep in their hearts that Melvin had always been hopelessly in love with Paula, even though nothing had ever been said.

CHAPTER 21

"On the advice of my attorney I have no comment" was what Vern said to Martin Torres when he sat down in his little office at the courthouse on Monday morning.

"Who is your attorney?" Torres shot back, looking at Vern antagonistically across an oak desk.

"That would be a comment, I believe," Vern told him.

The room was neat and clean, with none of the usual clutter that Vern associated with most police stations. A portrait of some long-forgotten Fresno sheriff with a long mustache hung on the back wall next to a shelf of law books. Two spacious leather chairs sat on either side of the desk. It resembled a lawyer's office. Vern knew that Torres was the top cop in homicide, although he'd never spoken with him personally.

Torres picked up a ringing phone and said "Torres" into the mouthpiece. He was dressed sharp. He had on a white-on-white shirt with chocolate-brown trim; a tan silk jacket hung from the desk chair that matched his slacks. Two-tone brown-and-white spectator shoes completed his outfit. Monday was his favorite dress-up day.

"This guy that got his lights put out up here in Coarsegold was affiliated with the Duboce White Boys, and we found some dynamite and blasting caps and one a them anarchist bomb books in the trunk of his car," Jack Silver, a deputy in Coarsegold, said into his ear.

"That's interesting, but affiliated with the Duboce what?" Torres asked.

"The Duboce White Boys. It's a prison gang of white Nazis and was started by a couple dirtballs that lived on Duboce in San Francisco. They are all over the fucking state now and they are pure vicious," Jack assured him.

"Did the broad get a make on either one of the assailants?" Torres asked, watching Vern, who was studiously inspecting his thumbnail as if it were fascinating to behold.

"Hah, the crazy bitch says one a them was a Chinese ninja dressed in all black. I asked her how she could tell he was in black and she said it was because she couldn't see him in the dark. We may as well forget any help there," Jack said despondently.

"Well, keep me up on it, pardner. I got to run," Torres told him and returned his attention to Vern.

"I don't think you killed Paula Coy, but I'm pretty sure you know who did. Or at the least why they did it," Torres said.

"On the advice of my attorney, I—"

"Okay, okay," Torres said, putting his hands up, palms out. "I get the idea. You don't have to say a word. But since we're talking murder here, what about your other girl's brother?"

"What about him?" Vern shot back.

"We picked him up off a beach over at Pismo. There's an awful lot of killing going on around you, Coy, and I believe where there is smoke, there is fire. You are involved in this shit up to your neck somehow," he said to Vern, who by now was engrossed again in his fingernail. He was holding it up like a small mirror, as if trying to see his reflection in it.

Vern had talked to cops before, and Weldon had drilled into him to just give name, rank, and serial number. He felt semi-comfortable because he knew Torres didn't have a lick of proof or he would already be in jail.

Vern was glad to hear him mention Curly's brother. Now he could go home and tell her the police told him Sam was dead. He couldn't mention it to her before without her suspecting him of being involved, as she might anyway. But he was prepared to deny it until his dying day. He didn't even bother to respond with the advice of my lawyer shit. Torres stood up, leaned forward as his chair rolled back, and placed both hands palms down on his desktop, looking intently at Vern, who could see a vein throbbing in the cop's smooth brown neck.

"I can get over that thug they found on the beach and I can live without that piece of shit that was burned down in Coarsegold. But that woman, your wife, someone's going to have to answer for that and I won't sleep good until they do. Now if you get cute or hinder my investigation in any way, I'll bust your fucking hump, homeboy. You'd better tell me you understand me, Vern," he added in a dead-serious tone.

Vern had never before talked to Torres, but he knew him by reputation and was scared some by what he'd heard. Torres was a mean son of a bitch who wouldn't be above putting lemon squeezers on a guy's nuts and making him rat on a friend if it came to that. But he was way too slick to get caught at any such conduct. It was time to put aside all games.

"I understand and I wish you good luck," Vern said, looking

Torres levelly in the eye.

"Okay. Get outta here. But if I call you back, bring your lawyer and a toothbrush. You'll be staying for an extended visit. Just make sure I keep liking your style and don't do nothing that would disappoint me," Torres replied.

"I won't," Vern said over his shoulder on the way out.

Torres sat back down behind the desk. It looked as if he came to the party a little bit late to get to meet the guy who did Paula. Right now this Little Joe looked like a pretty good candidate. So it would be on to the why of everything. If he could discover why all this mayhem was going down right around Vern's people, then he could probably get a line on who was doing what.

He remembered that Vern had a brother in prison and made a note to find out if the guy had been cooperative, but he probably hadn't since he ended up in the jug. Still, he intended to check it out.

He made another note to get some info on the DWB, which would be hard. Many cops assigned to report on these guys didn't have a clue as to how to get next to them. So they wrote reams of reports on their observations. Ninety percent of which was bullshit. The only known facts came from stoolies who were former members. Only about sixty percent of their observations were bullshit.

These gangs tended to branch off into cells of three and four and engage in scams they didn't even divulge to the rest of the gang. They kicked down tax to the leaders but kept the deal to themselves. Of course they could always call on the entire gang for muscle if they needed it. The deals they loved most involved large amounts of heroin. Over ninety percent of prison gang members are hard-core heroin addicts. Which made it even harder to tie this gang to Coy and his women. They damn sure never used heroin. So it had to be something else. Right now,

Torres was leaning toward thinking that maybe the DWB was trying to organize the white whores in Fresno. That's about all it could be, and he decided to work that angle until something looked better.

CHAPTER 22

Alan reached over to the nightstand beside his bed and scrabbled around in the confusion and disorganization for his ringing cordless phone. The pale light of early morning was just beginning to filter into his little room through the well-worn drapes that were trying to keep out the daylight. He couldn't see much of anything, but he found it on the fourth ring.

"It's Alan, talk at me," he mumbled into the mouthpiece. He hadn't really been sleeping anyway. Just nodding and napping in a long heroin dream.

"It's Tim, man. They put Little Joe's lights out last night," Tim Jones told him abruptly.

"They what? Who?" Young Alan said, and scooted up further in his bed. He slept on one of those hospital beds that can be cranked to almost any position.

His room was tiny, the bathroom almost as large as the living room. It was like a million other hotel rooms in San Francisco that rent for two or three hundred a month. Next to his phone on the night table was a dope cooker made from a shoe polish can lid. He had been a big man on a big frame but this eight-year run on heroin had taken its toll.

"I think that Vern Coy and maybe The Stepper did it. Joe was supposed to hit Coy but got his wife by mistake. I guess he underplayed the dude," Tim explained.

"Or that fucking Stepper. What the fuck is he hooked up with this Vern for, anyway?"

"I think he was Coy's brother's ace deuce in the joint. But we've got to put this shit right somehow."

Alan wholeheartedly agreed with that. Especially when his dope-laden brain took him back to a younger day in San Quentin when he had fought The Stepper on the handball court and got knocked out in front of about twenty convicts.

"I'll be there in an hour," Tim said.

"I'll be here," Young Alan said as he hung up the phone, turned on the night-light, and began cooking up a gram of tar heroin.

Tim was tall and slim, a good dresser with a fine sprinkle of gray in his once coal-black hair. They had met in reform school as kids, and been partners ever since. They had started the Duboce White Boys in the mid-seventies at Folsom Prison.

Tim, a health nut, had always been the brains of the outfit while Young Alan's barely controlled violence had kept respect and fear at a high level. Tim now lived with his wife and two children in the Sunset District while Young Alan went on doing his dope thing. But they still worked good together and neither of them had been to prison in over ten years, which was an impressive statistic in itself. The money was coming in well and steady from Mexican dope dealers and Young Alan still had enough sense to give Tim 20 percent of his to keep and invest. The rest he took in dope.

Tim seated himself on Alan's small couch and watched as Alan shoveled the cornflakes in the dimly lit hotel room. He got up and pulled a curtain back to let in some sunshine before sitting back down.

"How many Indians we got around here?" he asked Alan.

"Probably twenty right here in the city. Maybe fifteen more around the state that ain't in jail. I haven't done a count lately. Why?" Alan asked as he put the cereal bowl he'd been eating cornflakes from next to the dope cooker on the coffee table.

"Because we are going to have to stop Vern Coy if it takes every man we got. Not much we can do about Weldon now he's in the hole until he shows up somewhere on a mainline, but we got to stop Vern."

"Hell, he may stop himself. He may figure he's even after doing Little Joe. We can lay back and take care of him later when some of the dust clears," Alan responded.

"That don't work, homey. Nowadays I'm getting paranoid. Weldon hit Brian and Jack, the head people at Soledad. What if Vern is bound to go at the head people out here? Now that means us. Besides that, the fuckin' Stepper is down here with that fool."

Alan's head jerked up when Tim said "Stepper." He'd been about to go into a little nod as his chin dropped toward his chest. The Stepper was a worthy opponent and a dangerous one at that. He'd been in every joint that Tim and Alan had done time in, but they had never liked him and the feeling was mutual.

"Yeah, the way he thinks, his next thing to do would be to come up here and put a move on us," Alan agreed.

"That's the kind of thinking that is getting me downright paranoid," Tim said.

"You know, the thing I hate worst about a dope habit is that you can't ever go anywhere. At least not too far from your connection. But I've got an urge to get out and about. I'm tired of this fucking little room. It's like a cell," Young Alan said, looking around him carefully.

"So take a trip and take plenty of dope," Tim advised.

"That's what I'm thinking. I'll just go on down there to Fresno and take care of this. I'll take that gray van. If I run out of dope before I get done, you can send some by overnight mail," Alan told him.

"Yeah. It's about time we let these yokels know we ain't dead yet," Tim agreed.

"Yeah, and Brian and Jack were two good boys. I don't like the disrespect those clowns showed by that move. We need to straighten that out," Alan added.

"Do you plan to take anyone with you?" Tim asked, as he got up and brushed at his slacks.

"I don't see why. There's only a couple of them and I figure to just ease in and back out. If I take anyone, we could get made by them or the police before we could move. Just stay close where I can get in touch for the next few days," Alan said.

"If you need me or anyone, just call, and be careful, brother," Tim said as he hugged Young Alan. They were as close as any two brothers. They had been through a lot together, for a lot of years.

As Tim left the building and stepped out onto Polk Street, he was thinking about Young Alan taking this one by himself. No matter what Alan said, the bottom line for him doing it that way was Grady McCall. He had become determined to kill The Stepper before he died himself. The Stepper had been in their hair in a lot of prisons over the years. Young Alan didn't do much thinking, and when he did, it was bottom line. Tim had asked Alan not long ago what he thought about O.J. Simpson's guilt or innocence and he had replied, "If they had lived in Iran, the bitch would have been stoned to death for adultery, and O.J. wouldn't have had to kill her!" Alan didn't like any gray zones. It was all cut-and-dried with him. The Coy affair had given him a good excuse to kill two birds with one stone. McCall had once whipped Young Alan like he was a stepchild. Every convict in California knew about that.

CHAPTER 23

Yay-Yay and Weldon were taken out of their isolation cell, handcuffed, and escorted to the back of the cellblock where a small room containing a desk, filing cabinet, and several chairs had been set up as a disciplinary hearing and interrogation room.

They sat outside the room while two officers inside went about pulling files and getting ready for their hearing. Weldon was pleased to note that his lieutenant was one of the two. They knew that Jack had been dead on arrival, but Brian hung on to life and they couldn't find out for sure if he was dead or not. He hoped the proceedings would let them know.

The captain finally looked up and beckoned Yay-Yay in, calling his name through the door and actually using his nickname, Yay-Yay, which was unheard-of for a captain to do, but this one liked and respected old convicts and the codes and values they lived by. He was an old veteran of the prison wars himself, and some of these devious old thugs seemed more like comrades now than adversaries.

The escort cop checked on Yay-Yay's handcuffs as he helped him up and delivered him into the office. The captain slipped Yay-Yay some papers across the desk. Yay-Yay couldn't get them because of the cuffs, which were locked behind his back. The captain placed the papers where he was able to see them well.

There were two prison rules and two incident reports accompanied by a description of events and observations by institutional people and "confidential" remarks by prisoners nearby.

Killing—the first one said. Any inmate who takes the life of another is subject to six months of adjustment center and transfer. The hearing on these charges will be postponed until the outside courts have made their ruling.

"You understand, these are only a formality and will be dealt with after outside court has finished with you boys," the captain said.

"I understand," Yay-Yay replied while scanning the paperwork. All it said was that he knew he was the target of the investigation and charges were likely to be filed against them both.

He declined to sign anything and the captain sent him back to the chair and invited Weldon to join them while the scenario was played out again.

"Do you want to sign just saying you understand the charges against you?" the captain asked.

"Not until I see an attorney. How about releasing us from the hole until we are tried? We are innocent of these people's misfortunes," Weldon added.

"I doubt I can let you two go because there are about twenty-five more DWB on our mainline and they will all be looking for a shot to get even. I have to consider your safety. If you would be willing to enlighten us on what is going down, then maybe we could help. Otherwise, you and Yay-Yay are here for the duration."

Captain Brown looked like most other captains Weldon had seen. Overweight, nose blitzed by whiskey veins. A soft chair and cup of coffee at hand put him about where he wanted to be. Comfortable and secure.

The lieutenant had placed an unopened pack of Camels on the desk while the captain was talking. Weldon marveled at the nerve of the man, but took up the cue right away.

"Well, there are a few things I'd like to say, but not with both of you in the room," Weldon told him.

"Okay. Should I step out or should Bill here go out?" the captain said, nodding toward the lieutenant.

"I'll talk to the lieutenant here," Weldon said, and the captain got up and left the room.

"You'll need to think of something to report because I'm not telling you shit," Weldon said when the captain closed the door.

"I knew that. A few things I wanted to tell you is why I put the pack out and there are some goodies in there for you," the lieutenant told him.

"So they are both dead?" Weldon asked.

"Yeah, and that Ward done you all a favor before he died. Said it was two blacks come in on them. The cop was a fish and says he saw some blacks hanging around there and it looked like a little black who asked him to open their door from deadlock," the lieutenant said. "So you guys look like you got a way to go legally and I'll help all I can. Lose some papers if necessary. I'll tell the captain you're one of my boys and get some heat off you two. That's about it, though. You guys could still get convicted." As he spoke, he looked out the window above Weldon's head. "Curly will be coming up next Sunday to see you," he added.

Outside, Weldon could see that the captain was talking with

the cellblock officer and they were standing apart from Yay-Yay, who was leaning back in his chair, eyes closed as if he were near sleep.

"I know we still got problems, but thanks for the help." Weldon felt strange because he'd never in his life been helped by a cop.

The lieutenant reached over and put the pack of cigarettes in Weldon's coverall pocket. "Take these and good luck to you both," the lieutenant said, as they got up and headed for the door.

"What's this? You're not allowed cigarettes down here," the cellblock officer said and removed the pack from Weldon's coverall pocket.

"It's okay. I gave them to him from the hot drawer," the lieutenant said, and the cop grudgingly slid the pack back into Weldon's pocket.

Weldon's sphincter muscle tightened and his Adam's apple felt like a green tomato. Yay-Yay gave him one of the weirdest uncomprehending looks he'd ever encountered in the sea of faces from a lifetime.

"Easy, brother," Weldon mumbled to him, and saw Yay-Yay visibly relaxing somewhat. Weldon also thought about the lieutenant's remark: "I gave them to him from the hot drawer."

The "hot drawer" was a room where they kept cigarettes, coffee, candy, cash money, dope, and anything else of value they confiscated from other convicts. If they caught a convict with fifty cartons of cigarettes, they would take forty-six cartons because in the rule book an inmate is only allowed four cartons. The cigarettes and coffee were then handed out to stool pigeons or cons who mopped a floor or did any favor for a cop. Sometimes they gave a pack or two to cons in transit. A perpetual slush fund. When the drawer ran low they would have a series of shakedowns until it was replenished.

The Stepper had once burglarized the cops' "hot drawer" and taken all their cigarettes, coffee, and drugs. A deed that made the cops and everyone else miserable for the next few weeks. What with shakedowns, lockdowns, and rough interrogation sessions, the thought made Weldon smile.

The lieutenant had said the cigarettes were from the "hot drawer." So even if the cop opened them and found drugs, the lieutenant could have said that whatever convict the cigarettes were taken from probably had stashed the drugs in the pack. A story they would have to believe and accept as fellow cops. He could have just let it pass that the cigarettes were Weldon's. But he was letting Weldon know here that they had crossed the bridge that separated their worlds and were now working together for real. Let him know he would go right down to the wire with him. Weldon began to really trust this cop. Trust him more than he did many of his so-called gangster friends. This guy was for real and showed a lot of class. Curly did have good pussy. There was no doubt about that.

When they got back to the cell, Yay-Yay was almost beside himself. Still he kept his mouth closed and just watched as Weldon carefully opened the pack of Camels. It had been opened from the bottom, a space cleared for the two balloons, and then glued back as if it had never been opened. When one of the balloons fell out on the bunk, Yay-Yay exclaimed, "Chengow! Brother! You had me worried there for a minute!"

"Yeah, I know it looked funny. I feel kind of strange myself, but we do have a friend in the enemy camp. So watch for the man while I cook us up a shot."

"I got it," Yay-Yay said as he stuck a piece of mirror out of the bars far enough so that he could see down the tier. Usually they could hear the cop coming because of rattling keys and other small sounds. Still they had to be careful because some cops would tape down their keys and walk swiftly but silently down the tier. In isolation about all they ever discovered were sex acts and wine making. Many cops didn't care about such small stuff. But others stalked the tier day and night trying to bust someone.

They borrowed an outfit from a convict two cells away for a shot of the heroin. He sent along a small container of liquid bleach so that they could sterilize the needle. Bleach kills the AIDS virus and any other bug or germ that might be on or in the needle. After they got high they looked over the charge sheets they had received from the captain.

They were each charged with two counts of killing another inmate. Until now they had heard that one of the men was still alive. But it looked now as if Brian and Jack were both gone. Weldon didn't feel a lot of satisfaction, but he did feel some.

Their lives wouldn't bring Paula back, but in the future the gang might be more careful about who they killed. Nothing was settled for sure. Weldon and Yay-Yay had formally declared war on the DWB. For the rest of their prison terms, it would be kill or be killed by any DWB they ran across. Not exactly an easy way to do your time, but the die was cast.

"I sure appreciate your help, Yay-Yay, but I don't know why you insisted on biting a chunk out of this rhubarb," Weldon said.

"Ah, Cowboy, I was getting bored to death. This will give me something to do and think about," Yay-Yay replied.

"It will that," Weldon agreed, while thinking how easy it was to go from being bored to death to being stabbed to death.

CHAPTER 24

The Stepper thought he had heard Vern wrong. They were watching *60 Minutes* while Melvin dozed peacefully in the guest bedroom, and Vern asked during the commercial, "Do you want to help me rob a bank?"

Vern laid down a ballpoint pen he'd been doing some adding and subtracting with just before he asked Grady the question. The tone of his voice let the Stepper know it wasn't bullshit. It was late evening in mid-December, and the night was getting cool.

They had all calmed down a bit now. Melvin's stitches had been healing fine with no sign of infection, and from the news it was becoming obvious that the Sacramento police had not even a vague notion of who else had been involved.

"Hell, I hadn't thought about it, but my knee don't jerk against it. Do you think you are ready for that kind of action?" The Stepper asked.

"We've got to be, man. Weldon and Yay-Yay need the best

lawyers we can find them. Melvin would loan us money, but if any dust gets kicked up over that Sacramento thing, he's going to need all he's got, so we'd have to rob one anyway to pay for everything. Here, look at this."

He handed The Stepper the legal pad he'd been doing the numbers on and they looked dismal.

"You want part of it, hon?" he asked Curly almost offhandedly. It looked as if she had taken a healthy interest as she stood there with an iron she was using to press a pajama top for Melvin.

"Damn, man, how big is this fucking bank? Are we going to need a whole army? Why can't just you and I do it?" The Stepper demanded in a loud voice.

"Chill it, man. You'll wake up Melvin. We are using more people because we are going to get away clean. In fact, we need one more. It's going to take four of us to do it right."

"You'll need to convince me on that, Vern. I see doing the bank, but not with a bunch of people to baby-sit while we do it. That's dangerous, man," The Stepper told him.

"Okay. Just let me lay it all out and you all can say yes or no. No problem. If you want out, I trust you not to mention it ever to anyone."

"Lay it out, Vern," Curly told him, leaning forward to listen.

Vern laid out the scenario and even The Stepper was impressed. It would take four people, but they could get every dollar in the vault and with halfway decent luck get away with it. He decided he'd go if he liked the fourth party.

"I don't know of anyone we trust that much that has the nerve to do it," Curly told Vern.

"I'm number four," they all heard Melvin croak from the bedroom.

They all looked at each other.

"How long till withdrawal day?" The Stepper asked Vern.

"Two weeks, three at the most. I want it on Friday. This is Wednesday, say three weeks from Friday and two if things move along real good," Vern told them. He wanted to do it just before Christmas or New Year's.

"Hell, he's up and walking already, count him in," The Stepper said, and walked back to where Melvin lay on his back in bed.

"Look here. I've got a pretty good chunk of money you all can have if you want it," Melvin said as Curly and Vern followed The Stepper into his bedroom.

"I'd rather rob a bank than owe you, Melvin," Vern replied.

"Hell, we could get your money just by charging you half what the hospital would have charged you, Melvin," Curly added.

"Probably close to it," Melvin agreed.

"You're going to have to steal the car if you're going to drive, so you got to be up and about a couple days before the score," Vern told him.

"I'll get it, no problem," Melvin said. The Stepper could tell Melvin was in serious pain by the sheen of sweat that lay across his forehead right at the hairline. He shook two Tylenol and codeines out of the bottle and poured a glass of water from a pitcher next to Melvin's bed.

"Take these," he ordered, and Melvin sat up and swallowed them. His stitches had healed well except for the drains, and there was no infection anywhere to speak of. Melvin was already up walking around, even if just to the head and back.

Torres had been snooping around some, but it was obvious that he hadn't learned much that was useful.

Vern didn't see any real reason not to rob a bank. They were going to need a lot of money and it would be a good while before

Curly felt like getting back to work. He hoped to be able to leave Fresno soon anyway. Too many memories here.

He had a good bank picked out and didn't see how they could get caught unless they got really stupid. He didn't plan to do that.

CHAPTER 25

A heroin addict can make a major mistake very easily and that's what Young Alan did at the outset of his journey. He would have plenty of company on this trip, unwanted and unknown to him.

He entered a parking garage directly across from his hotel on Post Street, about six in the evening. A chilly wind blew in from the bay, mocking the orange ball of sun above the eccentric San Francisco skyline. Loud voices from the direction of the Polk Gulch Saloon at the corner of Post and Polk turned his head in that direction.

"The bitch came here with me and she's leaving with me!" one man said to another. It was two well-dressed businessmen arguing over a flamboyant transvestite, who watched the scene unfold, arms crossed over fake bosom, hip shot, feigning bored indifference at the crudity of jealous men.

Alan felt disgusted yet somehow intrigued with the scene.

Nowhere else in the world could that happen, he was thinking as he entered the garage and took the elevator to the fifth floor.

Flappers leaned against the trunk of Alan's black Cadillac, waiting for him. Flappers was a big man who bore a vague resemblance to Young Alan. The nickname was in honor of his oversized ears. Alan handed him the keys.

"Now look, there's probably only one carload of them. I'm coming down in the gray van. I'll follow you down, you hit the Polk Street exit and hang a left. I'll hit the Post Street exit and go right at Polk. They will follow you, so make sure you're clean."

"Go bring her down, brother. I'll be fired up and ready when you get down here," Flappers replied.

Alan went on up to the sixth floor and opened up the gleaming gray Dodge van. It smelled stale inside. It was a top-of-the-line van, packed with everything from an Uzi submachine gun to three fragmentation hand grenades. All the big stuff was stashed with strong magnets on the frame under the vehicle. None of the stuff could be spotted by a routine search. Tim called it "Our Batmobile," and they were the only ones who used it, although Flappers and two other members had seen it and rode in it a time or two. Dark-tinted windows completely blocked the view from the outside.

He swung down the ramp to the fifth floor and Flappers pulled in ahead of him. When Flappers went left, Alan went right, and they hit the two different exits at about the same time. The waiting police wouldn't have the time to think about anything. He made his left onto Post, a one-way street, and then a right at Polk and was on his way to the Oakland Bay Bridge freeway that leads out of town. It was a nice sunny evening, but he felt cold as he laid his left elbow on the window frame.

"Jesus Christ," he muttered to himself, realizing he had left the window down, and hit the switch that raised it back up.

"Pudgy" Whittaker, a member of the Special Services Unit, was standing in front of a liquor store on Polk and Post directly across from the Polk Gulch Saloon and had watched both Flappers and Young Alan enter the parking garage at intervals and was fine-tuning his two-way for the emerging black Cadillac Biarritz that Alan drove. A city street-gang task force car was observing the Polk Street exit.

"There they come," he said into his collar mike as the Cadillac swung left on Polk. The task force car pulled out behind it. Pudgy felt uneasy that the Cadillac contained only one person. He looked back toward the Post Street exit and was shocked to see Young Alan turning the corner in a new Dodge van. He was looking right at him. He yelled into his collar mike as he ran across Polk toward the hotel Alan lived in.

"He got slick, R. R. He just turned off Post onto Polk in a gray van. I'll catch you on the fly by the hotel. Let's move, partner!"

"R. R." Simpson, another member of the SSU team, fortunately had been parked up Post Street to cover that exit. He saw the gray van emerge, but all he could see was the tinted windows on the passenger side. It had just cleared the corner when he heard Pudgy's first communication, so he was cranked up and rolling when he heard the second and saw Pudgy running toward him across the intersection. He timed his speed so Pudgy would be behind the hotel and couldn't be seen in Alan's rearview and slowed enough to let him jump in. They picked up Alan right after they turned the corner. They were driving a nearly new white Toyota pickup.

They followed him across the Oakland Bay Bridge into Oakland and laid back on him until he took the Sacramento junction. At that point Pudgy called his supervisor on the portable phone.

"He's heading toward Sacramento. This turkey hasn't been

anywhere this far in five years. Requesting permission to go wherever he goes and camp out with him. I've got a hunch he's heading toward Fresno and if he is, we may nail him. You know about Little Joe down there. This punk is probably holstered up."

The permission wasn't long in coming. "Affirmative. Check in daily and don't leave the fucking state," was the reply.

"Why are you so sure he's headed for Fresno?" R. R. asked.

"Just a hunch, but Little Joe got took out down near there. Seems like a lot of drama in that town lately," Pudgy told him.

R. R. and Pudgy began to get the old adrenaline rush of impending action. R. R. stood for Roto Rooter, a nickname John Simpson had picked up in the early days of the SSU, when he had joined the force from the ranks of California prison guards.

A single sexy little blonde lived directly across the courtyard in the Sunset District, where John and his wife dwelled. John was a tall, dark man with sleepy brown eyes and the clean-cut looks of a Gary Cooper.

Three times in one week the blonde had rung their doorbell and asked if John could help fix her toilet. Her story was that she didn't have the money for a plumber. John was adept at fixing things. When she showed up the fourth time in less than two weeks, John's wife had said to her, "Call the Roto Rooter, you fucking bitch." His compadres had finally shortened his new name to R. R.

Pudgy had got his name from a tendency to overweight and he liked it better than Robert anyway. He and R. R. worked well together, probably because of two strong traits they had in common. They were both mean as hell and hated convicts. Especially those convicts who joined and ran gangs.

The Special Services Unit was formed by the California Department of Corrections. It started with four or five prison guards whose job was to follow recently paroled gang members. They stuck very close to the top-ranked members of the Mexican Mafia, Aryan Brotherhood, Black Guerilla Family, and the northern Mexican gang, the Nuestra Familia.

The SSU had a good success rate. They sometimes followed people and were on the scene when they pulled a robbery. As more gang members were freed, the SSU grew and became very sophisticated. By 1980 they were putting beepers on members' cars and sticking with them like glue. They tended to shun the glory and newsprint of their busts and faded back from publicity. Today there are many more of them and nobody in the public knows much about what they do and how they do it.

They are the California Department of Corrections' own police force and by extension the governor's force. All that gang members know is that they are stealthy, silent, and brutal, and probably somewhere very close by. They were the main reason for Alan's inept maneuvers at the parking garage. He knew they had stayed on him even after he got off parole.

The work that the SSU does is so inherently dangerous that they don't even use a central office, for the simple reason that some gang could take a notion to blow it up. They use a fully equipped motor home and park it around the state at different police departments. Usually somewhere around Los Angeles. They use it as a command center.

Even their budget is kept secret and administered by a state legislative committee, much the same way that the CIA is run by our national government. But none of that mattered as much as how effective they were at putting the serious bad boys back behind bars. And how much they liked doing it.

CHAPTER 26

Melvin stole a four-door Cadillac by pulling the entire ignition and hot-wiring it. He was in it and gone in less than five minutes and it felt good to be working again, although only a little over a month and a half had gone by since he was shot and he was still in considerable pain. He drove the Cadillac to the garage of a little cottage he'd rented near Palm and Shaw avenues, where he changed the license plates. Vern had specified a four-door and it had to be General Motors because of Melvin's method of hot-wiring. General Motors cars are the easiest to steal; GM cars were also the only ones Melvin knew how to steal. It didn't take him long to find one. He took it around ten on Thursday evening. When he finished switching plates, he threw an old sleeping bag in the trunk and took off for their rendezvous point in the woods near Coarsegold.

The Stepper had moved from Vern's house to a motel on Motel

Row. On Thursday he rented a little white Ford Probe from a Rent-a-Wreck place where a credit card wasn't required.

Vern and Curly went to bed early Thursday night. They slept well, considering they were going to rob a bank the next day—sleep that would have been more fitful had they known Young Alan had their address and after three frustrating weeks in Fresno had today learned that The Stepper lived out on Motel Row somewhere.

At six on Friday morning Vern loaded three full army duffel bags into Paula's Blazer, and with Curly driving they left for Coarsegold. Melvin was waiting, the Cadillac parked up under a big mulberry tree in a little clearing on the river about a mile and a half from town. The Stepper was ten minutes behind them.

They silently and swiftly donned combat boots, coveralls, and full head rubber masks made to resemble humorous likenesses of famous people. Ronald Reagan masks had been a big seller. Melvin and The Stepper both wore him. They put their own clothes back into the duffel bag. Vern turned Curly around to make sure she looked manly. Her tits were taped down as much as possible by ace bandages. He decided she looked okay. He handed each of their gloved hands a .30-caliber carbine with a thirty-shot clip.

"Well, folks, it's war from now on. If we get pulled over, we come out blazing," Vern told them grimly as they piled into the Cadillac and Melvin drove toward the bank right off the freeway in Coarsegold. No one said anything else. Curly was amazed at how the few people they did pass on the road never noticed anything amiss about them.

Vern had gotten the idea for this bank on the trip they had made to kill Little Joe. Years ago he had worked here at a sawmill for a couple of months and cashed a good-size paycheck every Friday at this bank where virtually all the millworkers cashed their checks.

There were three cops at most in the town. There had never been a bank robbery here simply because there was no place for a robber to go after he robbed it. One main highway led in and out of Coarsegold and the nearest town of any size was sixty or seventy miles away. They weren't really paranoid around here about getting robbed. Vern intended to unhinge that serenity and hoped they didn't have to hurt anyone.

The street was quiet as they glided up and parked the Cadillac right in front of the bank, an old sturdy building made of red brick. Vern bailed out of the passenger side and was the first in. The Stepper was right behind him from the back passenger side. Curly and Melvin slid over and came out the same side, leaving both side doors open and the motor running.

"Everybody on the fucking floor, jump!" Vern yelled as he entered the bank and whacked a customer who had been leaving on the shoulder with his carbine to show he meant business. He kept walking toward the back as employees and customers dropped to the floor. Two of the tellers hit their alarm buttons before they dropped, but Vern had counted on that.

"Who's the manager?" Vern yelled again.

"*Mmmmme,*" a terrified plump man in a suit replied with his face pressed to the floor behind the counter.

"Well, get up quick and get in that vault. Move!" Vern yelled as the man struggled to get up.

The Stepper leaped the counter with a kem tool attached to his army-surplus webbing belt. It was a little crowbar-type tool with a nail puller at one end. He slung his rifle over his shoulder and began popping teller drawers open with the tool and emptying the bills into a canvas bag that was also attached to the belt.

Melvin roamed the area out in front, guarding the few people who lay there trembling. He had a stopwatch in his hand that he kept glancing at while keeping up a running monologue.

"Okay, fellas, we're just past one minute, let's try to gear it up now. We're looking at a minute and a half," he was saying in a loud voice.

Curly stood just inside the door, rifle ready, watching both ways up and down the street, looking for any approaching police car. Vern had given them two-and-a-half, and no more than three, minutes inside the bank. To her it was already like an hour. Her job was to open fire on any police car that came, and although she dreaded the thought, she knew she would do it.

She was experiencing an adrenaline rush such as she'd never known, more powerful than snorting a big line of pure cocaine. The world had turned to a tension-plagued still life. When she heard Melvin say, "Okay, wind it up, two minutes and fifteen seconds, we got to powder," and glanced over to see Vern exiting the vault with a duffel bag full of money, she had to clinch hard to keep from pissing on herself. She turned back to the street as The Stepper came over the counter and Melvin came past her for the car. So far so good, she thought gleefully. She didn't relish the job of holding three people's lives in her hands. Not even for two and a half minutes.

She was the last one to get back into the Cadillac and her door shut of its own accord as Melvin screeched a U-turn. It was fuck-the-speed-limit time.

"Oh shit!" she exclaimed just before they hit the highway when she saw a squad car come around a corner near the bank, red and blue lights flashing and siren wailing. There looked to be only one cop in it, but there was no doubt he had zeroed in on them.

IN THE HAT

"He's on us like flies on shit," The Stepper said as he glanced back at the gaining prowl car. Melvin was up near one hundred miles an hour, peering intently into the rearview mirror.

"Just keep cool. He's a ways back yet and all alone," Vern reassured them in a calm tone of voice.

Melvin slowed to about seventy for a good long curve and when he got around it he slowed very quickly and pulled the Cadillac over on the shoulder of the highway.

"You all know the drill. Just go for his tires and motor. Try not to hit him!" Vern said as they all threw open the doors and exited the Cadillac, rifles ready, listening to the swiftly approaching siren.

The cop hadn't slowed that much for the curve, and when he roared around it, a hail of lead and tracers were hitting his tires and grille and bouncing off the asphalt, sparks flying, by the time he realized the Cadillac had stopped and all four of the thieves were standing outside it shooting at him. He slammed on his brakes and slid sideways into the brush at the side of the road not sixty yards from where they stood. He threw his door open and, shotgun in hand, bailed out into the bushes, intending to put as much distance as possible between himself and the still-groaning squad car sitting there smoking with three flat tires.

Vern and his crew jumped back into the Caddy and headed for the river, everyone hurriedly taking off the boots and coveralls and stuffing them into the proper duffel bags. The Stepper crammed his sack of money into the one Vern had the vault money in. When they finished, Vern had three bags. One with money, one with guns and tools, and the other with the clothes and masks, which came off last. All they kept was their gloves. Just before they turned for the river, Vern jumped out and ran into the underbrush with the three bags.

When they reached the clearing Melvin drove down the riverbank onto a patch of rocks beside the river. The car couldn't be seen from the clearing and the rocks would yield no footprints. He shut down the motor, threw his gloves into the river, and went along the bank toward where his car was parked about a quarter mile away.

Curly and The Stepper threw their own gloves into the river and walked swiftly to their own vehicles. The Stepper made a right toward Fresno on the highway and Curly turned left back toward Coarsegold in the Blazer. She pulled up at a drive-in restaurant on the outskirts of town, ordered two double cheeseburgers and a chocolate shake to go, and went back out to the Blazer to wait on Vern. She overheard some people talking excitedly about the bank robbery and the chase. They talked as if it were still going on.

You can forget this one, honey. It's done and over with, she thought to herself as she settled down with her food, eating and listening to the screaming sirens as more squad cars rushed by toward the long curve.

Finally Vern came walking around the back of the drive-in nonchalantly and got in beside her. She handed him a cold cheeseburger, cranked up, and pulled out onto the road in the direction of Fresno. A police helicopter came buzzing and chopping overhead from the direction they were headed in.

"These guys are a little swifter than I thought they were," Vern said before biting into the burger.

"Not swift enough." Curly smiled over at him.

The sparse traffic slowed way down around the curve, but it was just gawkers looking at the squad cars and cops surrounding their shaken comrade from the shot-up squad car. Two deputies stood beside the road impatiently waving them on. As they passed the path into the clearing, they saw two cars pulling in toward the river.

"They found that Cadillac already, so push it a little," Vern said, and Curly eased it up around eighty when the road was straight.

"We got a big bundle of cash, hon. That sack must have weighed seventy-five pounds, and there were a lot of big bills in there," Vern told her as they drove along. He had buried the loot in holes he had dug the previous week in the woods. He'd even taken the precaution of burying the money in one place and all the guns, clothes, and tools in another, so that if someone with a metal detector stumbled upon the guns, they still wouldn't be able to find the money. It was well stashed and brushed over carefully, just like the other bags. Vern intended to wait a week or more, then ease back up here one evening, pick up the money and bring it home to be divided among the four of them. Tomorrow's paper should give them a good idea of the size of their haul. Vern figured at least two hundred thousand, which was a good bit more than he had planned to get.

The trip back to Fresno was uneventful, but for some reason Curly didn't want to go home. The feeling of Paula was just too overpowering right now. Vern dropped her off at Melvin's, with Paul and the dogs, as Melvin wasn't home yet. He drove the Blazer back to the house in Fresno. Relief and a pleasurable feeling washed over him as he entered the drive. It was the first good feeling he had had in a while. Paula would have been proud of them. Especially of Curly, who had stood up like Bonnie had stood with Clyde. He resolved that this would be her last caper. No matter what the rest of them did.

CHAPTER 27

PAYROLL HEISTED IN COARSEGOLD BY FOUR VICIOUS BANDITS was the headline on the front page of the *Fresno Bee* on Saturday. The story went on to say that over two hundred thousand had been lifted from the complacent bank. The entire payroll for the mill and a deadhead railroad station. The FBI had no comment as yet, but local police avowed there was very little to go on.

"It was like a blitzkrieg," said the deputy who had been fired on.

"You know, I couldn't find a one of those fuckers on Friday," Martin Torres was telling Bud McClure of the SSU, who had set up shop in Fresno and brought in more men as it became obvious that Young Alan and a few local DWB were seriously hunting someone. Before long they knew it was Vern and The Stepper. But while they stuck right on to the gang members, they didn't have manpower for Vern's crew. Torres had them under loose observation. Plain cars checking their locations and reporting in every day. On Friday none of them could be located, but a bank robbery was the furthest thing from Torres's mind. He was hoping to protect them from the fate that befell Paula. He wanted to warn them, but McClure nixed that notion.

In spite of Torres's mean reputation, he wasn't as bad as people thought. Most of the thieves he'd dealt with wound up respecting him. Men and women who stole from desperation or got suddenly greedy and jumped into a dope deal weren't high on his list of no-goods.

Killers who did it for money or to advance criminal schemes were the ones he had it in for. He stalked them so tenaciously that some of them thought he was nuts.

But old thieves who shunned violence, and hustlers trying to get by, like Vern's crew, he didn't resent all that much, although there was something about Vern that did bother him. There was more there than met the eye. He was sure of it.

Paula's killing had hurt him personally. He'd run across her in the days he worked vice. She was a likable woman, so was Curly, and he hoped she didn't get hurt too before this was over. It frustrated him that he couldn't figure out exactly what the hell was going on.

The closer the DWBs got to them, the more excited McClure became. He was a big, tough-looking middle-aged man who had risen to the top ranks of the SSU from a notorious San Quentin goon squad created by Captain Carl Hocker in the early sixties. Their trademark had been black berets and a habit of beating tough convicts so bad that they clung to the wall like bats as they walked for the rest of their lives.

All he wanted was to become certain that these dirtballs were packing weapons and he was going to have Pudgy, R. R., and the rest take them down like young Christmas trees. He was even a bit fond of Vern and The Stepper for putting slimy Little Joe's light out. It was something he had yearned to do for years. But Young Alan and Tim were his obsession. He wanted their ass bad and had for a long time.

Young Alan was mad and frustrated as hell, which was probably the main reason he hadn't knocked off the tail. The three DWB he had for help in Fresno were all addicts like him, but they didn't have the dope money he had. Much of their energy was used on getting their daily fix and they weren't dependable.

He had been here over three weeks now. Vern had been easy to locate, but The Stepper wasn't with him as expected and was harder to find than a slippery old eel. Alan was determined to take him out first, because if he took Vern first, the old outlaw would be too hard to deal with. He had to get Grady first, and he was running low on dope and tired of living in fucking motels.

On Monday Joker Smith, one of his best boys, came to him and told him The Stepper's motel and room number. "He's in the Flamingo in room one-twelve," Joker said, and looked like a puppy who was about to be rewarded with a snack. Young Alan rewarded Joker with a huge jolt of stuff and they holstered up from the stash under the van and set off for The Stepper's motel. Pudgy and R. R. watched every move they made.

"They're strapped down and on their way to The Stepper's pad. We're dead certain of it," Pudgy reported in to McClure.

"Take them any time you see fit. I'll have some backup at the motel pretty quick," McClure told him.

"Ten-four," Pudgy replied and the line went dead.

The Stepper was walking with just plain bad luck that day. When Young Alan and Joker pulled into the motel lot in the van, The Stepper was walking on the sidewalk toward a back entrance carrying a bag of groceries. He glanced at the van but couldn't see behind the tinted windows.

By the time he entered the building, Alan and Joker had quickly parked and were right behind him. They both jerked ski masks down over their faces as they entered the building. Pudgy and R. R. caught the whole scene and Pudgy was foaming at the mouth and screaming into the two-way.

"Easy now, pardner, easy." It was times like this that R. R. worried about Pudgy because he became downright overwrought. He had once shot a Nuestra Familia member three times in the neck to keep him from swallowing a bag of heroin, a situation that had been extremely difficult to extricate Pudgy from.

"Get the front of this motel covered now! We're at the rear. The bastards got on ski masks in this weather, for chrissake!" he yelled into the mike as R. R. parked and they grabbed their stuff. R. R. had an AK-47 and Pudgy toted a thirteen-shot automatic 12-gauge with double-ought buckshot.

"Should one of us follow them in or what?" R. R. asked Pudgy as they eased behind the Mercury Cougar they were driving today.

"Hell, they got to come back to the car. We'll take 'em then," he said; then they both heard the loud report of a pistol shot from inside the motel.

The Stepper had put his bag of groceries down and was unlocking the door when he heard a scuffling sound and looked back over his shoulder just as a ski-mask-clad Alan shot him in the back three times using a .380 automatic with a silencer. The shots made very little noise. A *pssst pssst pssst,* as they slammed The Stepper against the wall. He bounced off and wheeled around, leaving splotches of blood on the white stucco wall and door.

Alan couldn't believe it when The Stepper plunged a buck

knife all the way to the hilt in his left upper chest. He knew he was close, but he'd just shot him three times point-blank. He sort of froze up chopping at The Stepper with his gun hand. Joker shot the old man in the temple with a short-barreled .38. But he didn't have a silencer and it sounded like a cannon. The Stepper dropped to the floor, bloody knife in hand, as gray matter and pieces of his brain leaked onto the soft blue carpet.

People began yelling, running, opening doors, and diving back into their rooms.

"Let's blow!" Joker exclaimed and they made for the exit.

"Freeze, slimebags," Pudgy yelled when they came out, guns in hand, and opened fire with the shotgun before they could even locate him. The chatter of the AK-47 firing four shot bursts accompanied the blam-blam of the shotgun.

Alan and Joker jerked like puppets as the lead found its mark. Even after they went down, Pudgy tried to roll them like tin cans. R. R. had to grab the shotgun to stop him. They both ran for the motel entrance as a squad car roared around from the front. They found The Stepper lying near his groceries, bloody knife in hand.

"Looks like the old fucker took a chunk out of one of them before he went," R. R. commented as people began to gather and Pudgy started herding them back.

"Jesus Christ! There's enough lead in these monkeys to build a good-size boat anchor," a deputy said, as he kneeled between Alan and Joker, gently tugging at their bloody ski masks.

CHAPTER 28

Curly and Melvin saw the aftermath of the incident on the local news less than two hours after it happened. The announcer said that the police had tailed the two men thinking they were going to rob the motel. They were surprised when they found they had bagged the leader of a notorious prison gang.

"That's bullshit!" Melvin and Curly said at the same time.

"You know, that's scary. If they had been following us last Friday, we'd of took them right to the bank with us," Melvin told Curly.

"You're telling me," she replied. Vern was in San Francisco talking to two lawyers for Weldon and Yay-Yay. She got on the phone trying to get hold of him. The news hadn't given any names, but they were both pretty sure The Stepper had gone down. She missed Vern and dialed The Stepper's room, just in case, but got no answer there either.

What remained of their day was filled with remorse, grief, and apprehension. They had loved The Stepper and were further bothered by the fact they didn't know what to do with his share of the bank money. Vern finally called in and Curly broke the news to him.

"Are you sure it was him?" Vern asked, hope leaving his voice.

"They just gave all their names about an hour ago," she told him.

"I'll arrange to have him cremated," Vern said and hung up.

Melvin and Curly smoked a couple of joints and killed two bottles of red wine. They felt a little better when they went to their bedrooms.

Melvin was mildly surprised when Curly eased into his bed before he got to sleep. She wore only a thin cotton man's tank top and said to him as she ran her warm hand down his chest, "Do you think you're well enough to fuck?"

"No, but I'm well enough to make love. If you just want to fuck, get on back to your room and jack off. If you want to make love, let's get it on," he told her, and before he finished, her warm, soft fingers were closing about his dick.

"Does it feel like a nose inhaler?" he asked her.

"Yeah, but I think I'll stay awhile anyway," she whispered and ran her tongue into his ear as she drew her fingernails across the head of his now-engorged penis.

He brushed against her hard nipples, got a grip on her back, and pulled her roughly to him as their lips frantically sought one another.

He rolled over on top of her and she took him in hand and guided him until he went deep, making her eyes flutter as she breathed out: "Oh . . ."

He raised himself to look at her soft face in the pale moonlight that filtered into the room. The sight of her large, hard-nippled breasts lying against his biceps almost drove him crazy, joined together as they were.

"My turn has been a long time coming," he whispered.

"Melvin, I'll love you and I'll live with you, but I'm spoken for, and when Weldon gets out, I'm going back with him. That's all you can get here," she replied earnestly.

"It's enough," he said as she drew him back to her and began moving her pelvis up and down, squeezing and relaxing.

They roared into a frenzied gallop that left them in blissful intertwined sleep at the finish line.

Vern had spent his entire bankroll hiring Weldon and Yay-Yay two of the best criminal lawyers in San Francisco.

Tuesday evening Vern was on his way to Coarsegold in the Blazer to pick up their money. He carefully checked every car he saw and stopped now and then to listen and look for a helicopter. He decided to leave the Blazer at the hamburger stand while he dug up the loot. He might beat them there even if they were following. Things were moving too fast to wait any longer.

They were elated when they counted two hundred and forty-three thousand dollars.

"Sixty thousand, seven hundred fifty apiece, not counting The Stepper's," Vern said.

"Man, I can retire," Melvin exclaimed.

"You always was retired, sucker," Curly told him.

CHAPTER 29

On Wednesday Martin Torres was helping McClure get his papers and gadgets from his office when it hit him like a bomb. The revelation coincided with a phone call from the deputy in Coarsegold.

"Just wanted to know if you closed Little Joe's file," he asked Torres.

"Yeah, we figure Vern and The Stepper done him. The Stepper went down over here on Monday," Torres replied.

"Yeah, well, I almost got my ass shot off Friday by four bank robbers. This fucking little burg is getting busy," the deputy replied.

"Four? Did you say four? Any description on them?" Torres asked excitedly.

"Nah, full masks. Two tall and slim, two short, one slim, one stocky. Fucked my Christmas all up."

"Goddamn! I've got another call. I'll get back to you!" Torres told him. The Stepper, Vern, Curly, Melvin, went the chant in his mind. "Where were they on Friday?" he asked, as he told McClure of his suspicions.

"Wouldn't put it past them, but we just do gang members, so good luck," McClure told him as he left with his box of belongings, on his way back to Los Angeles.

Torres got Vern on the phone. "Vern, I want some help here," he said.

"Sure, what's up?" Vern asked.

"I want a statement from you, Melvin Nix, Grady McCall, and Curly telling me where you each were last Friday. Where you went, what you did, who you saw. The entire day. If it's not on my desk by Friday, I'm arresting you all," he declared. The threat was intended to get statements from them that he could use in court to impeach them. An end run around lawyers.

"Well now, old Grady, he may not be able to ah—"

"Okay, okay." Torres cut him off. He'd forgotten in his haste that The Stepper was dead. "Just the three of you."

"I don't see any problem with that," Vern declared and hung up.

They held the little memorial service for The Stepper on Friday evening out near Clovis at the funeral home that had cremated him. Curly had opted to take the ashes, although she didn't know what she would do with them. Vern's Aunt May had insisted on coming. Vern had taken The Stepper out to see her twice.

"I wanted to marry that man so bad," she sniffled there in the pew as tears ran down her cheeks. May, Vern, Paul, Curly, Peggy, and Melvin were the only ones there. About all they could think to do was pass around a quart of Gentleman Jack Daniels, The Stepper's drink of choice. Very little of their association and reminiscing could be talked about at this point.

As Vern rubbed May's shoulders, trying to console her, he heard movement and looked around. A dark-haired man with a sprinkling of gray in his hair entered with two women. One looked to be in her mid-thirties and carried herself with the grace and dignity of a prima ballerina. The other was a girl of about sixteen who was absolutely gorgeous. They were all dressed formally in black.

The women took a seat at the back and the man nodded to Vern and Melvin as he walked up to the bier where the urn sat. The urn itself was a jade vase that Vern had paid twenty-seven hundred dollars for. The old man had had such a unique style that Vern wanted his remains to rest in splendor. Melvin and Curly readily agreed.

The man knelt down, but in Curly's eyes he more or less sank like a big panther getting ready to pounce.

What a sexy hunk of man, she thought and glanced back at the two women who accompanied him. The youngest met her eyes and smiled as the man reached up and laid his hands on the urn. The next thing that happened was Melvin's idea and it totally shocked and mesmerized everyone in the room, including old May.

The mournful music stopped and there was total silence. Then the music began in earnest, much louder, and Linda Ronstadt could be heard caressing and wrapping her voice around the word "Desperado."

As she sang the song they could all feel the man, know what and who he was, what he stood for, and where he made his stand. The man who wanted the sunshine so badly but had to seek it in the darkest pits and poles of the earth. Desperate for adventure and bound by no man's rules or laws. Champion to some, dirtbag to others, despised by the majority, he was revered by the outsiders—the ones who understand that the things you want are the ones you can't get.

The sleek man rose and walked back to his women. There was moisture glinting beneath his eyes. He's for sure not a cop, Vern thought. When the song ended everyone in the room was crying except the parlor manager, who kept anxiously shooting his cuff and looking at his watch. Vern walked back to the man and two women, holding the bottle in his hand.

"Did you folks know Grady?" Vern asked as he approached. The man didn't rise. He just sat and waited until Vern had spoken.

Then he said, "That was his favorite drink. He liked it straight over ice that was as hard and cold as they make it. He said regular ice melted too fast and . . ." The man just waved his hand and quit talking. Vern could tell he was about to choke up.

"Care for a drink in remembrance?" Vern offered the bottle.

"Don't mind if I do." The fellow tipped the bottle to his lips. To Vern's surprise the two women took a sip and struggled to keep a straight face. Vern liked this crowd instantly and there was no doubt the man knew Grady pretty well.

"Vern Coy," Vern said and stuck out his hand.

"Bill Malone," the man replied, gripping Vern's hand firmly. "This is my wife, Gail, and my daughter, June." They shook Vern's hand and he introduced them to everyone. It felt good to have more people at this sparse gathering.

"He once told me he wanted to be cremated and have his ashes spread on a nude optional beach called Baker Beach in San Francisco," the man told Vern.

"Would you take them there if I paid for your trip?" Vern asked him.

"I'll take them there, but I won't take any money. I can get them there, no problem. What should I do with the urn?"

"Keep it as a gift from The Stepper and all of us," Curly said, and broke down. Gail put her arms around her and held her tightly.

"It's so beautiful," June whispered.

"He was too," Malone whispered back to her.

On Friday evening Torres went into his den after supper, opened his briefcase and reread their statements.

Vernon Coy:

Dear Mr. Torres,

On Friday December 22, I woke up thinking it could be a bad day. I took a handful of sleeping pills, smoked a large size hooter and went back to sleep. I believe it was Saturday when I woke up. Thank you for your interest.

Vernon Coy

Angela Perry, aka Curly:

On Friday I woke up horny and grabbed my vibrator. The off and on switch malfunctioned, and the power surged. It was shaking me so bad I couldn't dial 911. I kept hitting 913 and 914. The phone fell and in a desperate lunge I fell. It drove me around the room until I passed out. Thank God the battery went dead and I woke up Saturday sore but alive. Please keep this in confidence as I come from a socially prominent family.

Sincerely,
Curly

Melvin Nix:

Right at this moment I don't recall where I was on Friday. Should I sober up at a later date I may recall with perfect clarity.

I remain your servant,
Melvin Nix

Torres shook his head. They were all essentially saying, "Fuck you, you can't prove shit!" And they were right. But cute stuff didn't set well with Torres. He decided to glom on these three like a wet T-shirt.

Saturday Vern Coy walked up the gangplank of a cruise ship preparing to leave from Terminal Island in San Pedro. He could see the Terminal Island Federal Prison from the deck.

There but for the grace of God go I, he thought, and shivered some in the balmy evening. Convicts out walking around the track at the perimeter of the recreation yard still had their shirts off.

The ship was bound for Costa Rica and other southern seaports. Vern's passport said Brendan Sullivan. He planned to jump ship in Costa Rica and switch back to his own name. He wasn't wanted, even though he felt kind of hunted. The chunk of money carefully hidden in one of his new suitcases gave him a healthy, secure feeling. Romance once again was trying to find him also. He knew Paula would want that but didn't know how to begin looking for another woman like her. He wondered if they fought chickens in Costa Rica.

He and Curly could no longer share a bed crowded with Paula's memory. Curly had flat out told him that and he agreed, even though part of him wanted to vigorously protest. Costa Rica looked good. San Francisco had soured him on big American cities.

On Sunday Curly sat in a special section of the visiting room reserved for men in isolation. All the charges had been dismissed outside. The DA in Salinas looked at the daunting legal teams he faced and the evidence he had, and dismissed all the charges against Weldon and Yay-Yay. But the institutional disciplinary committee had found them guilty over the lieutenant's objections.

They sentenced them to ninety days' isolation and a disciplinary transfer to Pelican Bay Prison, way out on the lonely coast. A hellhole of a prison where they would be confined to cement cells with no windows for twenty-two and a half hours a day. No contact visits. Phones with a big sheet of glass separating visitors from prisoners. Not a chance in hell of getting any dope or other form of relief.

"I can do it. It ain't really that much longer," Weldon told her.

"Melvin and I plan to move up there until you get out so that I can visit every week."

"You'll get bored as hell," he warned her.

"We'll see," she replied, and he knew it was no use arguing with her. She was coming along. Her loyalty was total and unquestionable.

Sunday evening Bill Malone walked across Baker Beach surreptitiously spreading The Stepper's ashes from a beach bag while naked and seminaked men and women played volleyball, lay in the sand, or roamed the waterline as he was doing. He threw the last handful while Gail and June waited up by a little pushcart of a hot dog stand, standing patiently, hair blowing in the steady forceful ocean wind.

"You old fucker. How did you let a punk like that idiot sneak up on you? You were getting old. Should have made a good score and quit the game," he mumbled as he turned back toward the waiting women.

He'd never know how close Grady had come to doing just that.

9 781451 636642